"Is something wrong, Steven?"

"Wrong?" he repeated, with a cynical smile. "Only that I find it strange to spend dinner with a lovely woman whose main purpose seems to be finding out everything about me while revealing nothing about herself."

"But I'm interested," Maggie insisted.

Steven took a step toward her. His eyes held hers as he spoke. "I hardly think dinner conversation about my life on the Double E Ranch or my exploits during the Civil War is that fascinating to a lady of your obvious sophistication."

"On the contrary," she insisted, "I find everything about you fascinating."

She lifted her hand as if to touch his chest, and he reached out and grabbed her wrist. She had no time to even register her surprise.

"This game has continued quite long enough," he said. "Who the hell are you, lady, and what's going on here?"

Dear Reader,

This July, Harlequin Historicals brings you four titles that you won't want to miss.

Texas Healer from Ruth Langan is the long-awaited sequel to *Texas Heart*. After years of study in the East, Dr. Dan Conway finally returns home to Texas . . . as a wanted man.

With *Temptation's Price,* contemporary author Dallas Schulze has turned her talented pen to writing a historical. Matt Prescott married young Liberty Ballard for the sole reason of preserving her good name, and promptly left town. But five years of haunted dreams have got Matt wondering whether life without Liberty is really worth living.

In Deborah Simmons's *Fortune Hunter,* set against the backdrop of Regency London, a viscount looking for a rich woman and an heiress looking for a title discover that they've both been had.

Dangerous Charade by Madeline Harper is the story of a prince who is unaware of his royal heritage and the headstrong woman who convinces him to rescue his birthright.

We hope you enjoy this month's selection.

Sincerely,

Tracy Farrell
Senior Editor

Dangerous Charade

Madeline Harper

Harlequin Books

TORONTO • NEW YORK • LONDON
AMSTERDAM • PARIS • SYDNEY • HAMBURG
STOCKHOLM • ATHENS • TOKYO • MILAN
MADRID • WARSAW • BUDAPEST • AUCKLAND

Harlequin Historicals first edition July 1992

ISBN 0-373-28733-X

DANGEROUS CHARADE

MADELINE HARPER

Madeline Porter and Shannon Harper have been writing since 1978 when their first book, a Gothic, was published. Madeline lives in Newport Beach, California, where she is assistant publicity director for the award-winning South Coast Repertory Theater Company. Shannon lives in Winter Haven, Florida. During their almost fifteen-year partnership, Madeline and Shannon have lived on opposite coasts, and they collaborate via the mail, fax machines and their computers.

Prologue

1841

She was running for her life, the baby wrapped securely in its blanket, clutched to her bosom. She didn't stop until she crossed the snow-covered clearing in front of the cottage and disappeared safely into the shadows of thick, towering trees. Then she paused and looked back.

The cottage from which she had escaped seemed to glow for a moment from within, a soft, golden radiance as warm as the sunrise.

Suddenly, as if the entire world had exploded, the glow became hot and greedy flames that lapped hungrily against the night sky. The freshly fallen snow gleamed bloodred as the fire intensified in its furious destruction of the simple wooden structure.

The young woman pressed the baby more fiercely to her breast, staring at the flames as if mesmerized. Her world was gone, destroyed by forces that she was powerless to combat.

From the darkness beneath the giant fir trees, a man

moved forward, his skin illuminated by the bright fire. He reached out, touched her arm and broke the spell.

"Come, we must travel swiftly. It is too dangerous to stay here." His voice was low, urgent.

Reluctantly she followed him to the safety of a waiting carriage and the beginning of a journey that would forever make her a stranger in a foreign land.

Chapter One

He noticed her the first moment he stepped into the observation car.

After pocketing his poker winnings, which were considerable, Steven Peyton was taking a much needed breath of air. The car was almost empty, only a few tables occupied, but even if it had been filled to capacity, she would have stood out.

Ordinarily, nothing caught Steven's attention after an all-day-and-all-night poker game. Not even a pretty face. Yet his gaze swept over the woman again, once quickly and then more slowly, before he finally turned away.

His head was aching, his eyes burned from the smoke of a dozen cigars, and he needed a shave. He didn't need the distraction of some unknown female who was traveling the Transcontinental for whatever purpose.

Steven steadied himself against the swaying of the train and crossed to the heavy walnut buffet. Nodding perfunctorily at the smiling white-coated waiter, he glanced up into the gilded mirror above the buffet. There she was again, a beautiful reflection staring into space.

She was at a table alone, a tea service before her. Sipping occasionally from the gold-banded china cup, she seemed to be totally engrossed in the scenery as the great train labored upward toward the Rockies on its long journey to California.

The waiter was still smiling when Steven looked back. "How are you this evenin', Mr. Peyton?"

"Just fine, Sam." Steven was a frequent traveler from Chicago to Cheyenne, and he often left his private railroad car to take advantage of other opportunities such as lavish dining and high-stakes poker.

"Business good in Chicago this time, Mr. Peyton?" Sam asked.

"Very good, indeed. We can hardly keep the beef moving fast enough back East."

"That's fine. Just fine. Now, what can I do for you tonight, sir?"

Steven pulled a roll of bills from the pocket of his tapestried vest. Peeling several off, he slipped them to Sam. "I'd like some information. The lady—at the table alone. Who is she?"

Sam's face creased in a broad grin. "Thought you might notice her, Mr. Peyton. Don't know her name, but she got on in Chicago, too. I hear she's royalty, a princess or some such. So they say."

"Princess, eh?" Steven's green eyes narrowed in disbelief, which he did not voice. "Thanks, Sam." After a thoughtful pause he added, "Bourbon would be in order now, I believe."

Sam nodded and reached for the silver siphon as Steven turned away, leaning against the buffet and studying the woman openly.

Moments later, a tall frosted glass was placed at his elbow, the golden brown liquid topped off with a sprig of fresh mint. Sam moved away, leaving Steven in his contemplation.

The woman now looked out the window at the towering pines and rocky cliffs, which were shadowed in the deepening twilight. Steven's lips curved in a smile. Her attempt to ignore him was so obvious that he had no doubt she was very aware of his presence.

Although he did not for a moment put stock in the rumor of her royalty, there was certainly something quite patrician about her. Perhaps it was nothing more than her demeanor, the way she held herself, proudly and yet with no hint of uneasiness, no attempt at haughtiness. Her elegance seemed quite natural.

Her hair was a pale gold and drawn back from her high forehead into a loose knot at the nape of her neck. Carefully noting and then dissecting each of her features, Steven saw that her eyes were deep blue, slightly slanted and set above high cheekbones. Her nose was strong and her lips firm and full above a rather stubborn chin. Steven had long considered himself a connoisseur of beautiful women, and he realized that hers was not a conventionally pretty face, but there was something about it that commanded attention. He found her fascinating.

Reaching for his drink, he quickly disposed of the mint and took a long deep gulp, not removing his gaze from the woman. Her neck was long, her shoulders more square than daintily rounded, and her breasts were full and firm. She wore a dress of deep blue that accentuated the remarkable color of her eyes and clung caressingly, provocatively to her waist. It was a woman's body, full and ripe; he could tell that even though they were separated by the width of the car, even though she was fully and fashionably clothed.

What he vividly imagined beneath the beautiful dress caused him to catch his breath and run his tongue over dry lips.

Then the train gave a lurch as they rounded a sharp curve, and she leaned forward to steady her teacup. As she righted herself, her eyes met Steven's in a long, mysterious gaze. Was it an invitation that he read there?

Never one to hesitate when faced with a provocation, Steven put down his glass and started across the car toward her. Just before he reached her table, she rose quickly and turned to the door. Sweeping past him, she was so close that her skirts brushed his trouser leg, and he could smell the heady musky scent of her perfume.

Then she was gone.

He could have reached out, touched her arm, even held on to her elbow long enough to delay her so that he could speak. Yet he hadn't done so, possibly because the gesture would have been too overt.

Now he had yet another choice. He could easily follow her, make a note of her compartment and plan the rest of the evening accordingly. He was well versed at initiating contact through whatever means available. No doubt he could find some way to manage a formal introduction.

Or he could leave well enough alone. Which is exactly what he decided to do as with a shrug he walked the opposite direction, pushed open the doors at the end of the car and stepped onto the observation platform.

It had been a long, hard trip, and he was tired. Within a few hours he would be back at the ranch. Now was not the time to be thinking about a woman. Still, for a long while the memory of her face and the scent of her perfume stayed with him.

The woman opened the door to her compartment and collapsed onto the green velvet seat, her heart pounding as loudly as the wheels along the rails. He had seen her, and he had been interested. But it was not the time. Not yet.

The wheels seemed to be repeating his name. Steven Peyton. Steven Peyton. Steven Peyton. It was no wonder, for the name, and the man, had long been in her every thought.

She had known him at once from the faded brown daguerreotype secreted in the bottom of her bag. She had often examined it, memorizing each of his features, imagining what the face would be like when she finally saw it. To the indistinct picture she had added her own version of the man, and it so happened that her version was more like the man himself than even the daguerreotype had been.

Even so, it was far from accurate. He had been larger than she'd imagined, much more imposing and what she interpreted as self-assured. Perhaps even dangerous? She could not know what there was about him that gave her that idea. Yet it persisted.

His hair was not dark, as it appeared in the picture, but rather a russet brown streaked with gold. His eyes, which had looked cold and colorless, were in life an intriguing green that seemed to see deep into hers and sum her up.

She had watched while his private car was hooked on in Chicago, and waited patiently ever since for a glimpse of him. During the long days as the train roared westward across the Great Plains, her wait had, seemingly, been in vain. Mr. Peyton had not appeared.

She had learned from the Pullman attendants that he was known to frequent the smoking car and join in a game of chance, but that venue was out of bounds for ladies.

He had his own steward and chef aboard, and his private railroad car was well equipped and beautifully appointed. In that case there would be very little reason for him to venture further than the smoker, especially as she had also learned that he entertained young ladies in his private car. Mr. Peyton was always a gentleman, according to the ladies who emerged, quite contentedly, from their long evenings in his presence.

She was not going to be one of Steven Peyton's visitors. The game she had in mind was much more serious than an evening's dalliance, no matter how charming her host might be. The stakes were far too high, and she was not about to fail.

So she had continued to wait, aware that it was his wont to take air occasionally on the small platform at the end of the observation car. Tonight she had seen him at last. The contact was made.

She pulled back the window curtain and looked into the darkening gloom. She would succeed, had to succeed. The great iron wheels continued to repeat his name, the name of the man upon whom everything rested.

She let the curtain fall back, closed her eyes and remembered. A small hotel room in Chicago. Uncle Viktor had been there with her. She could still feel the closeness of the room, the fetid odor, the faded colors in the wallpaper and in the curtains, all belying their great hope for the future, a hope that was explicit in the promise she made to her uncle and to herself.

"This is the most important role of your life, *Liebchen*," Uncle Viktor had told her. "Do not fail us."

Never, she had vowed. As the night flowed by, she repeated the vow aloud. "Never. I promise."

Steven Peyton swung to the ground, drawing in long gulps of cool mountain air. He was still dressed in city clothes: dark trousers, starched white shirt, collar and tie, embroidered vest, gold pocket watch, the trappings of success in which he clothed himself because it was expected that he do so when traveling on business.

It felt good to leave the stuffiness of the train behind. No matter how successful his ventures in Chicago had been, there was nothing like coming home to Wyoming and to the ranch. And there was nothing like getting back into the rhythm of ranch life, including the denim and leather that went with it.

He walked along the spur where his private car had been sidetracked. His foreman, Bert Laker, would be waiting for him at the station house with a horse for him and a buggy for the baggage. The buggy would be especially needed this trip. Steven, who always loaded up in Chicago with items that were not available in the rough-and-tumble town of Cheyenne, had overdone the shopping this trip.

To his usual cheeses he had added exotic French pâtés, rich Dutch chocolates, laces from Belgium, and bolts of cloth. The yard goods had been purchased for his housekeeper Faye Laker, Bert's wife, and would be greatly appreciated. The other delicacies were for various lady friends; and for himself, a French champagne which would be brought out on a very special occasion.

Steven looked up at the sky. There was no other like it, black as velvet with huge stars hung like miniature chandeliers. The full moon played hide-and-seek with the clouds and cast an eerie light over the scene. Everywhere, there was sky. Truly this was the big sky country. It gave him peace. It was home.

There were still a few hours until dawn, a few hours before he'd be back at the ranch. He liked to arrive just as the sun came up over the vast horizon. It gave him a good feeling, and tonight he particularly looked forward to that moment when his horse galloped beneath the wooded sign that proclaimed his land, his ranch, the Double E.

The cry he heard was muffled. At first he thought it might have come from the throat of a night bird or a threatened animal. Then he realized what it was—the cry of a woman in distress.

Steven broke into a run, his boots pounding on the hard-packed ground. On his left, the train huffed and smoked, ready to continue on its journey. On his right were empty cars and a woman in trouble.

He could make out three shadowy forms, a woman and two men, struggling. He flung himself across the tracks, rushing headlong toward the battling trio. The moonlight suddenly illuminated the scene as Steven plunged into the melee, his fists swinging.

The woman was pushed aside, and both men turned toward Steven. His fist connected with the bearded face of one assailant, who staggered as the other grabbed on to Steven, arms around his neck, viselike.

Steven sidestepped, kicking out at the man who was on the way down while riding the other on his back until he was able to dislodge him.

He did so lithely, and before either man had a chance to move in again, they were both on the ground, rolling away to avoid further contact, and then they were on their feet, running.

Only one blow had connected to Steven's body, a weak punch to his abdomen that caused little harm. He straightened up and caught his breath, his first impulse to chase the men down.

Then a low moan caught his attention.

He knelt beside her, knowing who she was even before he saw her face. Her eyes were closed, her hair disheveled, but she was breathing, erratically, but breathing nonetheless. He bent low, his ear on her chest, listening.

When he straightened up, her eyes opened and looked into his.

"Are you all right?" he asked.

Her eyelids fluttered, and she struggled to rise. "Yes, I—"

"Don't move," he said. "Stay quiet."

"Those men...it was horrible..." Her voice was low and husky, the accent slightly exotic, untraceable but certainly not American.

He cradled her in his arms, and she leaned heavily against him, her head resting on his chest, her body pressed close. In spite of the encounter that had just occurred, he could not stem his reaction to the scent of her perfume, which wafted through the night air.

He inhaled deeply and caught himself in a half smile. The woman was safe. There was no harm in enjoying the moment.

"Thank you," she murmured. "I am so indebted to you."

"Nonsense," Steven assured her. "Anyone would have—"

"No," she said. "You got here just in time. They grabbed me, robbed me. Who knows what might have happened...." A shudder shook her body.

"Who knows, indeed," Steven repeated, something in his voice denoting a doubt that he did not even realize existed until he heard it himself.

"Can you get up? We should get you to a doctor."

"No, no," she protested. "I am fine. If you will just help me to my feet."

One arm around her waist, Steven set her on her feet where she wobbled briefly and then found her balance.

"There," she said. "If I can just make it to my compartment—" She looked into the distance and let out a little cry. "The train—"

"Gone," Steven said dryly. As they watched, it picked up speed and disappeared into the distance.

"Everything I own is on that train," she cried. "My baggage, my jewels. I had a purse..."

Steven bent and retrieved it for her. Frantically she opened it and felt inside. "My money is gone, too. I have nothing, nothing!"

She looked up at him, her face pale in the light of the moon, which had just darted from behind the clouds.

Steven felt the wry smile about to invade his lips once more and managed to bite it back. "Don't worry," he said. "I'm sure that we can be of assistance to you, Miss..." He let his voice drop, waiting for her to come up with a name.

"Carlton, Margaret Carlton," she responded. "And you, sir? I have no idea who my champion might be."

The grin was avoided once more as Steven thought how amazing this woman seemed. She had just been attacked, her life threatened by robbers, murderers perhaps, and here she was practically flirting with him. Amazing, he thought, but also rather intriguing.

"My name is Steven Peyton," he told her. "I own a ranch nearby, and I have very substantial connections here in Cheyenne. I have no doubt that we can make some arrangements that will be satisfactory for you."

"How very kind," she said, daring to take an unsteady step forward, leaning heavily on him.

"There is one thing that concerns me, however," he said.

"And what is that, Mr. Peyton?" she asked, looking up at him, eyelids fluttering either prettily, fetchingly or distressfully, depending upon one's interpretation.

Steven answered in a steady voice that took no notice of the eyelids. "Why, Miss Carlton, did you leave the train to wander around the tracks in the middle of the night?"

She stumbled slightly and fell against him. He was immediately made aware of the warmth of her body, the curve of her waist where his hand captured and steadied her.

"It seems foolish now," she said. "But I was having difficulty sleeping, and I thought the night air might refresh me."

"I see," Steven commented.

"Then those terrible men—" Her voice broke off in a kind of sob.

"There, there," he said with a smile she could not see in the darkness. He patted her arm. "Everything will be all right."

They had reached the almost deserted station house, manned only by the sleepy stationmaster. Just as they started up the steps, a shadowy figure emerged from the darkness and moved toward them.

Margaret gave a little cry of fear and clutched Steven's arm more tightly. The man was in his forties, with gray streaking his coppery mustache and hair. He was several inches shorter than Steven but many pounds heavier.

"Howdy, boss," he said. "Welcome home."

"Good to be back, Bert." Steven extended his hand to his friend. It was easy to read the curiosity in Bert's face. "This is Miss Carlton," Steven satisfied. "She's had an accident of sorts. Seems as though two men attacked and robbed her back there." He nodded his head toward the deserted train yard.

Bert's rather shambling stance became immediately alert. His hand reached automatically for the gun on his hip. "Any chance we can catch the skunks who done it?"

"I suspect they managed to catch the train as it was pulling out and are long gone by now," Steven told his foreman. "However, we can make arrangements for the lady. If you'll take the buggy around and collect the luggage, Miss Carlton and I will wait here at the station house. When you return, we can deliver her safely to the hotel. I'm sure they'll be glad to be of assistance until she can wire for funds."

Bert nodded in agreement. "I'll go directly, boss. Won't be long."

Steven motioned Margaret to a bench on the platform and sat beside her. There they waited until Bert left the platform and headed into the darkness toward the

Double E buggy. Then Margaret turned to Steven, looking up imploringly at him.

For a moment, he was completely lost in the deep blue eyes. He searched for a color to describe them to himself but failed miserably. They were much darker than a summer sky and yet not as dark as the midnight sky. Something in between, something indefinable.

Her hand rested on his chest. He could see the little pulse beating in the smooth column of her neck. She was an amazing presence, and for a moment he was completely enthralled.

Then she spoke and once more her exotic voice captured him. "You have saved me once, Mr. Peyton, and I owe you my life."

He shook his head, denying her words, but she persisted.

"Now I must throw myself on your mercy again. I need your help, and I need it desperately."

The words seemed practiced, almost artificial, and yet her fear was real, so intense that for a moment Steven was caught up in the drama. "I'll do what I can to help you," he said.

"Then please, I beg of you, do not send me to the hotel. Those men—"

"Those men," he repeated, "are no longer in Cheyenne, Miss Carlton."

"How do we know that?" she asked. "Did you see them get on the train. Did you?" Her voice was frantic now, her eyes fearful.

He answered slowly, carefully. "No, I didn't, but I expect that was their intention, and the train was moving slowly when it pulled out of the station."

"But suppose they had no intention of reboarding the train?" she asked him.

"Why would you suppose that, Miss Carlton?"

"Because they want me dead."

"Miss Carlton—"

"It's true," she said. "We did *not* see them get on the train. They could still be here, and as long as they are loose my life is in danger."

Steven looked down into the lovely upturned face, wishing he could read the truth there. His initial belief that the woman was playing some kind of game with him persisted, but her seriousness threw him off. He didn't know what to think.

"Miss Carlton, you are making a very sweeping accusation. I can't believe you—"

"But you must believe me, Mr. Peyton. You must. I am telling the truth when I say that I'm being hunted. I need a place to hide, at least for a few days. If you turn me away, my blood will be on your hands."

Steven raised quizzical eyebrows. This was far more than he had bargained for, but certainly no more than he was capable of handling.

"Then who am I to turn down a lady in distress?" he asked. "Of course I'll offer you 'sanctuary,' Miss Carlton, for as long as you need it. My ranch is almost a fortress, and I assure you that you'll be safe there."

They heard the buggy approaching then, Bert's voice speaking low to the horses.

"Bless you, Mr. Peyton," Margaret said softly. "You will never regret this."

"I hope not, Miss Carlton. I surely hope not."

Chapter Two

She had never been in a land like this before. Undulating green hills rolled toward purple-hued mountains capped with white, for even now, in the early summer, snow remained on the highest elevations.

As far as the eye could see stretched a deep blue cloudless sky just beginning to darken in the late afternoon. It seemed to be grander and more vast than any sky she'd every seen, and Margaret had traveled across continents on her journey to this strange land called Wyoming.

She pushed open the heavy shutters of her bedroom window on the second floor of the rambling ranch house to get a more panoramic view of the land around her. The windowsill was so wide that she could sit on it and contemplate the scene.

Closer to the house, neat outbuildings of timber and stone clustered near fenced corrals where a dozen or more horses whinnied and stomped, crowded against the rails and then began to gallop along the fence, manes and tails flying in the breeze. She watched them for a long time, enthralled by their sleek coats, which lathered as they ran, kicking up their heels, playfully and yet with such determination that Margaret felt her-

self shiver as she watched. She had never seen so many
horses so close, and their raw power captured her attention; their massive strength gave her a kind of perverse thrill, their unbridled wildness calling to something untamed within her.

It was with great difficulty that she tore her eyes away
from the scene and looked again toward the mountains
as the sun began its descent, turning the green hills gold
and then orange and then magenta. It was a violent
sunset that blazed across the hills and plains, almost as
if daring the daylight to try to survive in its wake.

Darkness won over light as, quickly and with little
fanfare, night fell. The horses ceased their galloping and
moved toward the barn, anticipating feeding time,
Margaret supposed. She could hear the sound of a lone
cowboy, calling in a plaintive voice, beckoning to them.

Then all was quiet.

She moved away from the window, hugging herself,
for it had suddenly grown cool, and her cotton camisole and petticoats provided little warmth.

She was still standing in the middle of the large room
when she heard the sound of a knock. She turned toward the heavy oak door.

She couldn't ask him in yet. She was barely covered
up, but just the thought of seeing him caused her pulse
to quicken and her breath to catch in her throat.

Nonsense, Margaret said to herself. It wasn't like her
to behave in the manner of a silly schoolgirl. This was
nothing more than her reaction to a strange new place,
one she must get used to quickly if she meant to succeed. She crossed to the four-poster bed, pulled off the
quilt and wrapped it around her bare shoulders. Then
she was ready for him.

"Come in," she said, taking a deep breath, forcing a smile and putting aside the thoughts that had so confused her.

The door opened slowly to reveal the housekeeper standing on the threshold.

Margaret breathed a sigh, whether of relief or exasperation she wasn't sure. "Please, come in," she repeated.

The housekeeper did as she was told, stepping briskly, a broad smile on her face. "Good evening, ma'am," she said, giving a nod of greeting.

"Oh, Mrs. Laker," Margaret managed, "I see that you have my dress."

"Yes, and I've done the best I could with it. Mended the torn seam and sponged it off." She placed the navy blue traveling costume across the bed.

"I'm very appreciative, Mrs. Laker—"

"Faye," the woman corrected. "We don't stand on formality around here." She was short and almost square with a no-nonsense kind of face and sharp brown eyes. Her gray hair was pulled back straight from a high forehead.

Margaret expected that the brown eyes missed very little, and she found herself blanching momentarily under the intensity of their gaze. She willed herself to relax, aware that the circumstances of her arrival at the ranch would look suspicious to anyone, but of course the woman knew nothing about her. Faye could be handled.

Margaret smiled graciously. "Well, Faye, I certainly appreciate your going to so much trouble for me." Generosity of spirit could work wonders; and it did. "The lovely breakfast, cleaning my dress..."

"Why it was no trouble at all," the woman declared. "Now why don't you have a warm bath before dinner?" She nodded toward the adjoining door. "I had hot water brought up for you."

Yes, Margaret thought to herself. Faye could be handled.

"Dinner will be served when Steven and the men return."

"Return? Mr. Peyton has been out today?" Margaret asked.

"Why, yes. He was out on the range at first light this morning."

"I see." Margaret thought of her hours in the high four-poster bed, sleeping off the exhaustion and tension of the past day and felt guilty.

"But don't you worry. He needs less sleep than most people. Now, get to your bath," she advised, "before the water gets cold."

Margaret did as she was told. If it took being cared for and babied like a child to win over the housekeeper, so be it, Margaret thought after Faye left. Dropping the quilt, she stepped out of her chemise and padded to the bathroom. She would find the housekeeper a wealth of information.

Sighing, Margaret slipped into the warm water, settled down and let it cover the whiteness of her breasts. She breathed deeply, leaning her head back against the cool porcelain. She needed to remain calm and keep her wits about her tonight.

So far she had done well, she congratulated herself. She was here, at the ranch, a guest in his house. Tonight they would spend together. She reached for the sponge and began to wash, looking forward to the evening with a kind of nervous anticipation. Steven Peyton had been more than she bargained for, and that in itself was exciting. She could feel something going on between them, currents of unspoken emotion.

She was walking a fine line, however. She was not supposed to get involved, but he *was* rather irresistible. She could play the game and still achieve her purpose, she reassured herself, soaping the sponge and lathering her long legs thoughtfully. She had only to be careful and very, very clever.

She was rinsing off when she heard a sound from behind the door, faint but unmistakable, someone in her room!

It must be the housekeeper, she assured herself, calling out, "Faye...Mrs. Laker."

There was no answer. Margaret remained still, holding her breath, straining, listening. If it wasn't Mrs. Laker, then who could it be?

She stood up, grabbed a towel and tiptoed to the door. Slowly pushing it open a crack, she looked into the room. It was empty. She stepped inside, noticed that the shutters on her window were loose and crossed to fasten them, convincing herself that must have been the noise she heard.

She glanced around, noticing that everything seemed just as she'd left it, and then quickly checked her hiding place under the mattress—the daguerreotype was still there. Thoughtfully she began to get dressed.

Steven Peyton stood beside the tall marble mantelpiece in the living room of the Double E. He was very fond of the huge room that was as grand as the rest of the ranch house. It suited him perfectly, and he felt comfortable here, even though the house had been built by a man he had called father but to whom he was not related.

They could have been father and son, however, so similar were their tastes. The high-ceilinged rooms, heavily beamed, were just as Steven would have planned them. The decor was a mixture of western and European style that blended the diverse tastes and different backgrounds of his mother and stepfather. Some might find it incongruous—indeed, he suspected that many did—to see a stag's head over the fireplace near a delicate ormolu clock, a sheepskin rug in front of a brocade sofa. For Steven it was a satisfying mix, one in which he took great pride.

"Faye said you wanted to see me." Bert stood at the door, worn cowboy hat in hand. "So here I am, boss."

Steven smiled at the moniker that Bert, who was more like a relative than a hired hand, seemed to delight in using.

"Come on in, Bert," Steven said.

Bert strode into the room and down the three steps to where Steven stood. Then, imitating his boss's stance, he leaned against the mantelpiece.

"How about a drink, Bert?"

"I'll wait till later, boss. Need to get cleaned up first."

"Well, this won't take a minute. I have a job for you."

Bert waited.

"I want you to ride into town tonight and send a telegram for me. You can pick up the reply tomorrow."

Bert shuffled uneasily. Although he did not often question his boss, he wasn't much for these kinds of errands, which seemed to be more suited to one of the young cowhands. "Boss, there's five hundred head of cattle got to be moved down from the north pasture tomorrow..."

"Let someone else move them. I need you for this." Steven pulled a handwritten note from his pocket. "It's extremely important, and you are the only one I can trust it to."

Bert's eyes quickened with interest. He took the note, read it and then nodded. "Count on me, boss. I'll take care of this little problem."

"Good, and not a word to anyone. That means Faye."

Bert laughed as he headed back up the steps. "Especially Faye, boss."

Steven smiled to himself. He was lucky to have such a loyal staff. They were his friends, actually, Bert and Faye. They had been here at Double E long before Steven arrived. They had been devoted to the place, and with his arrival became devoted to him.

Steven moved aside the fireplace screen, struck a match and lit the kindling. Then he went to the sideboard and poured himself a brandy. He had just replaced the bottle and put the snifter to his lips when he sensed her presence.

Without turning, he lifted the glass from his lips and held it high, above eye level. The brown liquid swirled and then settled, catching her reflection as she stood behind him at the top of the steps.

Lowering the glass, he looked toward her. She moved into the light, her head held regally high, her golden hair a halo. The vision caused him to catch his breath. Indeed, she was a breathtaking woman.

"Miss Carlton, you look refreshed. And very lovely."

She drifted down the stairs, crossed the room and held out her hand.

He brought it to his lips briefly before stepping away. The light of the fire played along the creaminess of her skin.

Referring back to his greeting, she said softly, "I understand from Faye that formalities do not count here. So I am Margaret."

"Of course." Steven bowed his head slightly to acknowledge her remark. "Margaret," he repeated. "Would you like a glass of wine?"

"That sounds quite nice," she said in a voice low and husky.

Steven found its quaint phrasing and vaguely foreign overtones quite intriguing. Her skin felt cool as she reached for the wineglass and their fingertips touched.

She didn't seem to notice. "What elegant hospitality you display, Steven, for someone you scarcely know, someone who has taken advantage of you." She took a sip of the wine, let it linger on her tongue, looking at him over the rim of the crystal glass.

"I may not know you yet but I hope to soon, Margaret," he said. "As for your taking advantage of me, I certainly don't feel put upon." He smiled at her.

She returned the smile and followed it with a bell-like laugh. "You are very kind, Steven." She said his name slowly, savoring the taste of it on her lips.

"And you're very mysterious . . . Margaret." He, on the other hand, spoke her name as if he didn't quite believe that it belonged to her. "As for what happened last night, do you want me to contact the sheriff?"

"No," she said quickly before recovering and restating her response. "Not now, please." She turned to him and put her fingers lightly on his lips. Her touch was soft and far from offensive in spite of its unexpected boldness.

"Perhaps later when I feel more settled, and able to discuss what happened."

"Of course." He seemed constantly to be repressing a smile, and he did so once again.

"I had almost forgotten the horror of last night," she said, "and I do not think I can face telling it over again to a stranger." She seemed to feel it was necessary to explain herself once more, and Steven was willing to let her do so without reminding her that *he* had been a stranger less than twenty-four hours earlier.

As soon as her position was established, Margaret changed the subject abruptly. "Faye tells me that you had very little rest today."

"Enough," he said.

"I know a great deal of work is necessary to maintain a ranch of this size. Or should I say a 'spread?' Is that not what it's called out West?"

"By some," he replied. She was all innocence and charm and humor. He found her fascinating but didn't intend to fall under her spell, and particularly not when it was beginning to sound like she was interrogating him.

"Has it been in your family long, this huge domain?"

Yes, there it was. He could answer her politely but give little information, or he could tell her everything she wanted to know. There would be no harm in that, and yet Steven decided against it for whatever reason.

"I inherited the ranch from Virgil Peyton, my stepfather. Over the ten years since his death I've added to it, made some improvements...."

"Oh, you are far too modest, I am sure." Steven smiled again, not even bothering to acknowledge the remark.

Margaret moved around the room, stopping to admire, to touch, items that interested her, a leather-bound book, an objet d'art. She paused before a table crowded with photographs, looking up from them to Steven. "You were not born here?" she asked.

He shook his head. "No." He could very easily have told her that his mother was a European immigrant, that his father had died when he was an infant, and that his mother had moved to Chicago to become a companion to an older woman, who happened to be Virgil Peyton's aunt. "My mother immigrated to America and met my stepfather in Chicago," was all he deigned to say.

"And it was love at first sight." She picked up a small color miniature of a handsome couple framed in heavy, ornate silver.

"Something like that," Steven said.

"You do not believe in love at first sight?" she teased.

"What they had was very special," Steven evaded. "Most of us are not so lucky."

"Their pictures?" she asked of the miniature.

Steven nodded, and Margaret continued her slow, ritualistic surveillance of the room, pausing before a series of watercolors. "These are charming," she said.

Steven took a sip of his drink, withholding comment.

"They are signed E.E."

"Elyse Elinor. Double E. When they married, my stepfather renamed the ranch for her."

Margaret studied the paintings carefully. "There were several in my room, too. The landscape looks like the Rocky Mountains, and yet..."

"Not the Rockies. Judging from the chalets and castles, wouldn't you say the Alps?" he asked dryly. "She missed her homeland, and these paintings were her way of keeping in touch." He didn't choose to name his mother's homeland.

Nor did Margaret ask, saying only, "She never went back."

"No." He couldn't understand Margaret Carlton's surprising interest in his mother, and he wondered what information she was after. He intended to tell her less than she wanted to know. After all, everything about Margaret Carlton was a mystery and contradiction. For no other reason than inborn suspicion and instinct, he would keep his mother's background obscure.

"Family histories can be more interesting if they're not your own," he said. "The Carlton family for instance—"

Before she could answer, Faye appeared in the doorway. "Dinner's ready. Mountain trout, just like you asked for." Faye smiled her now-familiar wide grin and gestured toward the dining room.

"Open a bottle of champagne, will you, Faye? I think Margaret would enjoy it," Steven said, holding out his arm to his guest.

Margaret took it and walked beside him into the dining room, very pleased with herself.

The feeling of satisfaction and security lasted through the meal but not much longer. Everything began to fall apart as they sat before the fire after dinner, drinking the rich, thick coffee Faye had brewed for them.

"This is very different from what I expected," Margaret commented, not thinking that he would hone in on that seemingly innocent remark until the damage was already done.

Steven was immediately alert; in fact, he had been all evening, his senses alive, ready. Now was the time. He got up, a dark shadow silhouetted against the glowing fire. "And just what did you expect?"

Margaret, too, had become alert. She had no intention of playing into his hands. There was only a moment's hesitation before she answered. "When you said that you lived on a ranch, I imagined something rustic, a kind of prairie existence. *This* was not what I expected," she said, smiling over her coffee cup, satisfied that she had weathered the storm.

"I see." There was a dangerous quirk to his eyebrow. "I didn't realize that in your precarious situation last evening you had much time to think."

Ignoring both his comment and its tone, she rose from the sofa with a smooth, graceful movement and stepped toward him. "Here at the Double E, it is continental, so charming. I cannot believe how lucky I am to have found refuge in so lovely a place—with so understanding a host."

She touched the gilt clock on the mantel. "I imagine this was your mother's, brought with her from—where did you say she emigrated from?"

"I didn't." There was a hard edge to his voice, and Margaret knew immediately that she had asked one too many questions.

Her face changed, softened, lost its curious look. Their eyes met; hers were limpid, dark pools of concern in the half-light as she attempted to survive through innocence. "Is something wrong, Steven?"

"Wrong?" he repeated, his mouth in a cynical twist. "Only that I find it strange to spend dinner with a lovely woman whose main purpose seems to be finding out everything about me while revealing nothing about herself."

"But I am interested," she insisted.

Steven put down his coffee cup and took a step toward her. In just a few moments they seemed to have moved from friendliness to confrontation. They were facing off, and she became immediately on the alert.

Steven seemed to back off a little, but his eyes held hers as he spoke. "I hardly think dinner conversation about my life on the Double E or my exploits during the Civil War are that fascinating to a lady of your obvious sophistication."

"On the contrary," she said.

He looked down into her eyes and was for a moment spellbound. Then his eyes dropped to her lips, which were full and inviting, wetted by a quick movement of her tongue. He looked away.

But she moved again, back into his vision. He couldn't seem to avoid her. "On the contrary," she repeated. "I find everything about you . . . fascinating." She lifted her hand as if to touch his chest.

His own reached out and grabbed her wrist.

She had no time to even register her surprise.

"The game has continued quite long enough," he said. "Who the hell are you, lady, and what's going on here?"

Astounded, Margaret gasped for an answer. "I—"

"Yes?" he asked, holding on to her wrist more tightly.

"Please, you are hurting me." She twisted in his grasp. "Let me go."

Her eyes blazed up at his, and he read anger in them, determination, and perhaps just a shading of fear. It was the fear that made him loosen his grip slightly. "I'll let go when you tell me the truth about why you're here."

"I have told you. Someone is after me..."

He laughed mirthlessly. "Yeah, I know. Men want to murder you." He looked directly into her eyes as he spoke. "You avoided my questions during dinner, but you can't avoid them now, Margaret, if indeed that is your name. Assuming your life is in danger and you're hiding from that danger in my house, I need the truth."

"I will tell you if you let me go," she bargained.

"No," he replied.

She had an immediate response. "I knew very well that there was danger outside, but I did not expect to find it in this house."

He had to admire her. She was going to bluff and fight to the end, but he wasn't going to make it easy. "Why did those men go after you?" he asked again.

"I have information. They want it. They will go to any lengths—"

"Such as attacking you?"

"Yes."

He released her then with a half smile. "And these mysterious assassins also stole your money?"

"Yes," she said, pulling away from him and turning her back. "You were there." She rubbed her wrist. "You saw what happened."

"I saw what you wanted me to see, Miss Carlton." There was a sarcastic edge to his voice. "If your attackers had really wanted to kill you, I couldn't have stopped them. The fight was too damned easy."

"Surely you underestimate yourself." She turned back to look at him, her color high, her eyes flashing, on the offensive again. It seemed to be her best weapon. "I resent your insinuation, Mr. Peyton."

He noted that she had become as formal as he.

"I believe I'll retire now," she told him haughtily.

"I don't think so." He moved between her and the door. "Not until you explain the five hundred dollars I found in your purse. Or did the attackers leave you spending money?"

"How did you know—"

"How do you think?"

"You were in my room?" she asked, remembering, knowing the answer. The momentary flicker of anxiety in her face was replaced almost at once with one of feigned outrage.

"*My* guest room," he corrected. "And yes, I was there. Don't bother to look horrified, Miss Carlton. You played me for a sucker. That was a mistake. I believe the time is right for an explanation. There was no attack, was there?"

"Yes, but it was not as I described. I am desperate, a woman fighting for her life. Please believe that." Her eyes seemed to grow larger in her now pale face, her voice became tinged with the edge of a tremor.

"I'm afraid I have difficulty doing so, even though you *are* very convincing," he said wryly.

"Please, I need to sit down. I feel faint," she said, sinking onto the sofa.

Ignoring the theatrics, Steven went to the bar and poured her a brandy, which she drained as he stood over her.

"Are you going to remain standing," she asked, "looking down on me like a judge in a courtroom?"

"I believe so," he responded easily. "Now, talk to me, Miss Carlton, or whoever you are, and tell me what the hell is going on before I really lose my temper."

She looked up at him, her eyes narrowed, measuring. Then she shrugged. "I believe you have me, Mr. Peyton. I am not Margaret Carlton," she told him. "My name is Margarette Oblansky, Countess Oblansky, and I am running away from my husband."

Steven let out a deep breath. "Oh, I see."

"Count Rikard Oblansky is a cruel man, a harsh man. I could not remain with him. It was impossible." She raised her hands to him as if in supplication.

Steven's face was impassive.

"To escape it was necessary for me to assume a new identity," she went on. "I thought it would be possible to reach my friends in San Francisco, others from my country, but he had me followed, and those men were trying to kidnap me, to take me back to him."

"Not very successful kidnappers," Steven commented.

"You are right," she said disarmingly. "Rikard did not get his money's worth this time, and he likes to get his money's worth. He will be very angry."

Steven folded his arms across his chest and looked down at her, trying to gauge the truthfulness of her story. She seemed sincere, but with this one, who could tell?

"Then you appeared," she continued, "and I thought perhaps if you could hide me for a short time we could throw his henchmen off my trail. I took a chance, not knowing you, not knowing how you would feel about hiding another man's wife."

"Let's just say I'm not called upon to do so often." His smile was sardonic.

"I also did not know how you would feel about taking on an enemy as strong as the count. If he finds out where I am . . ." Her voice trailed off.

"I have no fear of your count, or of anyone else for that matter," Steven told her. "I have loyal hands who can handle guns, but I don't expect it will come to that. Do you?"

"No. . .no. He is more. . .subtle, but believe me, I am afraid of him. So once again, I must throw myself on your mercy. I need more time. And I do have money," she offered.

He stared at her for a long moment, aware that as her emotions became more intense, her accent shifted slightly, becoming studied and formal, even a bit theatrical. He knew there was a clue to the countess, not only in what she was saying but in how she said it. There was much about her story that still did not ring true, but something was going on with her. She was afraid, and for some damned reason he couldn't understand, she had chosen his house as her retreat. And his silence obviously concerned her.

"Yes, I lied to you," she admitted. "I understand if you do not trust me, but I have no one else to turn to. No one." Her look was long and intense; a trace of tears glimmered in her eyes.

Steven sighed and reached out a hand to her. Obviously the game was not over. He rather relished the continuance of it. "Of course you can stay here, Margarette. Or should I say Countess?"

"Margarette is fine. I am deeply indebted."

"Now we need to get one thing clear. This is not an indefinite invitation. I expect plans to be underway immediately to get you to those friends in Frisco."

Her lips curved in a perfect smile. "A few more days is all that I need, Steven. Thank you."

She stood up, quite steady on her feet now, he noticed, and put her hand against the rough fabric of his jacket. She was a woman who did not hesitate to touch, and certainly that didn't displease him. He covered her hand with his own, capturing it there just above his heart.

They were very close, and he could see the rapid rise and fall of her breasts and the little pulse that beat gently in her throat. The heated anger of the past few minutes was gone, but something still lingered between them, a residual emotion, a tension that was papable.

He could feel the warmth of her breath and smell the heady scent of her perfume. Their eyes met and held. He felt the pressure of her hand against his chest, and he could swear he heard the accelerated beating of her heart. Or was it his? His skin felt hot and tight, and for a moment he was lost in a dizzying desire for her. He wanted to kiss her, and he knew if he did, he'd never want to stop.

She raised her hand to his face and touched his cheek. Her fingers were warm and soft against his skin. "Thank you, Steven. You will not be sorry."

He reached for her then, but she slipped from his arms, and he watched her retreating shadow cross the room and ascend the stairs. It was over for now. Steven could feel the tension slowly draining from his body. He should have been pleased to have gotten the story out of her, but somehow he was strangely discontent.

Margarette Oblansky was many things—beautiful, seductive, intelligent, manipulative and very probably conniving. Yet one thing was clear: he wanted her and he wanted her badly. And she was a married woman. Or so she said. He crossed the room, poured a stiff brandy and then sank into the sofa where he remained for a long time, watching the flames burn down to glowing embers.

The next day Steven left the ranch house at sunrise and by noon had ridden his hands and himself to the edge of exhaustion. The cattle drive from the north pasture had been rife with the usual problems, hauling a calf out of a ditch, mending a broken fence, rounding up strays that had wandered for miles, splinting the leg of a cowboy who'd gotten thrown, all of which Steven usually took in stride. But not today.

He knew the men were cursing behind his back because he was working them so hard and fast, finding fault when there was none, and making unreasonable demands. They were right, and he knew it. Usually evenhanded and fair, Steven was being short-tempered and perverse, and he didn't give a damn. His head throbbed with an unaccustomed hangover, and his body ached with frustration and an undefined need. So he rode roughshod over anyone who crossed paths with him.

Bert found him in the corral, where he was administering a tongue-lashing to an unfortunate stable boy who hadn't cooled down the horses properly. When Bert rode up, the boy wisely took the opportunity to vanish into the tack room.

Bert eased back in the saddle and took off his hat, which he beat against his leg to knock off the latest layer of dust before settling it back on his head. "Hear tell you're mighty ornery today, boss, like an old gelding with a burr under his saddle."

Steven looked up and smiled for the first time that day. "I am ornery, Bert. Let's blame it on the trip and too much brandy last night and a certain mysterious lady who's living in my house."

Bert pulled a folded yellow piece of paper from his pocket. "Maybe not so mysterious now, boss."

Minutes later Steven was in the big Double E kitchen. It was redolent with the odor of baking, one tray of biscuits in the oven, another covered with a damp cloth, rising on the counter. Faye kept one eye on the pot of soup that bubbled on the stove as she rolled out dough for her pies. When Steven came in, she barely looked up.

"Where is she?" he asked unceremoniously.

That got Faye's attention. Usually Steven settled at the table, poured a cup of coffee and pinched off a chunk of pie dough to munch on, just like when he was a little boy. But now he was standing, muscles tensed, eyes narrowed, the look on his face hard and unsmiling.

"I kept an eye on her like you told me. This morning I helped her with something to wear. We altered one of my old Sunday dresses—"

"What did you talk about?" he interrupted.

"The house, your parents, your childhood. She asked a whole lot of questions, but I was vague just like you told me. She thinks she's won me over, and I let her think it," Faye said proudly. "Then, praise God, she decided to go upstairs and take a nap, and I was able to get on with my work."

"She's up there now, alone?"

"Far's I know, unless there's someone else living in the house I haven't heard about. Steven, don't you want one of these biscuits—"

But he had already left the room. Noiselessly, like a great cat, he climbed the stairs two at a time, his footsteps muffled on the carpeted treads.

The door at the top of the stairs was closed. Steven paused to listen. Silence. Pushing open the door, he found, not to his surprise, that the room was empty.

Quietly he moved down the hall to his own room. The door was cracked. He could catch only a partial view inside, but he didn't need to see. He heard her, quietly opening and closing his bureau drawers.

He took a deep breath and pushed open the door. She was wearing only her camisole and petticoat. Her feet were bare, and her hair hung loose around her shoulders, caressing the whiteness of her throat and chest. Her breasts were full and rounded, and through the thin material of the camisole he could see the round buds of her nipples. Her filmy petticoat clung provocatively and showed clearly the outline of her calves and thighs.

The woman was rummaging through his bureau, ransacking his personal effects, and here he was, looking at her as if nothing else in the world mattered. And when she looked up and saw him standing there, she met his gaze boldly and directly, making no attempt to hide her purpose or cover her body.

They stood for half a minute, watching each other, waiting.

Steven moved first. In three steps he was across the room beside her. "Waiting for me, Countess?"

"Yes. That's exactly what I'm doing." Her voice was low and husky, and without a moment's hesitation he reached for her.

Chapter Three

It was the last thing he'd thought would happen, and there was no rationale for it. She was a liar, a spy, certainly a mystery to him, most likely a woman of deceit. Yet his desire for her had been there since the first moment he'd seen her on the train, held in abeyance, waiting for the moment. And clearly the moment was now.

He reached out, grabbed her and pulled her close, taking her roughly into his arms. This was what she was here for, what she wanted. She'd said so herself.

He tightened his arms around her and drew her closer, crushing her in his embrace with a need that approached violence. Then suddenly another feeling came over him, and he paused for a moment, holding her at arm's length, looking down at her. He realized then that she was just as he'd imagined, her body lush with breasts ripe and full, waist soft and inviting, hips curvaceous, legs long and slim.

He was attracted to her as he'd never remembered being attracted to any woman. He touched her face, almost gently, before bending his head to find her lips.

He felt her start to pull away, and then he held tighter, his need greater than before. He would have her, and he would have her now.

She struggled, but his grip was too strong. One of his hands held the nape of her neck while the other pulled against the small of her back. His lips found hers, his hand twisting in her hair, holding her tightly against him while he kissed her deeply and thoroughly.

She could feel the rough cotton of his shirt against her breasts, the material abrading her tender nipples, which swelled and tightened under the pressure.

It was too late now. It had been too late from the moment he'd discovered her there in his room. She'd had no choice but to say that she was waiting for him, to imply that this was what she wanted. There would be no escape. She could have run then, or tried to, but he would have stopped her easily, and even if he hadn't, what could she do, what could she say? There was no explanation possible, not that this man would ever believe.

And then this, his holding her, causing a feeling of desire to quicken deep inside, a desire she had long thought was dead. Vainly she fought against her instincts, just as she fought her overpowering and irrational need for this man. She must try once again to stop it from happening.

"Steven, please," she murmured, managing to pull her lips away from his.

"You said you were waiting for me, Countess, and I must take you at your word." He pulled her close again, looking down, his eyes burning into hers. "I am not letting you go. Not yet."

His mouth was on hers again, hot and burning, his tongue seeking, touching, teasing. What happened then was like awakening from a deep sleep as the layers of her defense melted, dissolved around her. And in that awakening she responded to him, tightening her arms around the hardness of his muscular back, pushing her hips against his. The struggle with her conscience was over. Need won against convention. She melted into his arms.

His lips moved from her mouth to her chin and along the column of her neck. With a deep trembling sigh, she dropped her head back to expose more of her throat for his caresses. Steven slid his hand from her waist across the ridges of her ribs and cupped her breast. He rubbed his palm insinuatingly against the hardness of her nipple, and she felt her response tingling down deep in the pit of her stomach.

He drew back again, looking at her with green eyes mocking, lips curved into a satisfied smile. "It's good between us, isn't it, Countess? Just as it was meant to be." And with that he scooped her up in his arms and in two long strides was at his bed. He dropped her onto it, unceremoniously, startling her, making her wish again that she had been more circumspect. But then he lay beside her and was gentle once more, kissing her forehead, her cheek, her chin, tracing the lines of her face with his lips.

As he moved against her she could hear the quick intake of his breath, feel the wild pounding of his heart, and she knew that his rhythms were matched by hers. He ran his fingertips along the curve of her breasts, watching their rapid rise and fall before reaching to unbutton the tiny pearls of her chemise.

In one final gesture of denial, she raised her hand to stop him, but he grabbed her hand, forced it down and placed her fingers against him. She felt the male hardness of him, the arrogant need that boasted of his desire for her.

"I want you, Countess. I want you, and I shall have you." The words were defiant but his voice was husky, his breath hot against her ear. "Say you want me, too," he urged, pressing her back onto the bed. "Just tell the truth for once and say it...."

She hesitated for a long moment, trying to make sense of what was happening, trying still to fight against the dizzying spiral of desire that was enveloping her, making her forget her purpose—who she was and most of all who he was.

His touch burned along the sensitive nerve endings of her skin, urging her response and getting it as her body tingled and came alive for the first time in so very long. And his kisses, his mouth on hers, ravaging, seeking, made her lose all sense of what was right and what was wrong.

"Say it," he urged. "Tell me what you want."

She was somehow incapable of speaking the words, but she knew only too well how she felt, and she told him not with her lips but with her body. Her hands tangled in the silky texture of his hair, roamed across his face and to his chest, struggling with the buttons of his shirt, pulling and tugging, not caring if she tore it.

She knew only one thing now, that she wanted to be part of him, and while she was unable to tell him so, she pushed her body against his and held him close for a long time, until at last he drew away and pulled off her chemise, parting it from her feverish flesh so that he could kiss her breasts, use his mouth to tease her, to suck her nipples until she cried out with pleasure and frustration.

The rest of her clothes were bunched around her, her hair in a tangle on the pillow. She didn't care. All she could think of was holding him, touching him and at last possessing him. Boldly she fought his clothes, pushing away his shirt to bare his chest, tugging at his heavy belt, rubbing against the fabric of his trousers.

There was excitement in the struggle and the striving, and she could feel the tension building inside her, a wild drumming like the roaring of a river down a narrow mountain gorge or the thunderous rhythm of a train hurtling through a long dark tunnel in search of daylight.

At last their clothes were removed, tossed onto the floor, and flesh met flesh with an unrelenting urgency that cried out to be satiated. Her breasts were crushed against his pounding chest, her abdomen pushed against his manhood; their legs became entwined, and their mouths explored and then drank the essence one of the other.

"You're beautiful," he whispered. "So beautiful. The most desirable woman . . ."

She drew his mouth down on her. She didn't want to talk; she wanted to feel, to come alive beneath his touch, to give to him and become a part of him. She refused to think about the madness of what she was doing. For once she wanted to live for the moment, this glorious sun-washed moment.

Her tongue touched his, and she heard herself moan, call his name. "Steven, Steven." She repeated it again and again, denying that she eschewed words, for these were not words. His name was something else, something more, the answer to her need.

Steven slid his hand along her thigh, caressing her, arousing her until she was ready—and he seemed to know it—for his fingers to slip inside her waiting softness. She arched beneath him, begging him with her body, showing him just what she wanted now. She was prepared for him, eager and ready.

He slid into her, and for a moment the world stopped. Her eyes, open wide in wonder and disbelief, looked up at him and saw his face poised above her, his eyes dark with passion, unreadable.

He was a stranger, a man she hardly knew. And yet in a way she did know him. In a way, she had known him forever. But not like this, never had she imagined that she would know him like this.

Forgetting that, forgetting all else, she arched upward toward him and reached out, embracing him totally, digging her fingers into his back, urging him on to what could no longer be denied by either of them.

They made love fiercely and passionately, moving together as if this had happened to them a thousand times, and yet awed by the newness and wonder of it. The way their bodies fit together was a perfection of unity. She threw back her head and called out his name again, her answer to his long-ago question. Yes, she wanted him! Never had she wanted anyone more.

Letting herself ride on the long wave of spiraling pleasure, she dug her fingernails into his skin. Yet Steven felt nothing but the joy of her, her softness, her sensuality, the way she enveloped him and drew him on, further and further into the deep abyss of passion. It had begun roughly, almost defiantly, this need for her, but now it was something else, something more. It was as if she had become the only woman he'd ever wanted or needed, the compilation of all the women he'd ever dreamed of in his lifetime.

He moved with a frenzied passion, a wild rush toward release that he both wanted and dreaded. He wanted to dominate her with his body, to make her cry

out for him and call his name once more. At the same
time he wanted the pleasure of her never to end. Her
hands kneaded his shoulders, her legs arched around his
back as with a wild cry of surrender he thrust explo-
sively into her, reached for her, holding her, covering
her passion-damp body with his own.

They lay still for a long time, not speaking, listening
to the rhythm of their hearts and the slowing of their
breathing. He reached for a quilt at the foot of the bed
and drew it over them.

Her eyes were closed, but he didn't have to see them
to remember those beautiful blue eyes as clear and lu-
minous as a summer sky. He gave a rueful smile to
himself, knowing what she was and who she was and yet
wanting her even now. He propped himself up on his
elbow and looked down at her. Her cheeks were flushed,
her hair was in bright disarray around her face. He
couldn't resist sliding his free hand beneath the cover to
feel the smoothness of her shoulder, the firmness of her
breast. Her nipples were still hard, and he ran his finger lightly across one of them, smiling again as she
smiled, eyes closed but with him in her satiated desire
that he knew could still be aroused. It was something
between them that was unexplainable and had nothing
to do with who she was.

Indeed, he had no idea who she was. But he knew one
thing well enough. He knew that he was a fool. What
had happened between them only complicated the situation.

As he watched, her breathing became deep and even,
and he knew that she was sleeping. He thought of waking her, decided against it and carefully slipped out of
bed. Putting on his clothes, he left his room, with the
woman—whoever she was—none the wiser.

* * *

When she awakened, turned over in his bed and reached for him, she spoke his name again, this time quietly, tenderly. Discovering that he was gone, she sat up and looked around the room. It was familiar to her, this room where he had discovered her only an hour or two ago. Why had he gone so soon after their lovemaking ended? Was he sorry about what had happened? Surely not. It had been wonderful for her, and for him. She was certain of that. Yet he had left her here alone.

Uneasy and confused, she got up, pulled on her skimpy clothes and tiptoed to the door. She opened it carefully, looked down the long hall in both directions and then slipped out, quickly making her way toward her room.

She had just finished dressing when she heard the tap at her door. Relieved that he had returned to her, she called out for him to come in. The door opened wide, and he stood there, tall and handsome. He, too, had changed clothes and was dressed more formally. She couldn't help thinking how regal he looked, the epitome of who he really was. If only she could tell him. But not yet. The time was not right.

"Steven, I—" She crossed to him, unsure of what she meant to say, but his upheld hand stemmed her words.

"Please, Countess," he said cynically. "Let's not play out this game any further."

She felt as if he had hit her. The words were so abrupt, so dismissive. "What do you mean?"

"What do I mean?" he repeated. "Well, let me tell you as plainly as possible. To begin with, you, dear Countess, are a married woman. The count would probably object to what so recently happened between us."

He watched her closely, noticing her face redden. At least, he thought, she had the good grace to blush.

"The count," she fumbled, "that was over long ago. Anything romantic between us." She looked across the room at him, for he had not moved another step from the doorway. Innocence radiated from her face. "This isn't usually... I mean, it's not like me to meet a man and..."

"Take him into your bed? Or shall we say, lure him into his own bed?"

"You are cruel, Steven," she said, so softly that her words were hardly audible. "You were as much responsible for what happened as I."

He started to interrupt, but she continued quickly, "And you know that what happened was special. Once we kissed, there was no way to stop it."

This time he did respond, dryly. "As if it were meant to be. Isn't that lucky, 'Countess'?"

"Lucky?" She seemed puzzled. And Steven thought he read nervousness in her expression, too.

"Yes," he replied, "lucky that I fell for you, lucky that it was so easy, lucky that I found you in my room."

"What do you mean?" She started to go to him, but the look on his face stopped her.

"Just a moment," he said. "I'm asking the questions." He still made no move toward her, but something in his voice seemed to threaten her, and she took a step backward. "Oh, you are good, I'll admit that. The damsel in distress, so mysterious, so beautiful, so alluring. That story about the count..."

"I won't listen to this," she said, "not from a man I've just made love to."

She marched forward then, determined to pass by him to the door, but his arm shot out and grabbed her elbow. "Don't try that imperial royal act with me, countess. Countess Oblansky," he added with an insolent drawl.

"That is my name," she snapped.

"Yeah, and I'm Ulysses S. Grant."

She raised her chin defiantly. "I have no idea what you are getting at, Steven, except that you're behaving very rudely. One would think you had never had this kind of encounter with a lady before—"

His grip tightened. "We can talk later about whether you're a lady or not. First I want to hear the truth, and I want to hear it now."

"I have told you the truth. I am Margarette Oblansky, and . . ."

He dropped her arm and pushed her away. "The hell you are. You, my dear, are Maggie Hanson. You're an actress out of Chicago. You booked the ticket in your own name, a real mistake. Then the next day you boarded the train as Countess Oblansky. Which, I must say, shows you are not as smart as you think."

Maggie wet her lips nervously with her tongue, her head spinning as she tried to collect her thoughts. She felt a terrible sense of dread and foreboding, but she forged ahead with her story. "That is preposterous, Steven. Ludicrous. If this is how you treat all the women you've shared a bed with, by insulting them, by calling them liars . . ."

He stepped back, smiling as he began to clap his hands slowly and rhythmically. "Nice try, Miss Hanson. Good performance, but righteous indignation doesn't work with me any more than the fake royalty routine."

He knew something, she realized, but how, what?

She did not have to wait long to find out. "I sent a telegram to Chicago—to the Pinkerton Agency. They're very proficient. In fact an old army buddy of mine runs the Chicago office. Everyone remembers a good-looking woman in the station that night. The clerk who sold you the ticket as Maggie Hanson remembers, and so does the porter on the train who was tipped so generously by the 'countess.' It wasn't hard to fit all the pieces of your rather crudely designed puzzle together. Now what I want to know is why you're here and what the hell you want from me. And this time I'd like the truth because whatever your scam, it isn't going to work. So tell me everything."

"Or what?" she countered. "You'll beat me? Tie me up in the barn? Burn me at the stake?" It was all bravado, but she could carry it off; she hadn't lost anything. Perhaps she'd even gained. He was clever, and that was good; in fact, it suited her perfectly to know that he was as clever as she.

With as much dignity as she could muster, she gathered herself to her full height, lifted her chin and marched right up to him. "I will be happy to talk about this with you, but first I would appreciate having something to eat," she said, "perhaps some tea. Downstairs. I still need a little time to complete my toilette so if you will excuse me." She moved past him to the open door and, gesturing for him to leave, turned away.

From the corner of her eye she caught the expression on his face as he walked out the door. It was one of grudging admiration.

Half an hour later, when she felt she had kept him waiting long enough, she went downstairs where she was surprised to find that Faye was indeed pouring tea from a small blue teapot on a ceramic tray.

She started to speak, but an abrupt, "Thank you, Faye," from Steven sent the housekeeper scurrying from the room, curiosity ablaze over what was going on.

Tension vibrated in the room like thunderclouds on a hot, humid summer day. Maggie was determined to ignore it as she reached for the single cup on the tray and took a sip of the steaming brew. Over the rim of the cup she looked at Steven. "You are not joining me?"

He crossed to the sideboard, removed the stopper from a crystal decanter and poured himself a drink. "I need something a little stronger," he said, holding up the glass in a mock toast to her.

Maggie settled herself carefully on the sofa and drank a little more of the tea. She could still feel the tension but she chose to ignore it. After all, she was an actress, and this was just another performance, on a different kind of stage, certainly, but she could handle it. The quivering inside her was no more than the butterflies she often felt before stepping in front of the footlights. She would pull it off; she had to.

"I'm waiting." Steven was cool eyed, expectant, standing there in his fresh clothes, the blue shirt and dark trousers he had changed into. The elegance of those clothes could not hide the memory of the physical man they covered. In fact, she could imagine his lean legs and hips, the breadth of his chest, the wide strength of his shoulders beneath the clothes; she could actually see the outline of the body she remembered so well.

She closed her eyes against the memory. It seemed like a dream, what had happened between them on that tumbled bed, and yet it had been real. She would carry the memory forever. Instinctively she ran her fingers across her lips, wondering if he could see the bruises left there by his kisses.

Obviously Steven had something else on his mind. He addressed her sarcastically. "Countess? Miss Carlton? Maggie? I am not sure which name to use."

"There is no such person as Countess Oblansky," she admitted. "Or Count Oblansky, for that matter."

"Well, a partial confession. Now what of Margaret Carlton?"

"Invented, also. You know my real name. It is Maggie Hanson. As you said, I am an actress. A very good one, which you failed to mention," she couldn't help adding.

"Can't imagine how I overlooked that obvious fact, but I certainly concede to it," he said, taking a long sip of his drink.

"But the . . . the deception was all for a reason," she assured him, "a very good reason."

Steven pulled a straight chair away from the wall and sat down on it. He kept his distance, but his gaze never left hers. "I'm still waiting," he said, "and frankly my patience is growing thin."

She started to speak, and then suddenly he seemed to change his mind, waving her quiet with a motion of his hand.

"No, let me," he said, tipping the chair back. "You boarded the train in Chicago pretending to be Countess Oblansky. You faked the attack in Cheyenne along with your henchmen, whoever they may be, so that I would come to your rescue. I complied. Then you inveigled your way into my house and insinuated your way into my bed. . . ." He saw a flush cross her face but chose not to acknowledge it. "Am I right so far?"

"All except the last part," she said in a strong, even voice. "I conspired to meet you. I had to meet you," she said, "and I had to see this house. As for my being in your room, it never occurred to me that you would come in from the ranch at that moment." She was doing well, and she knew it.

Then he spurred her onward. "And the rest?"

"I'm not proud of what happened after that. But it happened, and it cannot be undone." She looked down at her hands resting in her lap, amazed to see that they were trembling. She'd played before audiences in London and New York, and yet his final prodding had caused her to shake like an amateur.

She grasped one hand with the other. "I did not come here to seduce you."

He raised a disbelieving eyebrow.

"But," she added with a wicked smile, regaining her performance skills, "you were certainly willing to cooperate."

"This conversation is about you, not me," he said pointedly.

"Oh, you're wrong about that, Steven," she shot back. "As a matter of fact, what I have to say is about you." She rose and moved away from the sofa, walking with graceful movements around the room. His eyes followed her every step, and she saw the questioning look in them, and seeing it smiled to herself. She'd make him wait a little longer.

"I was sent here to find out about you, to learn what kind of man you are."

"Why?" he asked flatly.

She countered with a question of her own. "How much do you know about the country of Mendorra?"

The question came out of the blue and surprised him, but he didn't reveal the surprise in his reply. "Very little. My mother was born there but left when I was quite young."

"And you were born there, too," she said.

He nodded. "But wherever my birthplace, I can't imagine what it has to do with your various impersonations."

"I intend to tell you, if you will answer one or two simple questions first."

He nodded. "It's your deal, as we card players say."

"What do you know about your father?"

"I'm afraid that I must shock you and say I'm illegitimate, Miss Hanson."

She smiled secretly. "You know that he was Mendorran?"

Steven nodded. "Yes, I do know that." In one gulp he downed the drink and put the glass on the sideboard. "Now that's all the information you'll get from me, Miss Hanson, which is certainly more than you deserve. You're a guest in my home, and at this moment an unwelcome one, so I suggest you go on now with your explanation. And no more questions," he added adamantly.

"I am Mendorran, too," she said.

"No, not again. I don't believe I can sit through another of your stories, Miss Hanson."

"This is not a story," she assured him. "I was born in London, not Mendorra. My parents were emigrants. There were quite a few of us in England—exiles. We always wanted to go back, but the political situation was too unstable."

"I'm aware of that, although what was going on in Mendorra was hardly of primary importance while we were fighting our own civil war in this country."

"Then let me refresh your memory," she said almost angrily. "There have been years of unrest there. First our people had to fight against the advance of the Ottoman Empire. When the Turks were finally driven back from our borders, we had to contend with the Prussians to the north and Hapsburgs to the east, always looking for more territory to gobble up. Franz Josef would love to add our country to his Austro-Hungarian empire."

"Yet Mendorra has remained independent," Steven inserted.

"Independent of Franz Josef and Germany's Kaiser Wilhelm, yes. So far. But there are other serious problems. After the prince died, his father became little more than a figurehead, and the people turned to the military to keep its enemies at bay. Now we are left with General Adamo, the worst kind of dictator." Her eyes narrowed in anger.

"I appreciate the history lesson, but it hardly explains what you are doing here in my house."

"I am part of the resistance movement," she said, her voice filled with pride and a strong defiance that he could not help but admire. "I want nothing more than to see Adamo deposed, but we must have a replacement for him, someone who can capture the sympathies of the people, make them believe, someone who is part of the history of our great country."

Steven studied her thoughtfully. "I must admit that I believe you are finally telling the truth, Maggie. Your country seems to mean a great deal to you, and I appreciate that. But I sure as hell don't know what I have to do with it. Unless you plan to enlist me into your cause, and if that is the case I must tell you that my fighting days are over. I have no plans to ride into Mendorra on my white horse and overthrow this General Adamo."

To his amazement, she dropped to her knees beside his chair. "But that is just the point, Steven. You could do it. You must do it. You have the courage and the daring and the bravery. I know that from your war record—and I have witnessed it for myself when you came to my defense—"

"In that sham," he reminded her.

"Even so, you were there to take on two men without stopping to weigh the odds. And there is something more."

"I was afraid there might be," he said with a sudden smile. "What may I ask is this final card you have up your sleeve?"

She smiled back as she spoke the words. "Your heritage, Steven. You have royal blood. Royal Mendorran blood."

For an instant, as he looked at her upturned face, Steven felt a shiver of foreboding run along his spine. She was good, so good she was almost able to convince him. But the idea was too preposterous. He shook his head as if to clear it. "Royal blood? Come now, Maggie, you can do better than that. A woman with your immense talent should be able to conjure up a more believable story."

"It is not a story. You are far from illegitimate, Steven. In fact, your mother was secretly married to the crown prince."

"This is ridiculous." He stood up and shook her away.

She rose beside him, undaunted. "As a commoner, it was necessary for her to keep the marriage a secret. Had the situation changed, perhaps it would have been easier. Perhaps not. Who is to say? In any case, the prince's enemies found out and tried to kill her. She escaped with you to America. Before your father could join his family, he was killed."

Steven turned away. "If what you say is true, why did my mother never tell me?"

"Perhaps she wanted to spare you, keep you out of trouble. As you grew up, I imagine she saw how strong—and strong willed—you were. She wanted to keep you safe. If you had known your birthright, you most certainly would have attempted to claim it. If you had known of the suffering of your people, you most certainly would have wanted to end it. Plotting against the monarchy in Mendorra has gone on for years, by those who seek power. But the people love the royal family."

Steven was no longer listening. He was caught up in what she said earlier, denying it to himself and to her. "No," he said. "My father a prince. That's impossible."

"It's true, Steven."

He reached for her, holding her again in his strong grip, and for a moment all the tensions of the day, all the feelings that had passed between them came to the surface. Their eyes met, and Steven was the first to look away, dropping her arms. "What's your proof?" he asked finally.

"I have no written proof, but I do have word of mouth, stories told by old family servants, stories heard from the priest who performed the marriage ceremony. I know that further proof exists, and if we could find it, bring it to the people, rally them around you, we could overthrow Adamo.''

"We?" he asked. "You and I, Maggie?"

"There are many others, an army of resisters. My Uncle Viktor is one of them. He has been tracing your mother, and through her we finally found you. It is true, Steven. Your family name is Von Alder. It has the ring of royalty to it. Your family crest—"

Steven had moved to the sideboard to pour another drink, stiffer than the one before. "Forget the family crest and the genealogy. I'm not interested, although I can see why you didn't just waltz in and hit me with this. I can understand why you wanted to soften me up first."

Maggie winced at that but stood her ground.

"Despite your very ardent—and very appealing, I must admit—lovemaking, I still don't believe you. The whole story strikes me as another of your scams, Countess."

Maggie had followed him to the sideboard and faced him, looking up unflinchingly into his disbelieving eyes. "Of course, I could not have barged in and told you about your parents. I would not have wanted to, not until I found out the kind of person you were, found out if you were Elyse's child, as we had been told."

"So you went through my room."

"As you went through mine," she retorted.

"Touché," he said. "Two of a kind, I suppose."

"I know you are being sarcastic, Steven, but that may be truer than you think. I believe you are a man of great integrity, passion and honesty. I believe that if you knew what was happening in Mendorra, what was happening to your country, you would feel the way I do. You would want to help."

He suddenly slammed the glass down so hard that she thought it would shatter. "I have a country. It's called the United States of America. I fought to keep this country together. I've been through a war, seen friends die all around me. I don't want any more battles, Maggie. I don't want another country. And even if I believed every word you told me tonight, I would never return to Mendorra."

"Even to find out if what I say has a grain of truth in it?" she challenged. "Unless you return, you will never know."

"You're persistent, I must admit. And you never, never give up, pushing, wheedling, lying—"

"I am not lying," she said hotly. "I am telling you the truth, and if I have had to use devious methods to get to you, then so be it. The end in this case more than justifies the means."

"Even making love to me?" he asked.

She held her head high and met his eyes squarely. "That was apart from all the rest."

"Not in your plan, Countess?" he asked in his old teasing, sarcastic voice. "Seducing me, making me fall under your spell, so enrapturing me that I would follow you to the ends of the earth, much less to Mendorra?"

His words stung, and Maggie wished she had the power to hurt him as much as he had hurt her. She could only reply sadly, "Well, obviously if that was part of my plan, it was not very effective, was it?"

She was surprised to find that he had no response.

"But it was not part of any plan, Steven, and I would appreciate your never mentioning what happened again."

Their eyes met, flashing in what was as much passion as anger, for they both remembered what had happened to them when their bodies were locked in lovemaking.

But now, suddenly, they were strangers.

"You have my word," he said at last. "It will be as though it never happened." He spoke the words firmly but so very slowly, knowing that making love to Maggie was something he would remember all of his life.

After another pause, he drew a deep breath and forced himself to sound businesslike, even brusque. "Now that I know your mission, I need to make arrangements to get you back to Chicago. There's a train late this afternoon. Can you be ready?"

"Since the only clothes I have are the ones on my back, it will not be too difficult," she answered. "But please forget how you feel about me, and think of your mother and father. What they would have wanted."

"Resorting to a little emotional blackmail, eh?" he asked. "That won't work, either, Countess."

"At least take some time to think about it," she begged.

"I don't need time. I've done all of the thinking that's necessary. My decision is final. I've just completed a long trip, and I have no intention of taking another, certainly not to Mendorra."

Chapter Four

Maggie sat in the buggy next to Steven, her eyes fixed straight ahead. He flicked the reins over the bay horse's wide back, and clucked softly as they left the ranch house and drove toward the gates of the Double E.

Without looking back, she suspected that Bert and Faye were still standing on the wide veranda, watching them drive away. Steven had said nothing when they left, offered no explanation, and Maggie had read curiosity in Faye's eyes and what she thought was suspicion in Bert's. It could have been her imagination, but she sensed that Bert knew something about what was happening, more at least than his wife. She wondered if Steven would explain everything when he returned home or if he would never mention her again.

She'd left a note for him on the bureau in her room, but she didn't expect him to read it, even doubted if Faye would show it to him. And yet there was still a tinge of hope within her; it was illogical, but it was there nonetheless.

She stole a glance at Steven, still stoic beside her, not looking her way, totally unaware of her scrutiny.

He had the profile of the Von Alder family with its high forehead, fine brow, deep-set eyes, strong nose and chin. It was a wonderful face, she thought, not only handsome but honest.

She glanced down at his hands on the reins. They were large with long, tapered fingers, tanned from exposure to the sun and wind of the vast open spaces. She closed her eyes and looked away, remembering how his hands had felt against her skin, how gentle, beguiling. As she watched, Steven flicked the reins again and they drove through the gates of the Double E.

The moment of remembered intimacy and passion they had shared in his bed was over. There was nothing between them now but distrust and coldness.

She had made a horrible mess of the whole situation. She had failed miserably in her mission.

"Easy, girl." The voice startled Maggie, and she looked over at Steven, who still stared straight ahead, giving gentle commands to the bay and not acknowledging her presence at all.

Maggie's thoughts returned to her mission. They had had such high hopes for it, she and Uncle Viktor, but neither of them had realized the kind of man she would be dealing with. They had both expected a strong man, a regal man, reflecting his royal birth. But neither Maggie nor her uncle imagined what would happen between her and Steven. They had no way of knowing that she would behave like a love-struck girl and fall into Steven's bed. The tension, the attraction, the magic of that moment when he took her in his arms was even now with her. Even now, she was far from the trusted agent her uncle Viktor expected. Even now, she was thinking of the Steven who had made love to her, not the Steven who belonged on the throne of Mendorra.

And that Steven was a man who felt deeply. She was sure of it. As stoic as he sat beside her, as forbidding and silent, she still hoped that the man she had seen briefly and lovingly was there beneath the facade. She hoped that man would change his mind.

Those were her lingering thoughts when it happened, when the world around her seemed to explode and she was thrown into a nightmare.

Suddenly, there was the thundering of hooves from a grove of trees bordering the road. Steven must have heard it first because he'd already pulled back on the reins, but the bay mare got her head momentarily and began to run.

"Whoa," he shouted, half-standing, pulling back violently on the reins. At the same moment, he reached out and pushed Maggie onto the floor of the buggy.

A deafening sound cracked through the air, followed by another, closer. The horse began to buck in its harness, and Steven, his gun drawn, pulled Maggie from the buggy, and they fell together onto the road.

She was jarred by the fall. Her head hurt and her knees buckled beneath her as they rolled over and into a ditch beside the road. She tried to get up, but he pushed her back roughly.

"Get down and stay down," he said as he moved away, his body in a crouch, his gun blazing.

Maggie crouched down as he'd commanded, covering her head as the shots continued. She couldn't tell which shots were from Steven, and which were from the assassin. For that was who was firing at them. Somehow a Mendorran assassin had found Steven, too, with a mission to kill him.

Then there was silence. She lifted her head and looked over to the place she'd last seen him. He wasn't there. She turned around. He'd doubled back to the opposite side of the buggy, which was now stopped by the road, the spooked horse grazing contentedly as if nothing had happened.

But something had happened, something terrible. Steven was staggering back toward her, his arm hanging limply. There was blood everywhere.

Not thinking of herself, Maggie stood up and reached for him.

"Get down," he shouted as he ran toward her, rolling back into the ditch. "I don't know if I got him or not."

He fell against her, forcing her down again.

"Steven," she cried, the bright red blood sticky on her fingers. "Oh, Steven."

"It went all the way through, I think," he said, holding on to his arm, "but it hurts like hell."

Maggie was ripping the material of her petticoat, pulling a long section free and wrapping it around his arm, hoping to stem the endless flow of blood.

For a moment she felt as if she were going to be ill. The fear in her stomach had risen to her throat and mingled with the smell of blood. She was sickened by it at the same time that she plunged ahead with the makeshift bandage until her own hands were covered with it.

She tied the knot securely and fell against him.

He didn't seem to notice anything, even the wound, but continued looking toward the woods, the gun still drawn and cocked in his good hand.

"I think I hit him," he said, pulling himself up to get a better look over the rise of the ditch. "He's behind those rocks. I'll double around and—"

"No!" she screamed, holding on to him. "No, he still may be alive. He could kill you this time."

Steven paused long enough to look at her, suspicion mingling with his pain. "What do you know about this, Maggie? Do you know who's after me?"

"No. That is, I'm not sure, but possibly someone from Mendorra has found out—"

He bit back a sharp expletive. "More of your intrigues, Countess. In that case, I sure as hell am going to find out who our friend is. Stay here and keep out of sight."

Before he could struggle to his feet, they heard hoofbeats thundering toward them. Bert, looking to her more like a knight on a white charger than a middle-aged paunchy foreman, was riding their way, fast.

"Watch out, Bert," Steven yelled. "He could still be alive."

Bert swung off his horse and dropped down beside them. One look at the bloodstained rag around Steven's arm told him something of what had transpired. "That wound needs some tending to, boss."

"Later," Steven said dismissively. "We have to make sure there's no threat from the gunman. He was over there in the trees, behind that outcropping of rocks."

Bert nodded. "I heard the shots back at the house and couldn't figure what the hell was going on. But I think you got him, boss, or he'd have fired at me for sure."

"I expect you're right," Steven agreed.

"I'll just have a look," Bert said, making his way across the road, zigzagging toward the woods.

He was back in no time, a smile on his broad face. "You got him, boss. Once in the heart and once in the belly."

Maggie felt her skin grow clammy. The sight and smell of blood was one thing, but death— Her hands were still red with Steven's blood and she looked around ineffectually for something to wipe them on, finally using the hem of her torn petticoat.

Steven struggled to his feet, his face pale with pain. "I want to see him for myself," he said. "I want to see the son of a bitch who tried to ambush me." Then he turned to Maggie. "And I want you to see him, too. After all, you may know who he is."

"Please, no. Please—"

Her words went unnoticed as Steven grabbed her with his good hand and pulled her to her feet. Gritting his teeth as the pain radiated through his body, he cautioned her, "You'll do as I say, Countess, because I intend to get to the truth. Bert can carry you over there or you can walk. Which will it be?"

Bert stood silently, taking it all in, and Maggie knew that with a word from his boss he'd toss her over his burly shoulder like a sack of flour.

"I will walk," she said, "but I do not think—"

"I'm not interested in what you think," Steven told her, pressing the torn section of her petticoat tightly against his upper arm. "I want you to look—and tell me what you know."

Bert slipped an arm around Steven's waist and supported him as they trudged up the side of the ditch onto the road. Maggie followed behind, dreading what she was about to see and yet knowing Steven would never let her back down.

They crossed the road and headed toward the stand of spindly trees. Behind the rock outcrop she saw the boots, scuffed and dusty. As they moved closer, the trouser legs became visible. Then, clearing the rocks, the whole body. She turned her face away.

Everything was still and quiet in the afternoon sun. No crickets chirping, no birds singing. It was as if death had enveloped the plains and silenced the usual sounds of nature.

Maggie, her eyes averted, heard Steven's voice, clear and positive. "I've never seen him before."

"Me neither, boss," Bert affirmed.

Both men turned toward her. "Come and have a look, Maggie," Steven insisted. He motioned her to move forward, and she had no choice but to obey.

Slowly she walked toward the body, hoping to get away with a quick glance. Steven would have none of that. He pulled her closer, forcing her to look down.

The body lay grotesquely sprawled on the rocky ground, a splash of blood across its chest. That was all she saw on first glance, but Steven had reached for her and prevented her from looking away.

There was a small hole in the man's ribs from which a fountain of blood still spewed. Another shot had torn through his stomach. Maggie put her hand over her mouth and looked quickly at the face, distorted in death but unblemished—an older man with dark hair and a graying mustache.

Quickly she turned away, bile rising in her throat. "No. I have never seen him in my life," she said, relieved that the dead man was a stranger, relieved that she could turn away now and not look back.

"Go through his pockets, Bert." Steven leaned against the boulder, his face drawn and white with pain.

Bert bent over, taking his time as he methodically rummaged through the man's pockets. Finally he stood up, jingling coins in his hands. "Just some money. No identification. A few bills and these coins. This is a funny one."

He showed it first to Steven, who shook his head, and then to Maggie.

"It's Mendorran," she said. "He must have overlooked it."

Steven's eyes caught hers, filled with distrust. "So. You knew," he said. "You knew a Mendorran was after me. Was that part of the plan—to set me up to be killed?"

Bert was alert and wary. Maggie could see his hand hovering near his holster.

"I did not set you up," she shot back. "It was only a guess that the man was Mendorran. Oh, Steven, do you not understand?" she asked frantically. "Someone else knew who you were. Someone who would do anything to keep you away from Mendorra."

"And how do you suggest he found out, Countess?" Steven asked rhetorically. "Could you have led him here?"

She ignored the questions, saying only, "Believe what you wish." She was sick with the sense of failure. "But I have told you the truth. I do not know this man. It is possible he could be an agent, one of Adamo's men. It is just as likely he could have been working alone."

"I'm not in the mood to second-guess, Maggie. All I know is that the man was a bad shot, which is lucky for me. Bert," he ordered, "get me up on your mount and then drive Miss Hanson to the train."

She looked at him, startled. "You still want me to leave after all this?"

"Especially after all this," he replied. "You have a way of attracting trouble. Trouble that I can do without."

"I'm not sure I should leave you, boss," Bert said.

"That horse of yours knows its way back to the barn blindfolded. I can hold on. Do what I say and get this woman to her train. And Bert, not a word of this to anyone. When you get back, we'll bury our friend here and decide what to do next."

What to do next. His words echoed in Maggie's head and gave her a glimmer of hope. But the look she saw in Steven's cold eyes and closed face told her that she was not part of his plans.

Bert worked on the bandage until Steven was satisfied. Then with a curt nod in her direction he said, "Bert will get you safely to the train and wait for you to pull out of the station." He looked pointedly at his foreman.

"Then this is goodbye, Steven," Maggie said.

"Yes, Countess, it's goodbye. And don't think that it hasn't been interesting."

They walked back to the road, Bert helping Steven get his foot in the stirrup and throw his leg over the saddle. With his good hand, Steven clutched the saddle horn.

Maggie stepped up onto the buggy and settled herself in the seat. Bert climbed up beside her, heaved a sigh and grabbed the reins. The bay responded, lifting her head, ready to resume the journey so recently interrupted.

Maggie looked expectantly toward Steven, but he'd turned the horse with a motion of his body and both man and mount faced away from her, toward the ranch.

She opened her mouth to speak but thought better of it. She faced forward, heavy with the unremitting knowledge that she would never see Steven again.

Bert slapped the reins and the buggy lurched ahead. Maggie kept her eyes forward, wondering if Steven had turned to watch but determined not to look back.

* * *

Maggie's train ride was lonely and interminable. She'd never felt like such a failure, not only in her mission but in her personal life, as well. Eventually Uncle Viktor would understand and forgive her, although his disappointment would be acute. They had always faced the risk that Steven Peyton would turn his back upon his heritage.

What Maggie had never considered was her own personal involvement with the man she had hoped would be the savior of his country. How could she have known that a kind of magic would exist between them, dark and powerful and irresistible? It had created a sensual whirlwind that caught them up in each other physically while drawing them apart emotionally.

As the train roared eastward, Maggie shivered a little and pulled her cloak more tightly around her shoulders. Outside in the inky darkness the great vastness of America flashed by. Inside in her compartment, a curtain of loneliness surrounded her. It would have prevailed in any case because she had not achieved her goal. It was all the more devastating because of what had happened between them.

So much time had elapsed since Maggie had opened her heart to a man. Not since her husband, Jack, had she felt a comparable closeness. And he had died three years earlier when she was barely a young woman, only twenty-two. Yet even with her husband, whom she had loved with all the devotion of first love, she had never known the passion that had been revealed to her in the person of Steven Peyton.

She shivered in remembrance of the moments they had shared in his bed, the intimacy between them. But the ending had been the reverse of passion; the ending had brought distrust from Steven, even hatred. She would never see him again.

There had been brave, hopeful words on her lips, words never voiced. She had meant to tell him that they *would* meet again, that this was not the end for them. "It is not over yet, Steven," she had almost said. But at the last minute the words had not come. At the last minute, she had known it was the end.

Alone in the compartment, listening to the clatter of iron wheels on iron tracks, Maggie cried silently in the darkness.

Viktor Beitel was waiting for her at the railroad station in Chicago, the wind rustling his grizzled gray hair and beard as he stood, buffeted against it, wrapped in a black greatcoat.

Maggie ran toward him. She was exhausted, dirty and drained of emotion, but just the sight of her uncle lifted her spirits.

The coat encompassed his stunted body and flapped around his short legs. She smiled to herself as they embraced, the willowy woman and the little man who held himself so proudly and drew her to him, the husband of her mother's sister. He was not directly related to her, but Maggie's ties to Viktor were as close as blood.

After her parents' deaths, Viktor and her aunt had taken Maggie in and reared her as their own. They had always been family to her, and she owed them everything.

"*Liebling,* my Margarette. I received your telegraph. You have come safely back to me," he said as he hugged her.

"Oh, Viktor, it is so good to be back, so good."

She had no luggage, of course, only a small bag with a few items Faye had thoughtfully included for the trip. Viktor took it from her, offered his arm and led her out of the bustling station into the raucous streets of Chicago. A light rain had begun to fall, and she looked disgustedly about. There was no cab, not a carriage in sight.

Vainly Viktor dashed into the street, waving his arms about, hoping to attract a distant driver rounding the corner. Instead, the old man was almost run down as the carriage, filled with passengers, passed him by.

Maggie pulled him back from the street. "Come," she said. "There is a café in the next block. We can have a cup of coffee and talk. When the rain stops, the carriages will reappear."

"Of course, you are right, my dear," he said, patting her hand as he linked arms with her once more.

The café was dark and crowded. In the air was a cacophony of languages, Polish and German, Italian and Russian. So different from the virtually unsettled West from which she had just arrived, this was a melting pot of many nationalities, immigrants who had begun to pour into the United States in search of freedom from hunger and tyranny. Pushing forward, restless, these foreigners had settled in the hub of Chicago and here found a life that was new in its hope for the future of this brave land and old in its ties with the past and the mother country.

They made their way to a small table in the back of the café, where Viktor ordered coffee and pastries. Maggie had chosen just the right place, that much she knew. Viktor was happy to settle down beside her, feeling at home. "Just like the old days, eh?" he said, wiping a bit of sugar off his beard. "Oh, these pastries remind me of the Mendorran sweets—nectar of the gods.''

Maggie had heard his extravagant praises many times, as he compared the Viennese food to the Mendorran. "I have never tasted either, Uncle," she said, "except here in Chicago."

"It is not quite the same, although in this café they come very close, I must admit," he replied, taking another bite and washing it down with a big gulp of coffee.

"Someday I will know for myself," Maggie said.

"And that day will be soon, my *Liebling*." He looked over at her with surprise. "But you are not eating. Oh, I imagine you are tired."

"Yes, Uncle, I am," she admitted. Then to please him she took a bite of her pastry, followed by a sip of the rich coffee.

"So, my darling child," Viktor said, "how does it feel to be so successful in your mission?"

Maggie put down the coffee cup carefully and looked at her uncle. Hope and expectation glimmered in his eyes. How she hated to have to disillusion him, hated to have to tell him what had happened on her mission, which had begun with such hope and ended with such disappointment.

"But I was not successful, Uncle," she began. "I'm afraid that I have failed."

"You call this failure?" Viktor asked, reaching into his breast pocket and pulling out a yellow envelope, which he waved triumphantly in her face.

"What—"

"A telegram, my Margarette. It arrived only one hour ago from Steven Peyton. He wishes to know more about our mission. He asks that I write and explain. If I can persuade him, offer more proof," Viktor said, almost laughing aloud, "then he will make the trip to Mendorra."

Viktor, caught up in his own excitement, ignored the stunned look on Maggie's face. She was trying to understand, trying to imagine what could have happened to change Steven's mind.

"Is it not wonderful?" Viktor asked her.

Maggie nodded, not yet willing to attempt to voice her own sentiments. How had it happened? Then she remembered the scrawled note she had left for Steven. So Faye had found it and taken it to him after all. It had consisted only of a few sentences, one an apology for deceiving him in the beginning, followed by a plea for him to reconsider. Then she had left Viktor's address.

She hadn't let herself think that Steven would contact Viktor, or even that he would read the note. Yet he had done both, and her wildest hopes had been realized.

"So you see, *Liebling,* our plan goes forward! I will write Steven Peyton a long, detailed letter, telling him all we know. Perhaps I should begin now to make arrangements for him to meet us in Europe and slip across into Mendorra."

"Uncle, I—"

"Say nothing, dear Margarette." He grabbed his niece's hand. "For there is nothing to say. Everything we owe to you. You won him over, just as I predicted."

Maggie nodded silently. She had been reprieved. Viktor would never have to know what happened between her and Steven. It would be her secret. And Steven's.

As she listened to Viktor making grandiose plans about Mendorra and its future, one thought kept replaying in Maggie's mind. It had nothing to do with Mendorra or with freedom, and for that reason it made her feel guilty. But the thought was there, nevertheless. It was simply that whatever happened now, she would see Steven again.

Chapter Five

Paris wasn't at all what Steven expected, at least not the Paris that he came upon in the dark of night.

He'd looked forward to seeing broad boulevards filled with strolling couples, beautiful women wearing the latest fashions, expensive carriages, cafés with customers overflowing into the streets. He'd read of the Bohemian life of Parisian artists, and he had a curious urge at least to gaze upon the Paris of Degas and Manet. But Steven was immediately disappointed.

Of course it was late when he arrived, and the address he gave the driver was not a familiar one. Even the famous boulevard Saint-Germain, which led to his destination, was difficult to discern in the rain and mist covering the city.

They turned off the boulevard, onto a winding street, and then another and another, each barely wide enough to accommodate the carriage. Lining the streets were rows of houses, which Steven hoped would look less desolate in the sunshine. The rain, which should have washed them clean and added a glisten to the dark bricks, only succeeded in making them look more forlorn.

That was exactly how Steven felt. After two weeks of traveling, he was tired, irritable and angry at himself for having ever agreed to take part in such a farfetched scheme. And he was homesick for the wide-open spaces of Wyoming that he had left behind when he'd agreed to take on this foolhardy venture.

It had once seemed romantic, exciting and adventurous. That Steven had to admit. Now it seemed only ludicrous.

The carriage rolled to a halt, the driver demanded his francs and Steven found himself deposited in a small square facing a narrow house. Number seven rue des Foles. Steven smiled ironically. He knew a little French, and that he translated effortlessly. Street of Fools.

Carrying his bag in one hand, he rapped the knocker impatiently with the other. The door opened a crack, revealing a thin man, so short that he seemed almost dwarfed.

"Viktor Beitel?"

"Yes."

That was all. No recognition, just a one-word greeting, affirmative, but suspicious and wary.

For a moment Steven considered turning on his heel and getting out of this drab and dingy place in some distant corner of a city that had nothing of the romance for which it was so famous. Then he heaved a sigh and decided to get on with it. After all, he had not come across continents and a great ocean only to be dismissed by this little man.

"I am Steven Peyton."

"Ah, yes, of course. Step into the light, sir."

Steven did as he was told, taking a long stride over the threshold into the hallway.

"Ah," Viktor said, "I recognize you now. From the photographs. Welcome, sir. Welcome!"

Viktor grabbed Steven's hand and pumped it furiously. "We have waited so long."

"It's been even longer for me," Steven said, thinking not of the wait to meet this little man who stood before him, but of the weeks he had been in transit.

Viktor continued, animatedly. "Just to think, a Von Alder in this house. The son of my dear friend Prince Gregor."

Steven smiled wearily. "Just a tired American citizen named Steven Peyton, who would like to get out of his damp coat and then get some questions answered."

"Of course, of course, how inhospitable of me." Viktor was all concern, helping Steven off with the coat, ushering him into a small, dark sitting room where a fire burned brightly in the grate. "Paris is supposed to be lovely in the springtime, but you see we have our showers, too."

Steven didn't think of the cold misty rain as spring showers, but he made no comment.

"Sit down, sit down, dear boy," Viktor offered. "May I pour you a glass of brandy which, I promise you, will have the taste of French sunshine in it?"

Steven wished the old man would stop hovering over him, but there was nothing he could do about that, so he gratefully accepted the brandy. Over the rim as he drank, Steven studied Viktor. He and the older man had exchanged letters and cablegrams during the past month, and gradually Steven had allowed himself to be drawn into Viktor's conspiracy. Now he wondered who was the most demented, the old man with his dream of a king without a throne or himself for falling into the trap.

Finally Viktor sat down, sipping his own brandy, shaking his head in wonder. "I cannot believe you have truly arrived," he said quietly. "I hoped and prayed..."

"Let's just say you intrigued me, Herr Beitel. And let's also say that I'm a man who doesn't like a mystery, especially one in which I seem to be involved—against my own will."

Viktor raised a questioning brow.

"I wasn't particularly pleased by the idea of being shot at by a supposed Mendorran gunman on my own damn property. You might say that got my dander up a bit. And then when you advised in your correspondence that it could very possibly happen again—well, it seemed like a good idea at the time to get to the bottom of it all."

"At the time?" Viktor questioned.

"Now I feel like an absolute fool, thousands of miles from home where I belong."

"But, according to what you have written to me, you have no home, at least for a while," Viktor responded. "Am I not correct?"

"You are," Steven agreed. "I'm a man without a country." He smiled wryly. "Maybe faking my death was somewhat extreme, but it served the purpose, didn't it? The Mendorran agents—if there are such men—now believe that Steven Peyton is dead, and my untimely demise explains my absence from the ranch to all but my most trusted employees."

Steven sat silently for a moment, staring into the flickering flames, remembering how simple it had seemed at the time. Bury the man he'd killed in a grave marked for Steven Peyton; turn the running of the ranch over to Bert for a while; stay hidden in the house while his wound healed and grow a beard and mustache as a disguise of sorts.

It was almost like a game, and Steven was a proficient gambler. When all had been arranged, he'd left Cheyenne, not on his private railroad car, but traveling as a night passenger on the eastbound train just like any other citizen of the West.

He'd met one of Viktor's trusted accomplices in Chicago, and after receiving his new papers and new identity had begun the long journey to Paris. It had been complex and secretive, but there had been an excitement and momentum that seemed to thrust him forward unrelentingly, at least in the beginning. Now there was only exhaustion and a kind of puzzlement.

Viktor's eyes were wary and watchful. "You have second thoughts, Steven. I hope I may call you that. I feel from our correspondence we are friends, even though of course your status in Mendorra puts you high above me."

"I have no status in Mendorra," Steven said quickly. "And I prefer first names, Viktor." He got up and stood in front of the fire. "As for second thoughts, yes, I have plenty of those. But I'm going to see it through. I've come too far. I guess part of me wants to know the truth and to settle this once and for all—"

"Which we shall do," Viktor assured.

"And prove the whole story is nothing but a fantasy of some well-intentioned but obviously misled men," Steven finished.

Viktor was not disturbed by that. "Sometimes fantasies do come true," he said with a chuckle.

"Not this time," Steven replied flatly. Then, sitting down beside the old man, he asked, "What grand plans have you in store for us?"

Viktor leaned back, sipping his brandy. "As you know, you will leave tomorrow morning on the TransEuropa Express for Vienna and points east. You will be traveling as Steven Englehardt, an American of European background. You will be visiting Mendorra to see the sights and perhaps to partake of its renowned waters—and to share a honeymoon with your lovely wife—"

"Wife?" Steven became immediately alert. "You mentioned nothing about a bogus marriage." He hadn't anticipated this, but the thought of it brought Maggie immediately to mind, and although his words belied his feelings, he couldn't avoid a tremor of excitement.

"Of course, you need someone to travel with you, someone who knows the language, someone..."

Of course, Steven realized, it would have to be Maggie. As Viktor's voice faded away, Steven got up and walked to the window, pulling back the heavy draperies and looking out into the dampness of the night. He'd tried not to think about Maggie during the weeks since he'd sent her to the station with Bert. He'd made it a point never to mention her in his correspondence with Viktor, but that didn't mean he'd forgotten her. At night, no matter how much he fought against it, she was there, beside him in bed, ephemeral, haunting, manipulative and seductive.

"Maggie," Steven said at last. "Maggie Hanson, I gather, has been chosen to play the part of Mrs. Englehardt, my beloved wife?"

Viktor beamed. "Who better? She knows you, she knows the language, and she is, of course, a consummate actress."

"That part is certainly true," Steven muttered.

"And I trust her more than any living person."

Steven bit back his retort, saying instead, "It isn't going to work, Viktor. I prefer to go alone."

Astonished, Viktor stood up, raising himself to his full height, which was a little over half Steven's. "But that is impossible," he began.

"No, it's not. You can coach me, tell me what to expect."

Shaking his head vehemently, Viktor crossed to Steven and looked up at him. "You must have someone with you, Steven," he insisted. "One of us, someone like Maggie."

"Then find someone else," Steven ordered, wondering why he did so, but determined nevertheless.

Viktor was genuinely concerned. "There is some problem with Margarette? I thought everything went so well in Wyoming—"

Steven realized then that Viktor knew nothing about what had gone on between them, nothing about the blinding passion that had bound him to Maggie and nothing about the distrust that had forced him to wrench himself away from her. For a wild moment, he thought of telling her uncle everything, that he had slept with her, made love to her, and that he hated himself for it just as he still hated himself for the lingering desire.

Instead, he told Viktor, "I can't agree to it. The risks are far too great."

"Much less great for her than for any other woman because she understands her duty to Mendorra, and she understands the danger. She is perfectly agreeable to the mission. My niece is a very brave woman," Viktor added.

"It won't work," Steven insisted stubbornly. "If I am going to do this, I must do it alone."

"Everything depends on our plan, Steven," Viktor insisted, "and your chances will be greatly enhanced by traveling with a companion, a 'wife.'"

"Then it must be someone else," Steven said, restating the argument smoothly. "Your enemies could be watching her. She could have led the assassin to me in the beginning."

"Led them to Steven Peyton," Viktor said. "And he is quite dead, is he not? As for this house in Paris, no one knows we are here. Not even our compatriots in England. No one, Steven."

"I'm not convinced," he insisted. For her safety, for his own sanity, for whatever reason, Steven didn't want her with him. "It won't work."

"I believe it will," Viktor said. "And so does my niece."

"Then let me talk to her first. I won't go any further with this scheme until I am convinced it will work, and at this moment I'm far from convinced. I must see her alone first."

"Well—"

"Or no plan, no trip, no grand design to free Mendorra. Do you understand, Viktor?"

The older man nodded. "Now I see why Margarette insisted you were the right man for the job. She said you were strong, and you are. She also said there was a ruthlessness in you that was needed, and she was right again. So if you wish to see her—"

"You can do so now, but not alone."

It was her voice, and at the sound of it, Steven turned away from the window and saw her standing at the top of the stairs. Another man in his place might not have recognized her, for Maggie was an actress, and tonight, she was a different woman.

But Steven recognized her immediately, even though her hair was much darker, a rich russet color that brought out the beauty of her eyes, and her makeup, her manner, her dress were that of another woman. To Steven, it was still Maggie, and he couldn't take his eyes off her.

Maggie was amazed at her calmness as she descended the narrow stairs of her uncle's rented house in Paris. Amazed at the way she smiled at Steven and extended her hand as if to an old friend. He could have no idea of how violently her heart pounded or her knees trembled at the sight of him.

When she spoke, her voice was low and modulated, her words carefully chosen—and practiced all afternoon in front of the mirror as she'd often done before when rehearsing for a performance. "Steven, it is good to see you again. You look quite handsome," she said, and indeed he did, more than handsome. He looked marvelous, tall and elegant in his traveling clothes, his tailor-made suit that fit perfectly across the width of his broad shoulders and chest. Yet he seemed somehow out of place in the small parlor, which was overpowered by his brazen masculinity.

"Your beard suits you," she added. It was lighter than his hair, the tawny color of the desert tipped with a golden hue. His eyes were unchanged, however, green and measuring and wary.

Steven rubbed his beard reflectively. "It makes me feel like someone else."

"Ah, that is good," Viktor said.

"And you are not the same, either," Steven couldn't help adding as Maggie crossed the room and took his hand. "Quite the consummate actress, as your uncle reminds me."

"Yes, yes." Viktor bustled around nervously. "A different couple entirely, Mr. and Mrs. Stephen Englehardt."

Maggie smiled and looked toward Steven for a response. There was none.

"Brandy for you, Margarette?" Viktor's darting eyes watched them both, and Maggie realized that she must be careful not to give anything away. She could tell that Steven would reveal nothing, either to her uncle or to herself.

"No, thank you, Viktor. Perhaps some wine, though, to celebrate Steven's arrival. And our departure," she said easily. "I see that my uncle has told you of the plan for us to travel to Mendorra as man and wife."

"I've heard," he said, "and I've voiced my objections. It's too dangerous, Maggie, even for someone as clever at disguise as yourself. You may look different to some. I would recognize you immediately."

Maggie wasn't sure whether the comment proved his powers of observation or referred to their shared intimacy. She chose not to ponder the thought.

"I knew the danger when I went to Wyoming, Steven," she said. "I know it even better now. Our plan has no chance of succeeding unless I go."

"No, Maggie," he objected.

"I am utterly determined," she said, looking him straight in the eye and fighting the trembling inside. "Perhaps you are the one who is afraid, Steven."

He threw back his head and laughed, and the sound chilled her and made her remember. She'd heard his laugh before; it had been mirthless then, just as it was now, mirthless and full of sarcasm. "Countess, you haven't changed at all, have you?" he asked. "Still fiery and full of defiance. Still determined to have your own way."

She wasn't sure what that referred to but couldn't help remembering that he'd once accused her of seducing him: "Not always," she said tartly, "but perhaps this time, because this time it is necessary. I think we can handle this venture successfully as partners. And I am certainly not afraid."

"It isn't fear that makes me hesitate, Countess."

Maggie realized that Viktor, unaccustomedly silent, was watching and listening. She didn't want to reveal too much, and yet she refused to let what had happened between her and Steven foil the plans Viktor had made for them.

"I hope not," she said. "But let me remind you that this is not about what happened...before." She glanced quickly at Viktor before continuing. "It is about now, about a country that deserves the truth. You are the one who can supply that truth. This is more important than three people hidden away in a house in Paris. It is more important than our fate, but without us, it may never happen."

"Are you saying that the three of us can change the world?" he asked sarcastically.

"Not the three of us," Viktor replied, speaking at last. "The two of you will change the world together. I have had a small part in the plan. You must carry it out."

"Our country deserves the truth," Maggie said. "You are the one man who can give them that, Steven."

"Maybe," he responded.

"But we will not know, will we, unless we go there? Unless we try? Or do you plan to back out?"

"I never said that," Steven answered.

"Nor have you said otherwise," she reminded him. "Well, I am not backing out, either. I am going to Mendorra, with or without you." She looked at him challengingly and was surprised to see a smile forming at the corners of her mouth.

"You're damned good, Countess. You know just how to bluff a man."

"I do not understand," she replied.

"Bluff, Countess—you know the word. It's a card player's trick. I can't imagine that you plan traipsing across the continent to Mendorra alone, or what would be accomplished if you did. However, in making the offer, you've challenged my manhood. Am I brave enough to go to Mendorra or will I back out and send the helpless lady on her own to face unknown dangers?"

"See it that way if you choose, Steven," she whispered silkily. "However, if I am bluffing, it seems to me you are playing out a bad melodrama."

Thoroughly confused, Viktor tried again. "Now, children," he said, looking more puzzled than ever. "Let us talk calmly—"

"It is all right, Uncle Viktor. For Steven and me, this *is* talking calmly, even though it might not sound that way to others. We seem to bring out the . . . the worst in each other. That does not mean that we cannot work together," she added hastily. "Of course, he may not be up to the trip." She cut her eyes toward Steven and let her words trail off.

"I have one important question," Steven said, ignoring her challenge for the moment. "I assume many people in Mendorra know exactly who Maggie Hanson is. They know she is related to you, Viktor, and they know your politics. From a gambler's point of view it seems like bad strategy for me to waltz into Mendorra with Maggie on my arm."

Viktor smiled. "You are clever, Steven, just as my niece said, and that is a great relief to me. You spoke earlier about the Mendorran who attacked you. Well, as we three know, he is now safely dead."

"True," Steven admitted. "But there could be others, as you warned me yourself."

"There is certainly that possibility. However, your assumption that many people know Margarette's identity is quite wrong. We do not believe that she is known to any of them. She has never been to Mendorra. Her family, bless their souls, were totally nonpolitical people and were never under suspicion by Adamo's men. As for the men who staged the attack at the railroad station, they were, of course, our compatriots."

"Of course," Steven said with a smile in Maggie's direction.

"There is one final argument, the best of all," Viktor said, his face alight with pleasure. "What better way to prove she is innocent of all intrigue than by sending her into the lion's den, as it were? I cannot imagine that she would be recognized as she looks now, but—"

"I would recognize her in a moment," Steven said, and, when he saw the twinkle in Viktor's eyes, he knew he had revealed more than he meant to.

"Nevertheless," Viktor continued, not acknowledging the twinkle that was now well hidden, "no one would ever believe that I, Viktor Beitel, would ever be so foolish—or hardhearted—as to send my own niece into danger. And there, you see, we have covered all of our bets. Is that not the expression, Steven?"

"Yes, it is," Steven said. "But there's still something I must know."

"Ask," the old man offered.

"Would you send her into danger?"

"If it meant the freedom of my country, yes."

The tone in Viktor's voice sent a shiver through Steven's blood. The man was a fanatic. Steven knew that now, and with or without his help, Viktor was going to send Maggie to Mendorra. She, equally fanatical, had not been bluffing when she told Steven she would go.

Maggie moved close to him and put her hand on his arm. There was nothing intimate about the gesture; it was one of pure innocence and commitment to her cause. She looked up at him and met his eyes evenly. "We are serious about this, Steven. Are you with us...or not? We need to know, and we need to know now."

Steven shook his head in defeat. "All right. Let's sit down, Viktor, and go over the plan. Hell, I've come this far, I might as well see it through."

The TransEuropa Express pulled out of the Gare de Strasbourg half an hour behind schedule. Steven and Maggie were well ensconced in first class, complete with velvet cushions, foot warmers and a complimentary bottle of champagne.

Maggie was dressed more flamboyantly than on her train ride through the American West, as befitted the wife of a rich cowboy, she'd told him.

Her dress was a deep rich wine color, like burgundy, Steven thought. It fitted tightly from her neckline to her waist, hugging every inch of the rounded figure he remembered so well. The overskirt was drawn back into an ornate bustle effect, exposing a darker velvet skirt beneath. She'd thrown aside her cape, velvet, too, but lined with rose-colored taffeta. And atop her upswept hair she wore the silliest hat that Steven had ever seen, tiny, tilted forward, and rife with bows and feathers. Not many women could have carried it off, but not many women had Maggie's style.

Other men, passing up and down the aisle outside their compartment door had noticed her; they couldn't help it, Steven realized. There was a kind of sexuality about her that was unstudied but extremely compelling, too damned compelling, he decided.

They sat quietly at first, sipping the champagne, watching the city of Paris roll by through the window. The day had dawned clear, bright and cool, more like Steven had expected. He'd awakened surprisingly refreshed, and he was enjoying watching the landscape change from city to country. It was a countryside that intrigued him, nothing like the wide-open spaces of Wyoming. Here the rich, fertile land was divided into small plots, filled with orchards and vineyards.

He'd never seen grapes on staked vines like this before, row after row, perfectly trellised, springing from dark rich soil. For a long time he watched, fascinated. Then he looked away and noticed Maggie watching him unabashedly.

"You never told Viktor what happened between us," he said, his words more of a statement than a question. He'd thought long and hard about them.

"It didn't seem important—at least, not to him. I think it was for the best," she answered.

He followed with the next item on his Maggie agenda. "If Viktor had known, he might not have dreamed up this charade we're caught in."

"Possibly not."

He nodded. It was just as he thought.

"But is it so terrible to be married to me, Steven?"

"I don't know," he shot back. "It's hardly been twenty-four hours."

"You needn't worry," she told him. "In public I will be charming and dutiful, and in private—well, in private you'll hardly know I'm here."

He wondered about that but said nothing.

"After all, we have a mission, Steven. One too important to jeopardize with our sparring. I can put the past behind me, in fact I already have. You should be able to do the same."

He rubbed his index finger thoughtfully across his mustache. The idea of facial hair was still irritating to him. "I'm not at all sure we can carry it off," he said honestly.

"Being a happy honeymoon couple?" she asked. "Of course, we can. Remember, I am an actress. I can easily make believe I am in love." She caught his gaze and held it for a moment. "Even with you."

Instantly Maggie regretted her sharp words. They hadn't come out the way she'd meant them. "I know you do not like me, Steven, or trust me," she added more softly.

"Let's say once burned, twice shy."

She answered immediately, still speaking in a quiet voice. "We do not have to like each other to work together. As for trust, it will come...perhaps. Or perhaps not," she added as an afterthought. "It could be that your innate distrust will keep us alive. At any rate, I do respect you, Steven, for your intelligence and bravery and even for your skepticism."

He looked at her through narrowed, measuring eyes, and sighed deeply. "I hope you're not acting, Countess, because I want to believe what you're saying."

Maggie held her breath, waiting. For the first time, she and Steven were talking without the pretense and the old biting sarcasm.

"I respect you, too." His words were grudging but honest. "God knows you can act, and you're clever and courageous. No," he amended, "more foolhardy than brave, but you seemed devoted to Viktor and his cause." He gazed out the window at the endless vineyards. "Although I'm not sure he deserves your devotion."

She prickled a little at that, but he paid no attention.

"I wouldn't send someone I cared about into danger," he continued, "but you seem to relish the idea so here we are, certainly an odd match."

"I cannot disagree with that," she admitted.

"Maybe if we concentrate on finding out the facts about my supposed father and stay out of Mendorran politics and intrigue we can achieve our purpose and come out alive."

"Thank you, Steven," she said simply. "I shall do my best to hold up my part of the team."

"Just remember, if it gets too dangerous, we're leaving Mendorra on the first available train. I'll be dealing that hand, Countess."

She was quiet for a moment and then shrugged. "I have no choice, do I? From now on, you're the dealer, as you say." That established, she went on. "Now, tell me all about Mr. and Mrs. Englehardt."

Steven finished his champagne and began. "We met in Chicago where I saw you on the stage in ... damn, I can't remember the play you were supposed to be in."

"Actually, I *was* in it. I played Kate in Shakespeare's *The Taming of the Shrew*."

He chuckled at that. "Certainly fitting. It was love at first sight, of course. We were married in New York."

He touched his breast pocket. "I have our forged marriage license if anyone is interested. Since I'm such a devoted husband I'm taking you to visit your ancestral home in Mendorra, after which—if we're still alive—we'll visit the Englehardt estate across the border. Sort of a grand tour to see each others' homelands. Odd that we both come from the same part of the Old World, isn't it?"

"Not really," she said. "America is a country of immigrants, many of them, like yourself, from Europe. I was an English actress touring in your country, also a European émigré. Our Mendorran heritage was part of what brought us together." She refrained from mentioning what other attractions might have been between them. "With a few little embellishments, it will work," she said positively. "We will need to flesh it out, add some details."

"For my benefit, why don't we do a little fleshing right now? There're some details I'd like to know. About you. Real details about who you *really* are."

"Will you believe me this time?" she asked slyly.

His answer was equally clever. "Without your Uncle Viktor here to corroborate, I'm not sure. But try me."

"My name is Maggie Hanson. You know that. I am a trained actress."

"Where does the 'Hanson' come from?" he interrupted. "That's hardly an old Mendorran name."

"My husband," she said briefly.

"Oh, so you *are* married, but not to poor old Count Oblansky," he said cruelly. "I knew you were a woman of experience—"

"I am a widow," she cut it.

Steven had the grace to look embarrassed. "I'm sorry."

"I married Jack Hanson when I was eighteen. He was an American actor, a brilliant one, working in London. We met and eloped, much to Viktor's despair. Jack taught me the fine points of acting, which cannot be learned in school. He had no training, only his innate talent."

Steven regarded her seriously as she spoke, not quite sure whether he believed her story or not, but at this point it really no longer mattered.

"Jack took me to the United States where he planned successful careers for us both. He was all brash and full of optimism. We were only married for three years when he died. A stupid tram accident. He lived for several days after, but the head injuries were so severe he could not talk at all."

Tears glazed Maggie's eyes and she looked quickly out the window. "It was awful for Jack not to be able to talk. Words were necessary in his livelihood, and he spoke them so beautifully." She pulled a handkerchief from her reticule and wiped her eyes.

"And now," she said finally, "you know all about Maggie Hanson." The words were overly bright and glib, as if she had no intention of dwelling on the pain of her past. "After Jack died, Viktor and I became very close, and it seemed important for me to do something with my life, something real, where the part I played had meaning. Life is so short to waste any of it."

Her voice caught and she broke off, fighting tears. They were, Steven now believed, real tears, shed over a tragedy that was true, and very painful. He was compelled by a sudden and intense desire to reach for her and hold her. Not to kiss her or make love to her but just to hold her, much as a father would hold a child. At that moment he had a feeling for Maggie that was so strong and pure it almost seemed to invade the space between them.

He tried to look away, back at the landscape flashing by, but he couldn't. His feeling was too deep, a feeling that was new to him, strange and unknown. For a moment he couldn't even identify it. Then suddenly he knew. It was tenderness, a desire just to take away some of the pain she'd felt as a young, frightened girl who'd lost the man she loved.

She was looking away from him, out the window at the scenery that no longer interested Steven. It was Maggie who interested him now. He'd seen something new in her, something fresh and untouched and vulnerable. It was a side of her he'd never expected to be revealed.

He watched her out of the corner of his eye. She looked very young, not at all the portrait of a sophisticated woman of the world she presented to everyone else and which she'd presented to him at his ranch. She turned slightly and looked over at him then, her eyes gleaming with unspilled tears, her lips fixed in a straight line to keep them from trembling. All he had to do was reach out for her, touch her, hold her.

Instead he got to his feet. "I think I'll walk back to the observation deck and take a little air," he said, more brusquely than he meant to. He could see the hurt on her face, but he didn't know what else to do.

They'd finally come to a kind of honesty that had been missing between them. Taking her in his arms would only lead to confusion and misunderstanding. It would be a step backward to the lies and pretenses of Wyoming. If he reached for her now, she'd misinterpret his feeling and pull away. He knew that. She wouldn't understand what he meant, what he felt, and he damn well couldn't explain it.

"Yes, fine, fresh air," she murmured. "Perhaps I will read or—"

Before she could finish, he was gone.

She closed her eyes and leaned back against the cushion. Clenching her teeth, she determined not to let it happen, not to get too close and become vulnerable to him. He despised her; it was obvious, an insidious little voice inside her head told her. He thought of her as a liar and a cheat, a woman of no morals, the voice went on. Even when she told him about Jack he turned away from her.

And yet for a moment she thought she'd seen real caring in his eyes; for a moment she had the feeling he would reach for her and touch her. If he had, what would have happened? A repeat of the scene in the bedroom at his ranch, complete with recriminations and anger?

No, she convinced herself. The look she'd seen in his eyes had been different. It was a momentary flash of pity, and she'd rather have his disdain than his pity.

Maggie opened her eyes and looked stonily out the window, where his gaze had drifted so often during their train ride from Paris. She willed herself not to let him get close to her. She had let that happen once before, and it had hurt her terribly. She would not go through it again; she would not let herself love him.

Chapter Six

Maggie and Steven followed the concierge of Le Grand Impérial Hôtel Delphberg up the wide marble stairs. Behind them trailed a retinue of bellmen with their luggage. Bringing up the rear of the procession were four maids, carrying trays of fruit, coffee, tea and pastry.

"We have, of course, reserved the bridal suite for you," Herr Adolph Bracken announced, as beside her Steven did not try to hide a wicked grin.

Throwing open the doors with a flourish, Herr Bracken ushered his guests into the room, which almost caused Maggie to gasp aloud with surprise, first at the immense size and then at the rich colors of the room carpeted with bloodred Turkish rugs, its walls hung with pale cream silks, and the sofas and chairs covered in deep rose satins. The chandeliers and candelabra were all heavy gilt, and gold tassels held back the velvet draperies.

Herr Bracken crossed the room and pulled back the draperies to reveal floor-to-ceiling French doors. With another of his imperial flourishes he opened the doors and exclaimed, *"Voilà! Mendorra."* Herr Bracken, Maggie realized, was fluent not only in English but—in the tradition of the French-named establishment he presided over—also in French. No doubt he spoke half a dozen other languages as well.

He turned and smiled broadly. "And there, my dear guests, lies all of Mendorra before you."

Through the opened doors, they could see the proud mountains of Mendorra rising above the rooftops of the city. Even though it was spring, the mountain peaks were snow-capped, dazzling white in the clear sunlight. Verdant evergreen trees clung to the steep slopes, and nestled among them were ancient chalets right out of the pages of a storybook. Smoke curled from the chimneys, completing the picture of serenity and beauty.

"Is it not *magnifique?*"

Steven agreed. "Quite spectacular." Turning to Maggie, he asked, "Don't you think so, my dear?" There was the wicked smile again, echoed by a gleam in his eyes. He had not missed the look of stunned amazement on her face when she'd been confronted by the overly ornate bridal suite.

"It is lovely," she said simply. "I look forward to seeing all of the Mendorran countryside."

That seemed to satisfy Herr Bracken. With quick dispatch, he had their luggage disposed of, dismissed the bellman and ordered the maids to set up a table for the guests' refreshments. Then he continued the tour of their suite.

"This way, if you please," he said, gesturing through a twelve-foot doorway into another massive room, "to the bedroom."

Maggie tried not to look Steven's way, but somehow her eyes were inadvertently drawn to him, and there was the grin once more. She ignored it, or tried to, as they walked into a repeat of the sitting room splendor—more thick carpets, heavy draperies and ornate furniture.

It was impossible to ignore the bed since it occupied a large portion of the room and was elaborately covered in white silk that was repeated in the canopy. Thrown across the foot of the bed was some kind of animal fur, white with black markings.

If Steven had tried that wicked smile again, Maggie decided she would be tempted to kill him, for the simple reason that she was about to giggle herself. She couldn't help thinking the bed looked like something fit for the wife of a medieval knight.

Steven managed to keep a straight face, and Maggie followed suit as Herr Bracken showed them the twin dressing rooms and private bath.

"All that is required," he said proudly, indicating a velvet bellpull, "is for our guest to ring, and the staff will bring up hot water for the bath."

With that pronouncement, he led them back into the sitting room and continued to hover until they took their places at the table to begin the elaborate repast. Only then did Bracken seem satisfied that all was well, and the expression on his pink, rotund face turned from concern to relief, even pleasure.

"I trust you will enjoy your stay here."

"I'm sure we will," Steven answered. "We're very impressed with the service."

The pleasure mounted as Herr Bracken beamed. "Then I shall leave you and your lovely bride." He bowed slightly, and then suddenly gave his cheek a little slap of displeasure. "How could I have forgotten." He slipped a pudgy hand inside his coat pocket and drew out a creamy-white envelope.

"For you," he said, half-bowing again as he handed it to Steven. "Delivered by the personal servant of Count Raymond Von Alder," he said proudly. "A very old family," he confided, "highly connected to the royal family of our late monarch."

"Thank you," Steven said, putting the envelope unopened on the table.

"You are acquainted with the Von Alder family?" Bracken asked, still hovering like a curious pouter pigeon.

"We have mutual friends," Steven said casually as he turned his attention from Bracken to a pastry displayed on white doily, cutting it neatly in two with a silver knife.

Maggie volunteered nothing, concentrating on adding lemon to her tea, which was exotically dark and rich.

At last with a sigh and one final bow, Bracken departed, but not without first assuring them that his staff was on call no matter the hour or the demand.

When the door closed behind him, Maggie was unsure whether to scold Steven for his insidious smirks or to give way to the giggles that had been building inside her since they'd walked into the incredible suite where they were now so comfortably ensconced. She really had no choice. The giggles prevailed.

"I feel as though I am being held prisoner in a baroque nightmare," she said, looking upward toward the carved angels that surrounded the base of the gilt chandelier.

"With some Louis Quatorze thrown in for good measure," Steven answered. "Do you suppose there's any more gold leaf in Mendorra—or was it all used to embellish Le Grand Impérial Hôtel Delphberg?"

Maggie leaned back against her chair and sighed. "I suppose this lavish display is intended to impress foreigners with the splendor of the postmonarchy Mendorra."

"Foreigners have eyes, Maggie," he said. "They can take in all of what we saw outside in the real Mendorra, those sights along the way from the train station to the hotel."

Maggie nodded, remembering the long lines of Mendorrans waiting for food, the children in ragged clothes, barefoot far too early in the spring, and the look of defeat on so many of the elderly faces. Their suffering was immediately apparent.

"It makes me glad to hear you say that, Steven. It shows... well, that you have become sympathetic with the tribulations of Mendorra—the real Mendorra."

"It just means that I'm observant," he corrected, his face becoming closed and wary. "I told you and Viktor that I was interested in finding out the truth about my parentage, not in taking on a civil war in Mendorra."

"Yes, I know but—"

He interrupted her sharply. "Enough, Maggie. I don't care to get into it any further."

Something in his eyes told her he meant what he was saying, and Maggie knew Steven well enough to do as he said. He was not a man to be challenged. Soon, she hoped, he would see the truth.

For now, Steven was concentrating on more immediate matters as he picked up the envelope Herr Bracken had left for them. "Aren't you interested?" he asked. "Or was curiosity limited to Herr Bracken?"

"Of course I'm interested," she said. "Von Alder is one of our contacts in Mendorra."

Steven turned over the heavy cream-colored envelope, holding it at the edges, studying it. "Our best contact, according to your uncle," he said thoughtfully, "one of the few monarchists left in the country."

"Are you teasing me now, Steven? Open it, please," Maggie said.

He used the silver knife to slit the envelope's thick fold, drew out a heavy, engraved card and handed it to Maggie.

She read the invitation aloud. "General Felix Adamo requests the pleasure of your company this evening at a reception at the People's Palace."

"So," Steven said. "Von Alder has gone right to the top for us."

Maggie's eyes were wide as she looked at Steven. "And he has wasted no time. Tonight…" She frowned as she felt a little shiver run down her spine.

"Nervous?"

"No, no," Maggie denied. "It is just that I—"

"We don't have to go," he said. "We can plead illness, fatigue. After all, we've traveled a long distance."

"Of course we are going," she said, rising and crossing to one of the room's many gilt mirrors. "And I am not nervous in the slightest," she assured him as she removed her hat and dropped it onto a table beside her reticule. "I am excited."

He was watching her carefully with a look Maggie couldn't quite interpret, so she continued to reassure him. "I look forward to tonight and the beginning of our plan which I feel sure we can carry off."

The confidence was real, but a sudden tiredness had come over Maggie that caused her to drop back into the chair. Steven half stood, as if to assist her, but she waved him away. "I am just a little tired." Quickly she got back up, glancing into the mirror to adjust the pins in her hair. "It was, as you said, a long trip."

For a moment Steven had almost reached out to her. Now he was glad she'd stopped him. She could take care of herself, and to show concern at this point would be absurd. They were partners in this intrigue and nothing more. Yet he couldn't contain his concern which was twofold, both for her safety and her health. It wasn't an easy task that lay before them. He hoped she would be up to it.

Maggie turned from the mirror, stretching her arms above her head as if to rid herself of the journey's aches and pains. "All I need is a warm bath to relax in," she said.

Suddenly Steven's concern turned to something else, something that he'd tried to avoid. It was attraction, and as she lifted her arms in that catlike gesture it swept over him completely, settling directly in his loins.

She breathed deeply and her breasts swelled above the fabric of her traveling costume, causing Steven to remember what he had tried so hard to forget. The flood of desire continued; he was powerless to stop it.

His glance moved from her body upward and their eyes met. She flushed slightly, and Steven knew why. She'd read the thoughts on his face, seen his need for her. He cursed to himself for letting it show and quickly looked out the open draperies across to the cool shadow of the mountains. Damn her, he thought, for making him feel first concern and then lust. Neither were emotions that needed to get in the way now.

He wasn't sure whether she'd turned away at the same time or not, but when he glanced back, she was walking toward the bath, her reticule in one hand and that silly hat she'd worn on the train in the other.

"I hope Herr Bracken is right about the availability of hot water," she said over her shoulder. "Unless you'd like to bathe first," she added.

"No, you go ahead. We have separate dressing rooms. There'll be no problem."

"No, of course not. I was not anticipating any." She was the old Maggie again, unflustered, coolly in control. "Separate compartments worked fine on the train. I am sure they will do so here, as well."

"I'm sure they will," he answered just as icily. They were at it again, adversaries, arguing over everything— and nothing.

"You will sleep out here, I assume." She gestured toward the plethora of overstuffed sofas and lounges artfully arranged around the room.

He was remembering the seductively lavish bedroom and didn't answer immediately. He could imagine her in the bed, and he could definitely imagine himself there with her. The inability to control those feelings angered Steven and in a perverse way caused him to take the ire out on her.

"Why would you assume that, Mrs. Englehardt? After all, aren't we the happy bride and groom?"

The old sarcasm had crept back into his voice. Maggie refused to respond to it.

That didn't stop him. "Am I to be banned from our marriage bed on our first night in Mendorra?" Before she had a chance to respond, he added almost cruelly, "I've waited so long."

She got her answer in then. "You were the one who was against this 'marriage,' Steven. I am surprised to hear you bring up the subject." This time she didn't give him the opportunity to form an answer. "Or have you changed your mind? Have you perhaps been swept away by the sight of this nuptial splendor, all of the lush velvet and gilt and satin?"

His eyes narrowed as he stared up at her. She played the game well; he had to admit it. No matter what verbal situation he thrust upon her, Maggie faced it head-on and brazened it out. She was a woman who wouldn't be intimidated. That characteristic both fascinated and infuriated him. One thing was certain: it added spice to their verbal encounters and kept him from dwelling too long on those other feelings. He was glad of that because he was not at all sure just where he would have chosen to sleep if she had been any less confrontational.

Steven got up and sauntered to the balcony door, pulling it open to catch a breath of cool spring breeze. She was still waiting for a response, and he turned with a smile to deliver it. "If I were to be swept away, my darling wife, it would have nothing to do with our surroundings and everything to do with the woman involved."

She stood watching him, her lips parted slightly. It was all Steven could do to complete his thought with the same coolness with which he'd begun it. "So you can feel perfectly safe in your bed tonight. Of course, I'll sleep out here."

He crossed to the door. "There's a taproom downstairs. I'll sample the local schnapps while you bathe."

Maggie stood looking at him, two bright spots of color burning her cheeks. When would they learn, she wondered, to leave well enough alone? Each time they reached an understanding, a truce of sorts, neither of them seemed content with it. On the train they'd been civil to each other, and now they were at odds again. She'd never experienced anything like this before, and she couldn't understand why they continued to push each other—or what they were pushing toward. He brought out the very worst in her; but she wasn't about to stand by and let him goad her without responding. All she knew was that it could not continue tonight. Tonight was crucial, and they had to act as a team, not as two angry children.

"Steven..."

He turned at the door and looked back at her. "Yes, my dear?"

"Tonight is very important."

"I believe we're both aware of that."

"We must try to...to *seem* like a happy married couple."

"You're the actress, Maggie. I'm sure you can pull it off."

"But I will need your help," she said.

"Oh, Maggie, you are a little fool. Do you think for a moment that I would risk my life and yours over these stupid arguments? Of course, I'll be the perfect husband, just as you'll be the perfect bride. In public," he added as he opened the door, stepped into the hall and closed it quickly behind him.

Infuriated, she looked for something to throw, picked up one of the gold-rimmed plates, and then thought better of it. She would *not* let him send her into a fit of overly dramatic fury. With all the calm she could muster, Maggie put the plate down, went into the bedroom, gave the hand pull marked Bath a tug, and began to undress.

By the time Steven returned, Maggie had completed her bath, and he could hear her moving about in her dressing room. He ordered his own bath, completed it quickly, dressed in a dinner suit and returned to the bedroom. Maggie still had not appeared. He knew this much about women—they took the longest time over their toilettes. He'd never known an exception to that, and damned if he knew what they did all that time. The results were usually good, however, as he expected they would be tonight.

Darkness had fallen, and the lights of Delphberg twinkled below, repeating those in the heavens. The night was clear and cool, a perfect night to do battle, Steven thought. And it *was* a kind of battle they were going into, not unlike those he'd fought during the war.

He stood at the window, staring into the night, edgy and excited, as if the rebel troops were just over the next hill and he was in command. He'd faced many such nights during the terrible civil war that had torn his country apart, faced them with a mixture of fear and anticipation. He'd expected danger then, known it would be there. He expected it tonight as well and didn't mind it, maybe even welcomed it—for himself, but not for Maggie.

She shouldn't be here. Shrugging off any personal feelings, Steven told himself that his concern had nothing to do with Maggie herself; no woman should be in this situation. It was unwise of him—and of Viktor—to have allowed it. He vowed to talk her into returning to Paris as soon as possible and leaving him to sort out the truth about his parentage—alone.

Still deep in thought, Steven heard a rustle and half turned as Maggie swept by him in a blur of black and white that took his breath away.

He followed behind, watching the movement of her slim body, tightly fitted into white silk that flowed into a full skirt caught up with a bustle and demi-train, which he almost stepped on in his hurry to get around and see her from the front.

"Maggie, stop a minute," he said. "Where're you going?"

She looked at him sideways. "Into the sitting room where there's a much larger mirror."

Indeed, it filled almost an entire wall and reflected the front view of her that he'd been so determined to see, revealed a low-cut bodice sewn with shimmering crystals and jet-black beads. The sleeves were mere caps, decorated with black ostrich feathers that lay like shadows against her pale skin. He watched as she put on dangling diamond-and-pearl earrings, examined her reflection and then pulled on her long black gloves.

Satisfied, she turned toward him. The deep russet of her hair brought out the creaminess of her skin and the startling blue of her eyes. My God, Steven thought, it's Maggie who looks like royalty, not me.

She remained still, looking at him expectantly, holding her breath, and Steven realized he'd been holding his breath, too. He let it out in a long slow stream. "Countess, you are spectacular."

"I feel more nervous than spectacular," she said. "I am not sure about the dress. I bought it in Paris, and Uncle Viktor gave me the earrings. They were my aunt's, but I am not certain that..."

He held up his hand. "No doubts. You'll be the most beautiful woman at the reception. It's an honor for me to escort you." He bowed toward her.

Suspicion darkened her blue eyes.

Steven laughed. "I'm perfectly serious, Maggie. Don't look for hidden meaning in my words. I assure you I have no cards up my sleeve with which to surprise you. I mean it when I say that you're lovely."

She sighed with relief. "I'm glad to hear you say that, Steven. I hope it means we'll work as a team tonight."

"You can bet on it." He reached out to take her gloved hand and bring it to his lips.

She stepped back to have a first good look at him, pleased with what she saw as, still holding hands, they turned to look into the mirror.

"A handsome couple, if I do say so myself."

"Yes," she agreed. "I would never believe you were a Wyoming rancher, Herr Englehardt." He did indeed look every inch the European aristocrat, but under her scrutiny, she could see him becoming uncomfortable, pulling at his waistcoat and smoothing the white studded shirtfront. "I feel like a damned fool," he admitted, "but I guess, when in Rome..."

"Exactly," Maggie agreed, "but don't fiddle with your clothes at the reception. That will be a dead giveaway."

Steven laughed. "Keep an eye on me, Maggie."

"My pleasure," she assured him, "so to begin with, we might as well have everything perfect. Your tie..." She stepped forward, peeling off her gloves and handing them to him. "If you'll be good enough to hold these." With a flick of her fingers she loosened his tie and stepped forward to retie it.

She was close enough for him to smell the scent of her perfume, exotic and heady, just like Maggie. It emanated from just behind her ears, Steven decided, and it was all he could do to keep from leaning forward, removing the dangling earrings, and kissing each delicate pink lobe. Even more tempting than the scent of her was the fleeting touch of her breasts against his chest, the sweep of her full skirt against his legs.

Steven took a deep breath as she fussed with his tie, and tried to control his heart, which thumped in heavy rhythmical beats. Finally he could stand it no longer and reached for her hand.

She stepped back then, but he didn't release her hand. "There," she said, "it looks fine now."

He held on to her hand, perhaps more tightly than he'd intended, because he saw her flinch. Still, he held on, forcing her to meet his eyes.

She seemed to read something there; he could tell by her look, something that made her pull away. He didn't know what it was; it might even have been fear.

She reached out and took her gloves from him. "It is late," she said.

"Yes," he answered, offering his arm, his face now a mask of politeness. "By all means, we mustn't keep the general waiting."

Chapter Seven

They stood beneath the great domed ceiling of the People's Palace, two men and a woman, dwarfed by the setting. Once the most elegant structure in all of Central Europe, it was even now a building of incredible splendor.

It had been for centuries the Mendorran Royal Palace and as such the prototype of elegance. Kings and queens, princes and princesses, dukes, duchesses, lords and ladies, all of the European royalty had assembled there during the height of the Mendorran monarchy.

"Yes, it was magnificent," the older of the men said, shaking his head in what seemed a mixture of wonder and despair. He was Count Raymond Von Alder, and it was his pleasure to escort Maggie and Steven into the main ballroom of the palace, but first he'd lingered under the dome, sharing the past with them and regretting the present. "So different now," he said.

"But it's still beautiful," Maggie assured him as she looked around at the palace that twenty years before had been taken over by General Adamo and his staff.

"Let us say they have done no visible damage to the structure. How could they?" Von Alder asked rhetorically. "It is a fortress unassailable. And yet," he added, "there is so much here that has changed."

As they entered the ballroom where the reception was being held, he gestured almost sadly toward the marble gallery. It was lined with statues of Greek and Roman deities, set back into carved niches high above the ballroom floor.

"The statues are still here," Maggie reminded him.

"Yes," he replied. "We have our beautiful statues, for they are in the main ballroom. To remove them—or to desecrate them—would be too obvious."

"What then?" Steven asked, as curious as Maggie about Von Alder's strange reminiscences. The ceilings were as glorious as ever, Steven imagined, painted with frescoes that had faded to pastels of peach and rose and turquoise. The very softening of the colors made them even more beautiful.

Von Alder followed Steven's gaze. "And it is not possible to take away a fresco," he said almost jovially. "Those will remain as long as our palace stands. But there is a greed here that cannot be denied. It far outweighs the attitude of indifference so evident within the army."

He moved closer. "They have stolen great works of art from the palace. Our very greatest treasures are gone—the paintings of Titian, Rembrandt and Vermeer that once adorned the palace's smaller suites. Gone. All of them."

"Where?" Maggie asked. "How?"

"It was announced that the paintings were decadent and did not serve the greater purpose of Mendorra. They were removed, put into storage, or so we were told."

"But you don't believe that," Steven said.

"Of course not," Von Alder answered. "The truth is, the artworks were taken to Paris or to Milan and sold. There is no doubt where the money has gone, for it now lines the pockets of our leader, General Adamo."

Von Alder had kept his voice low, but as they entered the grand ballroom it was no longer necessary. Even Maggie and Steven had to lean forward to catch his words over the murmur of the crowd and the strains emanating from the stringed orchestra that played continuous Viennese waltzes.

Count Raymond Von Alder, the most important, perhaps the only monarchist remaining in this military state was an impressive man, and yet Steven couldn't help feeling a little disappointed in him. Not that his physical presence wasn't exemplary. It was. As tall as Steven, he carried his sixty some years with an almost military bearing. A handsome, impressive man with a small, intelligent face, a large nose, inquisitive eyes, he was every inch an aristocrat. It was his manner, Steven decided, that put him off. He seemed frivolous and lightweight, not at all the kind of man to be depended upon in a crisis.

While they stood sipping their champagne, Raymond had digressed from his worries about the missing artwork and was delighting in the gossip he shared with them, finding a slight sadness in it, as well.

"Very few of the old families are left, my Margarette. Most have fled the country or retreated to their castles in the mountains. Adamo was not kind to them," he said, shaking his head sadly. "Adamo was never kind to those who favored the monarchy. These people here tonight," he waved a gloved hand, "some minor titles, but most are from the military, from Adamo's staff."

There was, Steven had observed, more than a sprinkling of uniforms among the crowd. "But you're still here, count," Steven remarked pointedly. "You haven't been exiled or forced to flee into the mountains." Steven realized as he spoke that he was not only wary of Von Alder's abilities but suspicious of his position.

Raymond smiled. "But do you not see, my dear man, I am the court jester."

Maggie looked up at him, puzzled.

"So to speak, Margarette. So to speak. Everyone, including Adamo, sees me as a silly old man who is interested only in fashion and gossip and parties."

"Surely you aren't—"

"That is how they *see* me, my Margarette. Who is to say what is the real man, the real Von Alder? Even I, myself, sometimes wonder."

Steven was silent, still waiting to be reassured.

"So, when Adamo needed a token, someone to prove that he had kindly feelings toward the monarchy, he chose me. I am like the pet dog." Von Alder's face hardened imperceptibly, and Maggie thought she saw a strength and caring there that was not immediately apparent. She glanced at Steven but couldn't be sure how he felt.

Then Von Alder smiled, his silly jester's smile. "So I play the game, and sometimes I hear things I am not supposed to hear, and I pass the information on to interested parties. And I continue to play the jester. Even now, as our beloved General Adamo approaches, I am the jester."

Maggie and Steven turned to see a man in his late fifties stride toward them. He was of medium height, although his heavy shoulders and broad chest made him appear shorter. His hair was dark and wavy, shot here and there with traces of gray, and he sported a thick black mustache. His dark blue uniform was bedecked with medals, and gold epaulets glowed on his broad shoulders.

"Ah, Von Alder," he said, speaking with a thick European accent, "you will please introduce me to your guests."

Von Alder's demeanor changed immediately to that of subservience as he bowed and smiled. "Most certainly, my general. May I present Mr. and Mrs. Englehardt from the United States of America, here to tour our lovely country and perhaps enjoy our hot mountain springs with their healing waters."

Dismissing Von Alder with a wave of his hand, the general looked toward Steven. His dark eyes bored deeply as he offered his hand for Steven to take. "Welcome to our country."

"We are pleased to be here, General," Steven said.

"You have enjoyed your stay so far?"

"Well, since we just arrived—"

"Of course, of course," the general said impatiently, dismissing Steven as he had done Von Alder. The formalities were over, the men had greeted each other, and he could now, according to protocol, turn his full attention to Maggie. He did so without hesitating, reaching for her hand.

"General," she said, curtsying gracefully.

He raised her gloved hand to his lips, and Maggie tried to control a shiver of distaste. She felt as though she were under the cold-eyed gaze of a reptile. Yet there was nothing reptilian in the appearance of the sturdy, dark-haired man.

It was the smile, she decided as he released her hand, the smile not of a man but of a snake; that is, if snakes could smile.

When he spoke, his voice was smooth and silky, but underneath the polite words there was a crudeness, a harshness begging to break through.

"How long will you be with us?" he asked, causing Steven to bristle. Since their arrival date had not interested him in the slightest, it would follow that the departure was of equal unimportance. However, now that he had his eye on Maggie, everything changed.

Steven took it upon himself to answer. "Until we see what we came to see."

In an instant he realized that his response set up an antagonism between him and Adamo, like two stallions defending their territory. It was ridiculous, he knew, a bad mistake and one that Maggie was quick to rectify with smooth, conciliatory tones.

"My wonderfully generous husband has brought me to Mendorra to see the country of my grandparents." She placed her hand on Steven's arm and gave him a shy smile. "This is really a journey of nostalgia for us."

Adamo's eyes sharpened. "You are Mendorran?"

Maggie laughed lightly. "Partly, I'm proud to say. My father was born here."

Steven stood silent and admiring. She'd made no mention of her father's emigration, nor of her mother, whose sister was Viktor Beitel's wife.

"And your father's name?" Adamo inquired.

"You're so kind to be interested," Maggie said, turning the full power of her deep blue eyes on him. "I'm afraid the name has long ago died out."

"Nevertheless . . ." Adamo insisted.

"It was Landsdoe."

Steven had no idea if she was lying or not but the answer seemed to satisfy Adamo. "Landsdoe," he repeated. "Not a name I know." Then he asked politely, "You will go to visit our old houses and villages?"

She nodded. "And churches, graveyards, monasteries. Wherever our paths take us in your beautiful country. Isn't that right, darling?"

She was looking up at Steven with an expression of adoration on her face. It was a look he determined to keep with him to remember later, when they were alone and the expression changed to a much less friendly one. "Anything my beloved wants is hers," he managed, trying not to choke on the words.

"And you, Herr Englehardt, what is it that you look for in our country?" Adamo's dark eyes glittered in the light from a hundred candelabra. "Do you, too, have family in Mendorra?"

"Not that I know of," Steven said honestly. "However, we hope to visit the former estates of a distant relative, across the Mendorran boundaries in Bavaria."

The general, Steven was glad to see, had lost interest in him completely and was saying something to Von Alder, who leaned over attentively, nodding in the sycophantic manner he'd warned them about. Steven wondered how he could pander so, but then he dismissed the thought. He wasn't involved in this country's problems; he had no right to judge.

But he had every right to react, which he did when the general spoke to him again. The orchestra had paused between waltzes, its members retuning their stringed instruments before beginning the next piece. Adamo reacted immediately, his eyes darting from Maggie to Steven. "They are playing one of my favorite waltzes. May I dance with your wife, sir?"

"My wife speaks for herself," Steven said. Again the response had been a little too quick, a little too cool, as if his manner could make up for Von Alder's pandering.

The general paid no attention, for Maggie held him spellbound as she responded. "I can think of nothing I would enjoy more than dancing with the general on my first evening in Mendorra." She rested her hand lightly on his proffered arm.

As the general led her to the floor, Steven heard him saying, "And you must tell me how I can help facilitate your travel plans so that your stay with us in Mendorra will be perfect in every way."

Maggie's reply was lost in the swirling strains of Johann Strauss's "The Blue Danube."

Standing beside Von Alder, Steven watched the couple whirl away and become lost in the flashes of light and color. Couples floated by, women in elegant clothes in the arms of their partners, their dresses shimmering like rubies and emeralds under the candelabra until the whole room was awash with movement and melody.

Then Steven saw them again, moving across the floor in perfect rhythm, the general a more graceful dancer than his physical appearance indicated. The feelings that surged through Steven at that moment were confusing. He admired Maggie for her aplomb with the general at the same that he was strangely jealous. Mostly, however, he feared for her.

"Is the general suspicious?" Steven asked Von Alder.

"Of everyone, dear boy, and of everything. Felix Adamo is a dangerous man." Surveying the dance floor, Raymond squinted slightly, removed his pince-nez and wiped it carefully on his white handkerchief before replacing it. "He did not rise to his position as head of the country through a trusting nature," Raymond added.

Steven lost the couple for a moment in the maze and then spotted them again, twirling expertly as other couples respectfully made room for their leader and his beautiful partner. They seemed to create their own performance. Somehow it sickened Steven to see it. He turned away and gave his attention to Von Alder, who seemed anxious to talk with him.

"We must meet privately," Raymond said, taking Steven's arm and leading him along the edge of the dance floor. "There are plans to be made."

"Come to the hotel tomorrow," Steven suggested, his gaze still on the general and Maggie, twirling in and out of his sight as the light from the candelabra picked them up, lost them and found them again, illuminating Maggie's white dress and intensifying the brilliance of her auburn hair.

"Not at the hotel," Raymond said, "for even the walls have ears in Mendorra."

Steven tried to center his attention. "Then where?"

"In the People's Park." He leaned forward and spoke softly. "Tomorrow morning at ten, you and Margarette will take a turn there. It is quite as beautiful as Versailles, they say, and as tourists you must not miss it. I walk in the park daily, so that our meeting will seem accidental."

"I understand," Steven said. "We'll be there at ten."

"Go to the Garden of the Gods," Raymond said, "in the north corner of the park."

"How will we know it?" Steven asked.

"There are bronze markers leading the way. I will be waiting for you. We have much to discuss." And then so softly that Steven wasn't sure he heard it, Raymond added the word, "cousin."

The waltz ended and another began, and still Adamo showed no signs of returning Maggie to Steven. Above the rich and evocative strains of "Tales of the Vienna Woods" he had no choice but to wait and listen as Raymond settled into his other persona, that of court gossip.

As each couple swept by, he filled Steven in on their backgrounds, families and love affairs, and then quietly commented on their affiliation with the general, whether friendly or not.

"Those who are not in his favor do not care to be here tonight. You can tell it in their demeanor," Raymond said. "But they dare not stay at home for fear they will seem suspect."

"Which of course they are," Steven said.

"Of course, but they must not show it."

Adamo and Maggie swept by again. Her eyes were on his, her head held proudly. One hand rested lightly on his shoulder, the other held her train as she twirled and turned to the wonderfully sensual rhythms of the waltz.

Steven could stand by no longer. "I'd like to dance with my wife," he said.

"It would be more politic for you to wait. At the end of this piece, perhaps, he will return her to you and—"

"I don't care to wait," Steven said. Ignoring the count's futile grasp at his sleeve, Steven stalked out onto the floor and tapped the general on his shoulder.

"Please excuse me, General, but I want to dance with my wife. We are, after all, on our honeymoon," he added, offering a hand toward Maggie.

There was nothing for Adamo to do but yield. He did so with a cold, stiff bow, which Maggie managed to soften with words of appreciation and a dazzling smile.

She'd seen Steven coming, realized what he had in mind and known that it wasn't a good idea. She'd tried to signal with her eyes for him to wait, but he hadn't noticed, or if he had, he'd chosen to pay no attention.

Her only choice had been to part reluctantly from the general with as much charm and grace as she could muster. It had seemed to work; he had seemed placated. As for Steven, she was just about to berate him for his poor timing when he took her into his arms and she was dancing again.

Yet how different it was now. Not that the general wasn't an accomplished dancer, more graceful than he seemed, but nothing could have made her enjoy having him as a partner. Not just the knowledge of who he was, what he had done to his country and his people, but the man himself repelled her, his smile snakelike, his voice unctuous, his gaze insinuating, an easy man to hate and yet a man Maggie had tried to charm—until Steven appeared.

"I'm afraid you've made him angry," she whispered.

"Oh?"

"We have a purpose here, you know," she reminded him.

"We sure do, and part of the plan is to convince the general that we're a newly married couple, very much in love, who've come to tour his country. Would such a wife spend the evening dancing with another man? Would such a husband allow it?"

"You have a point there," Maggie admitted.

"Then let's play our parts."

With that, Steven tightened his arm around her waist, and together they moved to the music, Maggie dazzled by Steven's unexpected flair. He swirled her across the room, his green eyes locked into hers, his long body moving in perfect harmony with hers, around and around in dizzying circles, driven by the compelling melody of the waltz.

Maggie was transported into another time, another place, where all she could feel, all she could see, was Steven, one hand warm on her waist, the other holding hers gently but with a possessive firmness that seemed to make them one. She wished that it would never end, that she and Steven could dance all night and into the morning, that the others would disappear and only they would remain, alone with the music.

But it did end, and the sounds of the ballroom came back to her, the sights invaded her vision—color and light, voices, applause and the tinkle of glasses.

Steven dropped his arm and stood looking awkwardly down at her as if amazed by what had happened between them, the feeling of oneness, of perfect harmony.

"I didn't know that you were such a fine dancer," she said softly.

"I'll wager there's a hell of a lot you don't know about me, Countess." There was challenge in his voice but it was lighthearted, and she ignored it, not answering in kind as she might have at another time.

"In any case, it was wonderful dancing with you, Steven."

She looked up at him and for a moment saw a rare softness and vulnerability flicker across his features.

Then his face seemed to close as if he were consciously blocking out his emotions.

"Like I said earlier, our dancing was necessary to make Adamo believe we're lovers on our honeymoon." With that he took her arm, as firmly but far less intimately than before. "Let's make our farewells. We have a busy day tomorrow."

Maggie's smile faded, but she didn't flinch. She was used to it. "One thing never changes about you, Steven," she snapped. "You know exactly how to ruin a lovely moment."

Chapter Eight

The entrance to the People's Park was almost deserted except for a large class of schoolgirls, apparently gathered for a field trip in the park. There were dozens of them, dressed in crisp blue school uniforms, giggling and jumping about, paying scant attention to their teacher.

Maggie and Steven passed by them quickly and followed the arrow on a brass plaque that led them along a gravel path toward the Garden of the Gods. On the way, they passed through a series of other gardens, each more delightful than the one before, laid out to surprise and amaze the visitors rounding a curve or corner or reaching the rise of a hill.

The Japanese garden was built around the edges of a clear stream where frogs croaked lazily from the crowded lily pads and the red roof of a pagoda glistened in the early-morning sun. It led to the topiary garden with its bushes and shrubs trimmed into fascinating animal shapes.

The way was well marked, and yet as they strolled along, somehow they took the wrong path and found themselves on a hill just above the schoolgirls.

"I can't believe we've gone in a circle," Steven said.

Maggie laughed, for she could easily believe it. They'd been enjoying themselves too much during the morning, which had dawned bright and clear. Thoughts of the evening before, both pleasant and unpleasant, had been put aside as they began the day afresh. They were anxious to hear what Raymond had to say in this meeting, and Maggie allowed herself to believe that Steven's curiosity was a hopeful sign for their mission.

Even getting lost and being able to laugh about it was a good omen, she decided, along with the perfect weather, the cloudless blue sky and the smell of spring in the air. There was no strain between them now, although she could never tell with Steven just when it might turn up again.

"We must have missed a plaque somewhere along the way," Maggie suggested.

"Should we backtrack?" Steven asked her.

"Oh, please," Maggie replied. "Anything to avoid the schoolgirls."

"Agreed," Steven said with a laugh, as he folded Maggie's arm through his own and started back down the hill.

Halfway there, Maggie saw the plaque, embedded in a tall granite slab.

"How could we've missed it?" Steven asked.

Maggie didn't answer, but she knew. Throughout their talk and laughter, they hadn't been thinking about their reasons for being here in the park.

"Head north, Raymond said," Steven reminded himself.

"Well, I'm afraid I wouldn't know north from south," Maggie admitted.

"The sun's position makes it pretty evident," Steven told her.

"Then why did you take the wrong path?"

"Entranced by your beauty, no doubt, my dear wife," he said. His voice was cool as he regained his composure—lost during their intimate stroll, just as it had been lost during the dance the night before—and headed north.

Following his lead as she'd done all along, Maggie changed her mood quickly from intimate to impersonal and carefully embodied the spirit of their project.

It was easy, because she was dedicated to the plan, but also difficult because of the mixed signals she received from Steven. She should be used to it by now.

As they approached the Garden of the Gods, they both shifted their thoughts and began to look around, watching for tourists and anything suspicious. Maggie was on her guard and found it easy to concentrate on the work and forget everything else.

"I wonder how much Raymond knows," Steven said as they reached the outskirts of a clearing.

"You'll have to ask him," Maggie said. "But I know Uncle Viktor trusts him implicitly."

"I worry about how many people in Mendorra know what Viktor's up to. Even now I wonder if we're being watched."

Maggie looked around, but all she saw was the sun, the greenery of the gardens and the spring flowers. Then the clearing widened and they were in the Garden of the Gods.

It was bordered by a thick stand of laurel and myrtle trees, interspersed with huge statues of Jove and Athena, Ares and Aphrodite, the gods of ancient Greece.

In the middle of the garden was a statue of Poseidon riding a dolphin that spewed water from its throat. Standing beside the dolphin was Count Raymond.

"It was much more beautiful here when the garden was properly tended," he said.

"What a surprise to see you, Count Von Alder," Maggie said in an overly theatrical voice that carried easily across the green lawns.

Raymond Von Alder stepped forward and bent to kiss Maggie's gloved fingertips. "More good fortune than surprise for me. Usually I walk alone. It would be a pleasure if you would join me this morning."

"Of course," Steven said.

Raymond took one of Maggie's arms and Steven took the other as they strolled along the perimeter of the garden.

"This is my favorite of all the gardens," Raymond told them. "It was formerly called the Queen's Garden, begun over one hundred years ago by the wife of Karl I. She scoured the world, bringing in the most beautiful statues from Greece and Rome—some of them perhaps illegally," he added with a chuckle. "She also imported flowers from around the world—azaleas from the Orient and those myrtles from Greece." He pointed to the wooded area they'd just passed by.

"There was a greenhouse here at one time. Your grandmother's idea," he told Steven. "Now it's gone—"

"Just a minute," Steven said, stopping in his tracks. "I'm beginning to be irritated by all your references to my 'family,' dear cousin. I know nothing about these people you refer to, and if you have some proof that they're my ancestors, I'd like to know about it here and now."

Raymond was unperturbed by Steven's attitude as he led them to a marble bench in the middle of the garden. Sitting down, he beckoned them to join him. No one could approach for fifty yards in any direction without being seen. Their conversation could be private.

"They used to hold the May Day ceremonies here," Raymond said. "So lovely, with the Maypole and—"

"Enough of Mendorran cultural life," Steven said. "Answer my question."

"Steven!" Maggie remonstrated. "Please—"

Raymond patted her hand. "Never mind, my dear child. He is simply eager to hear what I am privy to, and I suspect a little worried about whether he can trust me or not. The answer," Raymond spread his gloved hands out with a shrug, "is that only time will tell."

"I'm getting impatient," Steven reminded him.

"Of course, of course. What I know." Raymond pulled off one of his gray moleskin gloves and took out his handkerchief to pat his forehead, blotting a trace of perspiration.

Steven, silent, gritted his teeth.

"To begin with, I know what Viktor told me, that his niece was visiting Mendorra with her husband, who wished to trace his family. I swear to you, there was nothing more in writing, so you need not worry on that account. However, when I saw you, well—"

"Well, what?" Steven demanded.

"My dear boy, you are the very image of your father. Have you not been told so?"

"I have," Steven admitted, "but I can't verify it since there's evidently no photograph of the prince."

"Your *father*," Raymond said, to Steven's further irritation. "None exists, it is true. Adamo had them confiscated and burned after Karl died, all the photographs and portraits. It was said he wanted no reminders of the royal family, nothing to be compared to himself. Like 'Hyperion to a satyr,'" Raymond added, abstractedly pulling out a line from Shakespeare.

Steven made an impatient sound deep in his throat.

"But you see, I was part of the royal family. I knew my cousin Gregor very well and I can tell you that the set of the eyes, the profile, the chin—there is a resemblance in all of the Von Alders, even myself," he added, turning his profile toward Steven, who acknowledged nothing.

"I see no resemblance," Steven said.

"Margarette?" Raymond asked.

"The profile is similar—"

"For God's sake Maggie, don't be absurd," Steven admonished. "One in twenty men walking along the street could be said to have a similar profile to Raymond's. It means nothing."

"You are absolutely right," Raymond agreed, to Steven's surprise. "A resemblance is hardly proof, especially as royalty is known to give birth to bastards on a regular basis," he added with a grin. "However, in this case, with your father dying so young and your mother running away as she did...well, I believe the evidence is quite clear."

"What do you know of my mother?" Steven demanded.

"This much," Raymond said. "She was a companion at one time to Baroness Sophie Mendheim. Did you know that?"

Steven shook his head. "Not only didn't I know she was a companion to Baroness Sophie, I don't even know who that is."

"Forgive me," Raymond said. "I seem to take for granted that you are more familiar with our country than you are. Baroness Sophie was very close to the royal family, and it was through her that your parents met."

Steven ignored the reference to his "parents" and gave Raymond his full attention.

"Your father, Prince Gregor, and your mother, Elyse, met at Sophie's Schloss in the mountains. If you want to know more about your parentage, I believe you should begin there at Schloss Wolke."

"Is this Baroness Sophie involved in the resistance movement?" Steven asked suspiciously.

"I can't imagine that she is," Maggie told him. "She doesn't seem political at all. She's just a dotty old lady who lives in a huge castle in the mountains. Adamo leaves her alone because she is no threat to him."

"Then maybe we should visit her," Steven said.

"It is arranged," Raymond told him. "She will be expecting a young couple on their honeymoon, friends of mine who want to explore the country and find out-of-the-way accommodations."

"She knows nothing?" Steven asked.

"Nothing, I swear," Raymond assured him, turning to Maggie and adding, "This young man of yours is suspicious, is he not?"

"It's necessary, Raymond," Steven said. "You must realize that it's dangerous enough just for us to be talking about the royal family."

"Ah, but it is so difficult not to talk of them. They are still greatly loved," Raymond said. "These last twenty years under Adamo—"

"When did the old king die, Karl II?" Steven asked, "My supposed grandfather?"

"In 1855," Raymond told him, "the year after Adamo drove the Turks from our borders. But he really had died earlier than that, when his son—your father—was killed. Your father opposed Adamo, as well he should, for he knew the man better than most as they were in military school together. Even then, when they were young men in school, I believe Prince Gregor saw Adamo as a dangerous adversary."

"Do you think Adamo had something to do with the prince's death?" Steven asked.

"Who is to say?" Raymond replied. "Nothing can be proven, but after his son died, King Karl II spent his last years in seclusion as Adamo gained more and more power."

Steven got to his feet. "I have no fondness for Adamo, but I didn't come here to fight him. I came to find out if Gregor was my father."

"So do not fill your head with anti-Adamo propaganda?" Raymond asked.

"Exactly," Steven replied.

"I will refrain from doing so," Raymond assured him, "and will leave that task to Margarette."

Steven's gaze shifted toward Maggie, but he said nothing.

Getting to his feet, Raymond said, "We've probably talked long enough for Adamo's spies to become suspicious, so I had best continue my walk in private."

"What about the arrangements to this Schloss whatever it's called?"

"Schloss Wolke," Maggie injected. "Cloud Castle."

"Train tickets are waiting at your hotel," Raymond said. "The train is a small mountain cog that will take you part way up the mountain. Then a carriage will meet you." Raymond looked at Maggie and smiled. "The castle is near the village of Bad Mendheim. The hot springs there are quite marvelous. You will not want to miss them."

"Oh, yes," Maggie said, her eyes lighting, "Mendheim. I have heard that it is a lovely village."

"Indeed it is, my Margarette."

Steven looked quickly from Maggie to Raymond. Something was going on between them, something about the village. That much he knew, but if he asked, they wouldn't tell him. That much he also knew. Instead, he'd have to bide his time and find out for himself. And he'd have to be very cautious.

Their luggage was loaded into the carriage with much wringing of his hands and official supervision by Herr Bracken.

"I cannot believe that you, our most favored guests, are leaving us so soon," he said. "Something must have disagreed with you. Our service—has there been a problem?"

"Certainly not," Steven assured him, but that didn't seem to placate Bracken, who turned to Maggie.

"The service was superb," she told him, "and the accommodations were perfect. It's only that," she looked up at Steven, transforming her face into a mask of loving adoration, "my husband and I really wish to be alone—somewhere frightfully romantic. When the baroness offered her castle to us, well..." Maggie sighed.

Steven looked away.

"But she is always there, the baroness, she never leaves," Bracken reminded them.

"Yes, but the castle is so large, it will be as if we're alone. Will it not, my darling?" She touched Steven's arm.

"All alone," Steven said, "darling."

Maggie ignored the inference of that last word, or tried to.

"Now I think we better be on our way," Steven said. "Herr Bracken, you've been more than kind to us." He slipped a wad of bills into the concierge's hand, and before Bracken could lapse into a round of fulsome thanks, the carriage was on its way.

"You enjoy it, don't you?" Steven asked Maggie.

"What?" She was all wide-eyed innocence.

"Tormenting me."

"Tormenting you? Steven, whatever do you mean?" There was a hint of a twinkle in her eyes, but her face was serious.

"Playing the loving wife, telling the world how much you adore me, when privately you probably want to slit my throat?"

"I am only playing the role that I was assigned," she said brittlely. "If I have to pretend to adore you, then I'll do it, and do it well. As for your pretending . . ."

"Yes?" Steven asked.

"You do it well, too. Better, I suspect, than I. Indeed," she added, "it sometimes seems quite believable."

"Oh?"

"Until it turns, and you become cold again," she said bitterly.

"Like you," he noted.

"Perhaps," she replied, wondering if her reactions to him was as confusing as his to her. "This plot we're involved in is very complicated," she told him.

"Indeed."

"And personal feelings should—"

"Should, what?" he pushed.

"Should be—kept in abeyance." That was the only answer she could come up with. She didn't mean it, but there was no other possible response.

"I see," Steven said, turning away and looking out on the passing scene.

"Steven, I—"

"Never mind, Maggie," he said.

Through the carriage window, they saw two men in uniform stopping someone on the street. The officers grabbed him, holding on roughly as the lone man struggled, and then punching him in the stomach until his knees buckled beneath him.

Then the carriage turned the corner and the incident was out of sight.

Steven heaved a sigh and turned back to Maggie. "There's nothing we can do about it," he said.

"Not now but someday..."

Steven studiously ignored her remark, and they rode in silence until Maggie finally referred back to their earlier conversation, saying softly, "I never wanted to slit your throat, Steven."

He smiled. "Maybe that was an exaggeration."

"In fact, I do not hate you, either, if that is what you think. I never have."

Before he could answer, the carriage stopped, and the driver came around to open the door.

"The train station already?" Steven asked.

"No," Maggie answered. "I asked the driver to make a stop along the way. It is the royal cemetery," she said as Steven helped her out of the carriage. "I thought you would like to see where your father and grandfather are buried."

"You're devious and clever as always, Maggie, but playing on my emotions won't win me over to your cause."

She held her head high and met his eyes. "I am well aware that your emotions are out of bounds, Steven. I brought you here as a matter of courtesy."

"Oh?"

"Yes," she said emphatically. "If Gregor is your father, then it is important for you to see his grave. If he is not your father, we have wasted nothing in visiting the royal burial ground."

With that, she marched ahead, holding up the hem of her traveling dress as she climbed the marble stairs to the royal tomb. There was nothing for Steven to do but follow.

The tomb was simple yet beautiful with the sarcophagus of Karl I dominating the space. His queen was beside him and his descendants along the wall.

Steven moved quickly along, stopping to study the bas relief on the tomb of Karl II, father of Prince Gregor. He studied the sculpture carefully, thinking about what Raymond had told him: there was a similarity between his profile and that of the king, in the long forehead, straight nose and square chin. But that in itself meant nothing.

He moved along to the simply decorated sarcophagus of Prince Gregor, the man who could possibly have been his father. Again, he studied the marble profile, finding similarities—and differences.

Hesitantly he reached out and touched the cold marble, outlining the silhouette with his fingertips. And he felt—nothing.

"Let's go," he said to Maggie. "There's nothing here for me. I have no feeling for these people."

Maggie looked at him long and hard, her russet hair gleaming in the sunlight that poured through the open rotunda of the memorial. "Maybe that is because you do not allow yourself to feel anything for anyone, Steven."

"Maybe," he agreed. "But those are my reactions, and I can't change them simply because you—and Raymond and Viktor—have a romantic idea of who I am. I'm myself—nothing more and nothing less. And at this moment I don't feel in the least bit royal."

With that, he took her arm and led her back down the marble steps to the carriage.

Three hours later another carriage bore them through the streets of Bad Mendheim. "This is like something out of a fairy tale," Maggie murmured.

"There's certainly a sense of unreality about it," Steven agreed, looking out through the window at the village.

The houses and shops were constructed of timber and stucco with sharply gabled roofs, doorways and windows framed in bright colors, each opening decorated with a window box that spilled out spring flowers. There was a tavern called Café Legel, a butcher shop, a bakery and a greengrocer.

"This whole afternoon has been idyllic," Maggie reminded him as she settled back against the seat and let the sun bake her skin. She thought of the ride up the mountain in the cog-wheeled railroad on a grade so steep that the engine pushed from behind instead of pulling from the front. As they'd climbed higher and higher into the mountains, the scent of evergreens had been overwhelming in its pithy fragrance.

Steven watched through the window and, like Maggie, enjoyed the idyllic scene. Yet something about it puzzled him; he couldn't quite decide why. Looking over at Maggie, he analyzed her reactions and found them strangely pat. Too accommodating, too enthusiastic, even for a new experience in the European mountains. Something was wrong. Something was missing.

He watched carefully as they drove through the streets, for a clue to the puzzle, and found nothing. It was all clean, beautiful and picture perfect. Then Steven realized what was missing: people. There was almost no one outside on this beautiful spring afternoon when the streets should be filled with townspeople.

"Maggie?"

"Yes, Steven?"

He searched her eyes for some secret but found none. "The Schloss," he said finally, "is it a real castle?"

"It is, from what I've heard," she answered. Something in his inquiry bothered her. It didn't seem completely forthright, and it made her wonder if he suspected.

Maggie turned away, looking out the window, trying to convince herself that no one, not even the suspicious Steven, could imagine that Mendheim was anything but what it seemed, a sleepy mountain village, something out of the stories of Hans Christian Andersen.

She glanced quickly over at him, satisfied to see that he was drinking in the scenery. It was all right so far, but Maggie wondered what his reaction would be when he found out the truth. Anger, certainly, and distrust. But they had to risk that, she and Raymond. If he had known the truth about Bad Mendheim, he would never have agreed to come, never have met Sophie, never have found out about his parents. All that had to happen if they were to achieve their goal. And they would never achieve it without Steven. He was the key.

"Look," Steven said suddenly. "Just beyond that peak."

Maggie saw it then, rising from amongst the trees, a magnificent edifice.

"My God," Steven said. "It *is* real."

The foundations of Schloss Wolke dated back to the time of the Crusades when Count Mendor Mendheim had returned from the East with a sack full of Saracen gold and built a fortress on the mountain to protect it. Though in crumbling disarray, those walls and turrets remained. Each successive Mendheim heir had added to the castle, with no fixed plan of architecture. The great hall was pure Gothic, with soaring spaces and twisted spires; the small church was simpler, more Romanesque in style; while some of the living quarters emanated a romantic rococo feeling. Yet the disparate parts fitted into a whole that gave forth an aura of timeless elegance.

A retinue of servants met their carriage, and the majordomo—a giant of a man, over six feet tall with a huge head that sat uncertainly upon his narrow neck and eyes that scrutinized them with a beady distrust—led them into the house.

"The baroness awaits you upstairs in the family parlor," he told them.

"Thank you," Maggie said uncertainly, not sure whether to go ahead or wait for the giant to lead the way.

Steven took her arm, holding her back until, after satisfying his curiosity about them, the giant moved forward, lumbering toward the staircase.

Their footsteps echoed hollowly on the stones of the curved stairway as they climbed to the top and then made their way down a long, dark hallway filled with paintings of the Mendheim ancestors.

"A barbarous-looking lot," Steven whispered, catching a glimpse of one particularly fierce countenance.

"Shh," Maggie warned as the giant glanced back at them before stopping in front of a pair of huge carved double doors. Then, flinging them open, he announced, "Her Grace, the Baroness of Mendheim."

"Come in, my dears," a frail, throaty voice instructed. "Do not be intimidated."

Steven and Maggie stepped into the cavernous chamber. Heavy draperies were drawn over the windows, the room was lit by numerous tapered candles, and the heat was stifling.

"Come, come," the baroness ordered from her thronelike chair at the far end of the room. Maggie squinted to get a better look, but she was too small and too far away, a gnome of a woman, encased in blankets, her dark eyes bright sparks in the distance.

"There is tea here," the baroness said, "if you will venture forward and not linger back there in the doorway."

They did as they were told, inching forward in the semidarkness until they stood within a few feet of her. A table was set, and two chairs were pulled up to it.

They seated themselves and Maggie offered, "Shall I pour?"

"Now there is a well-brought-up young lady," the baroness chortled. "Already making everything easy for me."

Maggie poured fresh cups of tea, aware that the baroness's sharp eyes were on her.

"So the young honeymooners wish to get away," the old lady said. "Well, this is the ideal place."

"We're very appreciative of your hospitality," Steven said.

"Count Raymond is an old friend. A very close friend," the baroness responded, smiling a little wickedly. "We still look out for each other, and I am always willing to do him a favor."

"You are very gracious," Maggie murmured.

"Not at all," the baroness retorted. "I am simply selfish. I like company, I like young people around me, and most of all I like romance." Again she gave forth one of her hoarse laughs.

"Well, your castle is certainly very romantic," Maggie said. "I imagine the walls could tell many stories."

Steven looked over at Maggie appreciatively, for the stories, if they were forthcoming, might very well have something to do with his mother.

"The walls!" the baroness sneered, "they know nothing compared to what I know."

Maggie and Steven exchanged amused glances.

"I was quite a belle in my day, sought after by numerous young men. Even after I was married to the baron—well, if you must know, he was quite a bit older than I." She emerged from the enveloping blanket just enough to sip gingerly at her tea. "Life was not always so militarized in Mendorra. Once it was gay and exciting—before the advent of that infamous general."

"So you are not a supporter of Adamo," Steven said.

"Pfft," she spat. "He is a pig, do you not agree?"

Steven realized immediately that the old woman was not as politically naive as Maggie had indicated. "We met him only briefly in Delphberg," he said.

"A pig," she repeated contemptuously. "Nothing to compare with what came before him—ah, the royal family. The men so good to their people, so fair and equitable—and so dashing," she added. "They were often visitors here."

"Were they?" Maggie asked innocently, trying to keep the excitement from her voice.

"Oh, yes. The old King Karl and his son, Prince Gregor, came often to the Schloss. Ah, there was a romantic and exciting young man, the prince." She preened, pushing back the blanket and touching her faded hair. "Many thought that he and I were lovers."

Steven flinched but said nothing.

"Were you?" Maggie asked boldly.

"Alas, no, but the gossip persisted. Even the baron suspected. At one time he tried to coax the prince into a duel, but nothing came of it."

"Who did take the prince's fancy?" Steven asked bluntly.

Maggie kicked him under the table, but her warning was too late. The baroness had been offended.

"Well, if not me, then I cannot imagine," she said airily with a dismissive wave of her hand. "Oh, bah, these stories are old and boring. I would prefer to hear about you young people and your travels. But now not," she said. "I am tired and need to have my rest. We will talk over dinner. Then you can tell me everything," she advised. "All about your visit to Delphberg and that terrible Adamo."

Pulling the blanket closer around her, she shut her eyes, and Maggie knew the interview was over. She and Steven got to their feet just as the voice instructed them one more time. "We will dine in the great hall at nine o'clock," she said. "Heinrich will show you to your rooms."

As if by magic, the giant materialized.

Silently they followed him along one hall, down another and up half a flight of broad stairs. "Your room," he stated, opening the door. "You will please to ring if anything is needed." He gestured to an elaborate bellpull and then with a nod turned on his heel and disappeared, leaving them standing on the threshold.

They stepped inside and closed the door. "Do you think she'll sleep there wrapped in the blanket?" Maggie asked.

"No, I expect Heinrich will go back and put her to bed," Steven said. "She can't weigh more than eighty pounds, which would be nothing for old Heinrich."

Maggie laughed nervously. "He is rather frightening."

"Harmless, I expect," Steven said. "If you can just forget his size."

"Which is not easy when he is looming above me." Maggie crossed the room, pulled back the curtains and opened the casement windows, trying not to think about the giant.

"He's really rather childlike," Steven said, following after her.

"Hmm."

"What does that mean?"

"It means I would prefer not to meet him in the dark hallway."

"I'll be sure that you don't." He stood beside her, looking out at the view of mountains and sky as far as the eye could see.

"It is lovely," Maggie said.

"But it can't compare with the other view."

"What?" Maggie looked up at him.

Steven took her hand and led her over to the ornate bed. It was painted cream and blue and studded with gilt angels.

"Well, it is lovely, but—"

"No, Maggie, I don't mean the bed. Look up."

Above the bed was a huge mirror.

Steven couldn't conceal his amusement. "The baroness has quite a sense of humor. I wonder if in her heyday she made use of this bed—and the mirror?"

Maggie stood beside Steven and looked up. They were perfectly reflected in the beautiful leaded mirror suspended above the elegant bed. Steven was still laughing, but Maggie couldn't join in his amusement. This wasn't like the hotel in Delphberg. There was no drawing room or parlor, no overstuffed furniture where Steven could spend the night. There was only this room, this bed and the mirror overhead.

The bed was made for one purpose and one purpose only. It was designed for making love.

Suddenly an image flashed into her mind, white-hot and unbidden. She and Steven were on the bed. His tanned hard body covered hers. Her hair was undone and flowing wildly across the satin pillow. Her arms were wrapped around his back. Her body moved fiercely with the rhythm of his . . .

"Maggie," his voice insisted. "Are you all right?"

"Of course," she said, dismissing the image from her mind.

"You have the strangest look on your face."

"I was just thinking," she said.

"About what?" he insisted.

"Nothing. That is—"

"You're tired?"

"Yes," she agreed gratefully.

"Why don't you rest while I take a walk around the castle grounds?"

"Thank you," Maggie said. "I would like that very much. But do you think Heinrich will allow you outside?"

"We'll see," Steven said with a smile.

Maggie sank down onto the bed. "Perhaps when you come back we can map out a strategy to get the baroness to open up."

"Oh, I don't think we'll have any trouble," Steven said. "Something tells me our friend the baroness likes a little nip or two. A couple of bottles of wine and one of brandy and I think we'll find out everything we need to know."

Chapter Nine

Maggie sank down onto the bed, fluffed the pillows under her head and heaved a sigh. She *was* tired; that much was true, but she was also nervous, high-strung and on edge about what lay ahead for them. There were things that she hadn't told Steven, things that she felt it necessary to keep from him for a while longer.

There were also feelings that she hadn't revealed to him—and never would. Furthermore, she would keep them out of her own mind whenever possible. If they managed to invade her sensibilities, she would be sure that Steven never knew. But it was becoming more and more difficult to keep her emotions under check, and being in increasingly intimate situations with Steven didn't help. They had been lovers, no matter how they tried to deny it; it had happened, it was real, and she never could forget. Never.

A nap was what Maggie had hoped for, but it soon became very apparent that she wasn't going to get it here in this bed, staring up at the huge mirror that reflected her every mood and move. It saw too much, and she couldn't help wondering about what it would see later that night.

She closed her eyes, but it was hopeless. Finally Maggie got up and rang for the maid. She'd take a bath while Steven was out; that would make her feel better.

But the maid who answered her ring arrived without the expected hot water.

"I would like to have my bath," Maggie said.

The plump-cheeked girl curtsied with a quick movement. "My name is Helga," she said, speaking English proudly.

"How do you do, Helga," Maggie said politely. Then she repeated, "I would like to have my bath now." She was not at all sure how well the girl understood.

She must have, though barely, because she responded, "It is outside," slowly and carefully, her cheeks reddening at her struggle with the language.

"Outside?" Maggie was sure she had the wrong word.

"Yes. You will come," she advised.

Maggie hesitated and then, deciding she really had no choice—and certainly nothing to lose—followed Helga through the door and down the long hall to the back of the house. Helga descended a narrow stairway and Maggie, more and more doubtful but feeling adventuresome, went along.

They exited the house and followed a winding path toward a hollow at the foot of the garden. There before them was a beautiful grotto.

Helga turned and smiled. "Yes?" she asked, apropos of nothing.

"Yes!" Maggie repeated.

The grotto was a perfect cavelike hollow in the side of a rocky hill fed by a hot spring and covered over by natural foliage that clung to the latticework of a columned pergola. At the foot of the grotto were two small bathing houses made of stone. Bubbling up from the rocks was a deep pool of steamy water. The heat that rose from the pool formed mist in the cooler air and gave the grotto an eerie, mysterious feeling that somehow made Maggie very peaceful.

Through the columns of the pergola, she could see the natural beauty of the mountain forest, pines and balsam with their heady aroma, oaks just coming into bud, vines blossoming and stretching through the trees and over the roof of the pergola.

The sun was setting, and there was a chill in the air. Maggie shivered slightly, which caused Helga to advise, "Is warm water, madame. To bathe."

"I understand," Maggie said.

Helga led the way around the pool to one of the bathing houses, which looked like a miniature mountain chalet. The furniture was simple, and it sparkled with cleanliness. In a way, the little house was more welcoming than their room in the overpowering Schloss Wolke.

There was no need for Helga to explain the procedure. It was obvious. A heavy white robe and a pile of fluffy towels had been laid out for Maggie. There was an open closet for her clothes, which she had the feeling Helga would retrieve and return to her room, neatly sponged and pressed.

Helga stood in the doorway, an expectant smile on her face. Maggie returned the smile and felt obligated to let the girl know that she understood what was expected. "I shall undress here and bathe in the pool," she said slowly.

"Yes, yes," Helga replied. Whether she had translated properly or not was unimportant. They had communicated well enough, and with another quick curtsy, Helga was gone, closing the bathhouse door behind her.

Maggie undressed and hung up her clothes. Then, wrapped in the robe, she went outside and moved across the cool stones toward the pool. Carefully stepping along the rocks that led into the pool, she tested the water by splashing it as she walked. It was warm, almost hot and very pleasing.

She'd just untied her robe and was prepared to toss it aside when she heard a splash and a long, drawn-out, "Ahh."

Startled, she looked across the pool, and in the mist that swirled above the water, she saw a man.

Quickly rewrapping the robe around her, Maggie turned and began to run back toward the bathhouse.

"Maggie—"

She stopped in her tracks. "Steven?"

"Yes, I'm here in the pool," he called out. "Don't run away, for God's sake."

Maggie walked back, squinting in the mist as she tried to make out Steven's form in the water.

"What are you doing here?" she asked.

"Having a bath. Heinrich directed me to the grotto. And you?"

Maggie laughed. "I was about to do the same, directed by Helga."

Steven leaned back in the pool, his arms resting along the ledge behind him. "Do you suppose this is a plan cooked up by the baroness as a honeymoon surprise—"

"Or is it really the way everyone at the Schloss bathes?" Maggie finished for him. "I will never find out from Helga."

"Her English isn't any better than Heinrich's, I gather," Steven said.

"No, and she has no German. But she's not as frightening as Heinrich."

"Don't worry. He's really quite friendly," Steven assured her. "Aren't you coming in?"

Maggie realized that she was still standing ankle-deep in the warm water, the robe pulled around her. "Should I?"

"Of course. It's very relaxing," Steven said. "I hadn't realized how tight my muscles were."

"Well, I could wait until you finish your bath...."

"Hell, Maggie, the staff of the whole castle is probably watching. We're purported to be honeymooners very much in love. Let's don't disappoint them—or make them doubtful," he added.

She realized he was right. It would seem very strange for the young lovers to bathe separately. Still, she was hesitant, and that hesitancy involved the feelings she wanted to keep from him.

"Maggie," he warned, half-rising from the pool, "if you don't get down here, I'm going to drag you in."

"I am coming," she said, "but close your eyes. Just for a second."

"For God's sake, Maggie..."

But he did as she asked, and in the instant when she saw his eyes close, she tossed aside the robe and slipped into the water.

Steven was right, she realized immediately. The water felt delicious against her skin, warm and comforting. "Oh," she marveled, sinking down into the warmth until only her head remained above the surface. "This is heavenly."

"And in a down-to-earth way, very good for the muscles," he advised. "Move over here. There's a rock bench of sorts underwater where you can relax."

Remaining submerged up to her neck, Maggie made her way to the underwater seat beside him.

"Come closer, and you can see the sun begin to set. Look, it's like a giant fireball."

Maggie peered through the trees toward the horizon. The sun's radiance streaked the sky with purple and blue and gold which did, indeed, look like a heavenly conflagration caused by the huge red sun.

As they watched, the sun sneaked behind the horizon, the bright colors softened to pastels, and the fire seemed to extinguish. The wind whistled softly through the tops of the trees, and somewhere nearby a bird called out in the gathering dusk. Maggie closed her eyes and let the heat seep through her, deep into her muscles, relaxing them completely.

"Don't fall asleep," Steven warned in a voice as soft as the wind. "Maggie..."

"Yes," she replied dreamily.

"Wake up, Sleeping Beauty. We need to be at our best tonight."

She opened her eyes slowly, saw him beside her and groped for the mental shield she'd hoped to keep between them. But here in the pool, so relaxed, so peaceful, she wasn't able to summon it up. They were very close, only inches apart on the underwater stone seat. A little movement by either of them, and their bodies would touch.

"We will be at our best," she said quickly. She was trying to maintain a professionalism, but the water prevented it. Relaxing, peaceful, yes; it was that, but it was also sensual, calling up every deep feeling within her. "When we work at it, we are a very good team," she managed.

"And as a team we can find the answers about my family."

"Yes," she agreed softly.

"And then get the hell out of Mendorra."

For a moment, Maggie was jarred from sensuality into reality. There was more at stake, more that would be required of them after Steven learned the truth. She wanted to tell him that, but she couldn't. Not yet. Instead, she tried to cover her concern with a question. "You dislike being here so much?"

"In a way, yes. Oh, I like the countryside, the beauty of it, but I don't like what's happening here, and I like even less the pathetic hope that I'm some kind of royal hero who will change things, who will save the people. I'm not."

"I—we—had hoped—" Maggie attempted.

"No," he said. "Not a chance, Maggie. So you might as well take advantage of the hot springs, relax and forget your dreams of intrigue."

"But—" she tried again.

"I know, it's like asking you not to breathe. You're all caught up in the cause of the Mendorran people. It's made you nervous, anxious."

She didn't answer, because she knew he was right.

"Well, tonight, I'm going to see to it that you relax, my darling wife. Now, turn around," he ordered.

"What?" she asked, mystified.

"Turn sideways on the bench." She felt his warm, heavy hand on her shoulder, repositioning her on the seat.

"Like this?" she asked throatily.

"Exactly," he answered. Then without another word he began to massage her neck and shoulders in an easy rhythm with his strong, long-fingered hands. But Maggie was not prepared for what was happening, and she fought against it, tensing, instead of relaxing, at his touch.

"Hey, this is supposed to be pleasant, Maggie," he said. "Enjoy it."

"I am," she lied, and then as his hands continued to work on her tense muscles, the lie became a truth. She could no longer resist his magic. He rubbed her neck, her shoulders, moving his hands slowly along her flesh until she began to melt under their touch. Combined with the heat of the water, the heat that emanated from his hands was exquisite torture. She gave in to it.

"Now, that's better," he said as she rolled her head back and let out a sigh of contentment. "It feels good, doesn't it?"

All she could do was nod, for she scarcely dared to breathe as she waited to hear what else he would say.

He didn't disappoint her with his carefully chosen words. "Being here with you like this is so quiet and peaceful. We've never had that, have we? Peace and quiet."

"No, I guess we never have," she agreed. "We have had nothing but fireworks from the first moment we met."

"Countess Oblansky," he said teasingly, "whoever would have thought we'd end like this. Married, at least in the eyes of Mendorra, sharing a honeymoon in a mountain hot spring."

She wasn't expected to respond, which was lucky because Maggie couldn't have found her voice. He'd stopped the massage of her shoulders and had begun to run his hands up and down her arms. Despite the heated water, she could feel a cool shiver of delight run along her skin where he touched her.

Then, slowly, deliberately, he slid his hands around her waist and let them linger there for a long moment before moving one hand upward to cup the roundness of her breast.

Maggie felt as though she were suspended in time. Her heart had begun a wild, erratic pounding, so violent that she didn't think she'd be able to take another breath. Yet somehow she managed to breathe, managed to inhale gulps of air that kept her from turning toward him as she wanted to.

Yes, she wanted to, but she fought the impulse. Once before she'd fallen too easily into Steven's arms, and her impetuousness had brought nothing but pain to both of them. She'd promised herself not to let it happen again.

Maggie had to keep her emotions intact for one simple reason. She didn't trust them. They could betray her very quickly and easily. Nor did she trust Steven, when she let herself think about him. Everytime in the past when she'd felt close to him, he'd turned on her. She couldn't afford to let that happen again.

She put up her mental defenses, asking herself if this was a trick, a trap of some kind to discredit her. She wouldn't put it past Steven, whose behavior had confused and puzzled her all along. Wild thoughts about him careened madly through her mind while her body tried vainly to fight the sensations that his touch continued to arise in her.

"Maggie, Maggie." He leaned closer, and his breath was warm and soft on the nape of her neck. Slowly his fingers caressed her breast, teasing the hard orb of her nipple. Maggie sighed and leaned against him, her body no longer able to control the feelings that coursed through it, her mind no longer able to think rationally. She was overpowered by him, mentally and physically. There was only Steven and his touch; everything else was gone.

He was saying her name again, whispering in her ear. "Maggie, Maggie. Look at me."

She remained turned away from him, her eyes downcast.

"Then listen, Maggie," he said. "When I saw that bed and mirror, I couldn't help but think..." He took a deep breath. "I couldn't help but think of you there, lying on the bed, beneath the mirror—with me beside you."

She held her breath, still silent.

"I know that it's foolish, maybe even dangerous for us to be lovers again. That could get in the way of your plans. But Maggie, what will it be like for us tonight—in that room, in that bed together? Answer me," he demanded.

She'd thought about the night, too, thought of little else. "I do not know," she said. "It will not be easy."

"No, it won't," he repeated. "In fact, it might very well be impossible for me not to hold you." He held her now, warmly, eagerly. "To love you. All night long."

Maggie remained immobile, fearing to move, fearing to breathe, fearing to let him know how she felt. Then she allowed a sigh to escape her lips, and she knew he heard it.

"Does that mean you feel the same? Tell me, Maggie. If it's wrong of me to want you, let me know." Steven moved away from her. "If I've spoken out of turn, tell me. Tell me now, Maggie." There was a raw edge of urgency in his voice.

She turned toward him, ready to answer but not able to find her voice.

"I can ask the baroness for another room," he said. "If that's what you want. I can tell her—"

Maggie stood up. The water cascaded down her shoulders and between her breasts. Her skin shimmered and shone with a damp, golden glow in the last rays of sunlight. It painted her whole body in a soft radiance that took Steven's breath away. He'd never seen anything so beautiful, so ephemeral and otherworldly. To Steven she looked like a goddess, like Venus rising from the sea.

She looked at him directly, smiling a tentative smile.

That was all Steven needed. He rose and stood beside her, hip-deep in the warm, bubbling water. Putting a hand around her waist, he pulled her close. Her breasts were wet and slippery against his chest, and in order to hold on to her he had to grip even tighter, enveloping her in his arms. Her soft breasts were crushed against him, and he hoped he wasn't hurting her, but he couldn't stop pulling her closer and closer.

Maggie's reaction was as intense as his when their lips met and she allowed him to drink deeply of her in a long kiss while she clung to him, her arms tight around his neck.

"I want to make love to you, Maggie," he said. "Right here, right now, to kiss your breasts and touch you everywhere." He whispered the words against her mouth as their kisses continued. "All I can think about is making love to you. I know you feel the same. Remember that day in my room at the ranch—in my bed?"

"Yes," she murmured. "I remember."

"Remember this?" His hands caressed her, and as he moved them over her body, she returned his kisses with a fervor that imitated his own, a little moan escaping her lips whenever their mouths parted for an instant.

He let his hand stray along her back to her waist and then cup her bottom and lift her partially from the water.

Maggie gave herself completely to every move of his, every touch, every murmured word of need that escaped his lips. She allowed her hands to wander restlessly up and down his back. With the tips of her fingers she traced the scar on his upper arm, the fresh scar from that terrible gunshot wound. It brought everything back in a shimmering wave of remembrance. Their passion and their anger, their beginning and their ending.

"I am sorry," she murmured. "I am sorry you were hurt because of me."

"It doesn't matter now, Maggie." His voice was low and husky. "Not now."

She wanted what he wanted, and his need was apparent to her. She felt it hard against her abdomen and as he lifted her, her legs opened slightly to welcome the touch of his manhood.

She couldn't believe she'd responded so easily and with such abandon, but she'd not been able to stop herself. The feeling of him against her in the warm water was more than she could bear. It sent shivers throughout her body, intensifying the heat of the spring that bubbled around them.

"This can't be wrong, Maggie, not when we both want it so much," he whispered.

"No, it cannot be," she agreed. There was nothing she wanted more than to make love to Steven, here under the gathering twilight, beneath the rays of the rising moon.

"And yet..." Those two words lingered coolly in the air.

"And yet?" she repeated, her heart stopping for a moment, catching a beat.

"Every damn thing about us is wrong."

Maggie felt her stomach churn, unable to believe that his shifting feelings were changing again just when they'd reached out for each other. She moved away slightly, as if to let her defenses slip back into place.

"It was wrong from the way we met right up to this plan we're involved in. It was all pretense and lies."

Suddenly she shivered despite the warmth of the water. Pretense, lies . . . she didn't want to hear it.

His voice was low and soft in her ear, each breath tickling a strand of her hair against her neck. "If we had any sense, we'd get on the first train to Paris, wouldn't we?"

"I suppose so," she whispered. Her mouth was dry, her throat tight. She had no idea what he was going to say or do.

"But we don't have any sense, do we? Not about each other, not tonight."

She looked up at him, her eyes passion dark, her blood singing in her veins,. "No sense at all," she said softly, flowing back to him, letting herself melt against his chest.

"And no more lies and pretending," he said. "That's all behind us now." He looked down at her, the planes of his face gleaming in the last rays of sunlight, drops of water glistening on his beard. Maggie was gripped by a strange sense of unreality, wrapped in the misty steam rising from the water, held in Steven's arms. She heard him telling her what she'd wanted to hear from the first night she'd met him. She heard him saying that he wanted her....

"No matter what, this can never be wrong," she said, closing her eyes and raising her face to him.

He wrapped his hands in her hair and tilted back her head so he could kiss her more thoroughly, his tongue touching hers, sucking, drawing her into his mouth.

Maggie moaned and pressed against him. She was losing all sense of time and place, of what was right and wrong, of what could be foolish, even desperate. None of that mattered. Steven was right. Whether anything else made sense or not, what was happening between them now could never be denied.

In the distance, lights were flickering in the castle, great lanterns being lit outside the doorways, and from far away they could hear the hustle of a house preparing for the evening. A voice, perhaps a maid calling out, drifted to them.

Forcing herself back into reality, Maggie said, "Steven, the castle—"

"I know," he answered with another kiss.

"The baroness—"

"Yes," he said, pulling her close.

"She will have dinner waiting."

"Hmm."

"Steven!" She pulled away, or tried to, struggling to put distance between them. "We should go back to the castle."

"Or we could go into the bathhouse," he murmured suggestively.

It was an idea that tempted Maggie sorely, especially when he touched her again, one hand lightly on her cheek, but it was enough to bring back the tremors she'd felt just moments before.

"Yes, we could," she said tentatively.

Steven was very still, devouring her with his eyes. His hand lingered on her cheek. They'd moved into deeper water, which now lapped around their shoulders. "This just shows what a beautiful woman in a hot springs can do to a man. It can turn his thinking all around."

"A woman's, too," she said slowly, wondering if her life would ever be the same again.

"The baroness can't be faulted as a hostess," Steven said with a low, teasing laugh. "She knows how to keep her guests happy and satisfied."

That's when a small hesitant voice called out from the other edge of the pool. "Madame—"

Maggie and Steven turned together toward Helga, both of them automatically submerging a little deeper until they were neck high in the spring.

"Well, almost satisfied," he whispered to Maggie.

Helga's round pink face was wreathed in a smile. "Is time," she said, gesturing toward the brightly lit house. "You dress for dinner now."

Steven laughed and called out, "Your timing is marvelous, Helga."

"Please?"

"It is all right, Helga," Maggie said quickly, nudging Steven. "I understand. We will dress for dinner now."

With another smile and a little bob of her head, Helga was gone.

Holding Maggie's hand, Steven led her to the edge of the pool and reached for their robes. "I guess the bathhouse plan will have to be put aside," he said.

"I suppose so," Maggie replied.

"Well, we still have our bed tonight," he said.

"Yes," Maggie agreed. "That marvelous naughty bed."

Chapter Ten

The dining hall of Schloss Wolke reminded Maggie of the Tudor mansions she'd visited near London. There was a gallery above the room, complete with banners bearing the coats of arms of Mendorra's titled families. The baroness, not one to eschew flaunting her own background, was quick to point out the Mendheim banner—a hawk rampant on a field of scarlet clutching a dove of peace in his talon.

"The baron's family were always warlike," she said with a chortle, "and always attempted to hide the fact with their pretenses at peace." Baroness Sophie gestured toward the dove. "There is blood, we cannot help observing, where the talon holds the bird."

"Fascinating," Steven said, looking more carefully at the coat of arms before letting his eyes circle the room. In corner niches suits of armor were displayed, the very ones worn by Mendheim men on their various crusades against the Moors, the Turks and the Saracens. Weapons—spears and sabers and swords—decorated the walls.

They followed the baroness as she strode past the huge fireplace, high enough for her to walk into, deep enough to roast an ox, she commented, which had happened often in the past.

Although she walked with a cane, her gait was remarkably strong for so small and delicate a figure, no more than skin and bones and penetrating black eyes. "I am old and I look it," she told them, "but there is life in me still, at least for an hour or so at a time. Now let us take our places."

The solid mahogany table was at least twenty-five feet long. "So heavy it would take an army of servants to lift it," she told them. The baroness had a way of commenting on each item they confronted—the coats of arms, the fireplace, the table—as if discussing old friends.

They grouped at one end of the table, Sophie at the head with Steven to her right and Maggie to her left. The light was provided by two heavy silver candelabra holding twenty candles each. "I like to have enough light to see my food properly," she told them. "I detest dinner parties where one must constantly grope around with one's fork, never sure what it might find upon the plate."

She chortled again as she lifted her silver goblet to toast her two guests with white wine from the Rhine country. It was the first of many glasses of wine that the steward would pour during the evening as course after course was brought out of the serving pantry. Maggie couldn't believe her eyes as the fish sautéed in wine was followed by a roast pork loin, delicate squabs wrapped in pastry, crusty bread served with liver and mushroom pâtés. More surprising still, she managed to eat at least a portion of each course, ending with fruit and cheese and another wine, this one from Italy, Sophie explained.

"Your wine cellar must be extraordinary," Steven complimented.

"More than extraordinary," Sophie replied with not a trace of timidity. "It is the best in all of Mendorra. In the old days, when the baron and I entertained, our hospitality was the talk of the entire country. Everyone wished for an invitation to Schloss Wolke."

"Even the royals," Maggie added.

"Especially the royals." Sophie's eyes sparkled. "Oh, our dear Raymond, he cut quite a swath then. No woman was safe in the same room with him."

"And the prince?" Steven asked.

Maggie held her breath. She could feel the tenseness in his voice, and she knew he was hoping to hear more than the baroness had divulged earlier in the day.

"Prince Gregor." She said his name with a kind of familiar authority. "He was quieter, as becomes a royal, but no less dashing, and of course the rumors persisted about his conquests, but they were kept very quiet, as befitted his station and his destiny in life."

"So he was not a saint," Maggie prodded.

"Of course not, my dear. No man is." She chortled again. "As for his admiration of me, well, as I mentioned, a duel was nearly fought because of it. Yes, the prince came here often, to see me, of course."

Maggie glanced at Steven, wondering if he was as dubious as she, but his expression, serious and attentive, told her nothing.

"You see, there was no possibility of an affair between the prince and myself," she assured them, "even though, I am certain, he wanted me for his mistress," she said confidentially.

Once again, Maggie looked toward Steven, noticing not just the hint of a smile on his lips but something else, a deeper inquisitiveness, in his eyes.

"No, he was not a saint," she repeated, "and he did stray once that I know of. Of course, I was the cause of it," she bragged, "however unintentionally."

"How is that?" Steven asked. He'd gestured to the wine steward, and their glasses were filled again with the rich, ruby port. The baroness drank deeply, her bright eyes beginning to glaze a little.

"He visited often because of me," she said, "and as I was not available to him, why, he found someone else, right here at Schloss Wolke."

This time Steven was silent, but he had leaned forward, intent upon her words.

"Gregor's eyes fell on a young woman in my employ. Is that not interesting?" she asked rhetorically. "She was working as companion to my children. She had come to me highly recommended, the daughter of a school teacher in the village, a widower who was himself in poor health. She was virtually an orphan so we took her in."

"And the prince became enamored of her?" Maggie led the old woman on gently.

"Indeed, what was he to do? He could not have me," she reminded them. "I suspect the girl pursued him. In any case he always seemed to be here, hunting with my husband—once the thought of a duel passed out of their minds—or taking the waters or attending a ball. I would see him occasionally slipping out, to meet her, I believe. It was summertime when their affair took place."

"How long ago?" Steven asked, his voice tight.

"How do I know? Many years ago, too many for me to remember," she said, dismissing the question.

Steven was insistent. "Baroness," he said urgently. "You have to—"

Maggie interrupted. "I imagine there was quite a scene when the affair was discovered."

She shot Steven a quieting glance. Now was not the time to attempt to get detailed dates out of the baroness. It was all she could do to follow the conversation.

"After all," Maggie added, "the woman was a commoner."

"Indeed, she was," Sophie agreed. "It was all hushed up, of course, but Gregor was ordered back to Delphberg by the king. As for... now, what was her name?"

Again, Maggie's glance urged Steven to be patient. If the baroness was going to remember, she would do so more easily without prodding.

"Was it Alicia? No," she decided. "Lise," she tried, and then shook her head. "Now I remember!" The black eyes lit up. "It was Elyse. Elyse Contrand." She rewarded herself with another sip of wine.

Steven didn't allow himself to react when he heard his mother's name. Amazingly, he remained stone still. But his eyes were darkly thoughtful, and Maggie knew he was beginning to believe.

"What happened to her, to Elyse?" Maggie asked.

"Oh, I cannot remember. I believe she just left. Yes, that was what happened. She left me without a governess for the children. I had to spend most of the summer finding a replacement. She just seemed to vanish. And then of course, so soon afterward, less than a year, Gregor was killed in that accident."

"I thought he was assassinated," Steven blurted out.

"Well, of course, we all suspect that he was, but it was purported to be an accident. Most of us, at least those who are not afraid to speak up, blame Adamo. He was commander of the army, and Gregor was inspecting one of the battalions near the front—we were fighting against the Turks on the Eastern Front at the time," she remembered. "That is when it happened, arranged, I am certain, by the pig Adamo."

Ready with his next question, Steven ignored the fact that the baroness was fading fast. "If everyone knows the prince was killed, how can the Mendorrans allow Adamo to rule their country?"

The baroness gripped her wineglass with her gnarled, heavily ringed fingers. "Fear, my dear boy. Fear. None of us wishes to die like Gregor—and the others."

"So no one investigated Gregor's death?" Steven asked. "Not even the king?"

That elicited a quick response. "Ah, the poor king. He was so bereaved, so despondent. I do not believe he knew what he was doing when he appointed Adamo to investigate."

"What?" Steven asked.

"Yes, it is true. Setting the fox to guard the henhouse, eh?" She sipped a bit more wine. "But the old man could not be held accountable for his actions because of his grief. So there was no opposition to Adamo from any quarter. But now—now we have the opposition we need. Now we have some hope. The rebels—"

"Baroness, may I get you something?" Maggie interrupted. "After-dinner coffee?"

Steven looked sharply at Maggie. After urging the baroness to talk all evening, Maggie now seemed anxious to change the subject. Immediately he felt something was wrong. He tried to remember the other times he'd felt this uneasiness. It had been especially noticeable in the looks Maggie and Raymond had exchanged when the village of Bad Mendheim was mentioned, and there had been other hints, as well.

"You're interested in the rebels?" Steven asked the baroness, ignoring Maggie's coffee ploy, which Sophie had not, in any case, considered.

She let out a whooping chortle. "Well, I would have to be, would I not, living in the midst of them?"

"In the midst of them," Steven repeated, his voice low and cold. "I don't know what you mean."

"Few people do," the baroness Sophie replied sadly. "Raymond knows, but he is very discreet."

"Are you telling me that there're antigovernment forces in Bad Mendheim?" As he spoke, Steven looked across the table at Maggie, who had the grace to look away.

"I am not going to tell you," Sophie responded drunkenly, wagging her finger. "Not going to say. Discreet." With that her head wobbled slightly and then dropped heavily forward onto her bony chest. She had spoken her final words of the evening.

The wine steward clapped his hands. And Heinrich appeared out of the shadows.

"The baroness is ready for bed," the steward announced.

"I think we'll make our good-nights, too," Steven said as Heinrich stepped forward to attend to the baroness.

Maggie tried to catch his eye, but Steven would have none of it as he stood up abruptly, pushing back his chair with a grating sound that carried across the stone floor of the huge room. "We'll thank the baroness for her hospitality in the morning. My dear," he said, looking for the first time at Maggie.

She got to her feet and walked silently from the room with Steven following behind her. They spoke not a word as they ascended the wide staircase and made their way down the hall to their room.

Once the door was closed behind them, Steven turned on her.

"You knew!" he said angrily, and in those two words were all the bitterness he'd kept pent up inside. "You knew the rebels were in Bad Mendheim and you used my curiosity about my parents to get me here. When were you planning to tell me, Maggie?"

"I—" she stammered.

"Never mind," he said, "I see what you had in your head. You were going to make me the damned king of the mountain, weren't you?"

"Not the king of the mountain, Steven," she said honestly, "but the King of Mendorra."

"And when did you intend to tell me?"

"When the time was right," she answered.

"After we made love? After I was softened up and besotted with you?" He turned suddenly, slamming his fist against the door. "Dammit, Maggie, why do you keep this up?"

"What?" she asked tremulously.

"Seducing me into believing in your crazy schemes."

"It was no scheme, Steven," she said, more evenly this time. "We are here to find out about your parentage. I am not responsible for the fact that the baroness lives near Bad Mendheim, where the rebels are hiding. Steven, there are rebels everywhere, all over Mendorra," she shouted.

He turned back to her, his face still angry. "Don't lie to me, Maggie. Just tell me the truth for once. You and Raymond weaved your own plan, at some point when we were in Delphberg, and I was out of your earshot. It must have happened at the ball or in the park," he mused to himself. "Your plan was for me to meet with the rebels and be wooed into helping them."

"No, I—"

"Maggie," he insisted.

"All right," she said, almost shouting. "Perhaps that was part of the plan."

"I see." His voice was coldly understanding.

"Well, what is wrong with that?" she asked. "You *are* sympathetic with their cause."

"Wait a minute," he interrupted.

"You are just too damned stubborn to admit it."

"Have it your way," he replied disinterestedly.

"There is nothing wrong in your meeting with them, Steven," she insisted. "It would not be a commitment. But you are afraid to become involved."

"This has nothing to do with fear," he replied.

"Oh, it no longer matters, Steven," she answered, turning away from him and clutching the bedpost, her shoulder dropping as if the life had gone out of her. "I am tired," she said, "tired of you and your stubbornness. Do whatever you wish. Leave. I do not care anymore."

Steven took a long stride, closing the gap between them. "I can't leave," he said slowly, "as you well know. Not now, not when just half an hour ago I learned that a woman named Elyse worked in this castle and supposedly had an affair with Prince Gregor. Elyse was my mother's name, Maggie," he reiterated.

"I know," Maggie responded weakly.

"That's the first solid information I've had. My mother was here, in this village. So was the man who was my father. I don't know if he was a prince or a villager, but I know he was here, and I'll find out. I won't leave until I do."

Maggie's face lit up. It was going to be all right. "Then we will stay," she said.

"*I'll* stay, Maggie. You can do whatever you like." His voice cut through her like a knife.

"I do not understand you, Steven." She turned back to look at him. "Each time we begin to become close, everything falls apart. You become so cold and angry and . . . heartless."

"Heartless?" He laughed bitterly. "Well, Countess, I wonder where *your* heart is in all this? But I really shouldn't wonder because after all you're a fine actress. When we were in the hot springs tonight, that was all an act, too, wasn't it?"

She had no chance to respond.

"Sure it was, your warmth, your . . . ah, hell, you don't have to tell me. I know. It was all a damned act to keep me around, but you excel at that, don't you—lying, pretending?"

"Get out," Maggie said suddenly, furious with him. "I refuse to talk about this anymore. I refuse to listen to your accusations. Just get out."

"Gladly," he said. "I'm sure somewhere in this castle I can find a bed—alone, without a mirror," he added in a nasty voice as he turned on his heel and left the room.

With a thunderous crash the door closed behind him. Maggie stood beside the bed, holding on to the bedpost. Finally she looked up toward the mirror on the ceiling. Her pale face and her sad eyes reflected in it, mocking her until she looked away.

Steven was gracious enough to acknowledge Maggie as she entered the sunlit morning room where he was having coffee and ignoring a plate filled with the ubiquitous Mendorran pastries.

"Good morning," he said. "I hope you slept well."

Maggie glided into a seat at the charming little table that had been set up for them and poured a cup of coffee. "I slept marvelously," she lied. "And you?"

"Like a baby," he said, although the circles under his eyes belied his words.

Maggie occupied herself with her coffee, adding cream and sugar, tasting, and deciding on more sugar. It was a careful routine designed to avoid more conversation. She wasn't going to be the one pushing and prodding today.

"So are you staying?" he finally asked.

Maggie stirred her coffee, took a sip, smiled and replied, "Of course. I gave my word." Pleased with herself and the coffee, she took another sip and asked, "And you?"

"I told you last night. I want to find out more about Elyse Contrand. I think the village would be a good place to start."

"The village," she repeated. "Why, what a surprise, Steven. I should not think you would want to be in the village with all those rebels running around. You might even see one, or worse, be confronted by one." Sarcasm dripped from her words like the icing from the pastry she nibbled on.

"I can handle it," Steven said dryly.

"Good. Then perhaps we should begin at the cemetery next to the church. Someone might remember the Contrands—the priest, a deacon, an old attendant. One never knows who—"

"What do you mean 'we'?" Steven interrupted, raising an eyebrow.

"Of course, 'we'. For good or ill, you and I are in this together, Steven." Maggie was determined to be as coolly polite and aloof as he. "Unfortunately, it is too late for us to drop our guise of a happily married couple."

He shrugged. "That's fine, Maggie. I'm ready anytime you are."

She took another sip of coffee, another bite of her pastry and carefully wiped her lips. "You are not having any pastry?"

He shook his head.

"It is delicious," she reminded him, but when he didn't respond, she shrugged and got to her feet. "I will fetch my hat and gloves."

"And tell the baroness where we're going," he suggested as she crossed the room.

Maggie paused at the door. "Unless I miss my guess, the baroness will be sleeping until noon. But I will certainly leave word with Heinrich."

Two hours later, after an exhausting and fruitless search through the cemetery at Saint Luke's Church, Maggie and Steven relaxed within the cool darkness of the Café Legel on Bad Mendheim's main square.

They chose a round, battered wooden table beside high arched windows so that Steven could look out onto the street and the square. Maggie would have preferred the smaller, more deeply recessed windows, which allowed glimpses of a sunny interior garden, but she deferred to Steven, whose unsuccessful trek through the myriad of tombstones had left him irritable enough.

The view didn't help. "I'm surprised to see so many soldiers out there," he said. They'd spent their time in the cemetery alone except for a few words with the priest, and entered the café from the side street, so this was Steven's first glimpse of the town life in daylight.

Maggie looked out the window to see scattered groups of soldiers milling about. "It is eerie. They seem to be watching for something."

"Tourists, maybe," Steven told her half-seriously as the waitress approached.

The waitress smoothed her printed dirndl skirt and tugged a little self-consciously at her scoop-necked blouse, greeting them effusively in German.

Steven raised a questioning eyebrow to Maggie. "It's up to you. I'm lost."

The girl laughed merrily and tossed her head of long black hair that cascaded down her back. "You are Americans," she said excitedly.

"Yes," Maggie responded with relief that she wouldn't have to translate the conversation.

"We are pleased to have visitors from England and America so we practice our English. I am Maria," she announced.

Maggie jumped in quickly, introducing herself and Steven as "Margaret and Stephen Englehardt, exhausted from our exploration—"

Steven gave her a negative shake of the head, but she ignored it.

"Yes?" Maria asked.

"Of the church and graveyard."

Maria was clearly confused.

"On a hunt for ancestors. We both have family from this part of the world."

"Oh," Maria said, "I understand. It is possible that I can be of help. My family is here in Mendorra for many generations."

"That's very interesting," Steven interrupted. "But maybe we could have our coffee first."

"Oh, yes," Maria exclaimed. "I am so sorry to forget. May I please to tell you about our choice of coffees?"

"Just coffee," Steven said, "of whatever kind."

Now it was time for Maggie to telegraph the silencing look. "But, of course, we would like to hear about the coffee you have to offer," she told Maria.

The waitress looked questioningly at Steven, who nodded in agreement with his "wife."

"There is much to offer," Maria said. "First, the Melange. Is half coffee and half milk. Then we have Einspanner, rich coffee with whipped cream. Is very nice," she assured them. "And last, our Turkischer. Is the Turkish coffee, black and much strong."

Maggie laughed. "I am afraid 'much strong' would be too much for me. I will have the Melange."

"Turkish," Steven said, "and the stronger the better."

After Maria exited toward the kitchen, Steven leaned across the table and asked angrily, "What's all this heart-to-heart with the waitress, telling her our business? I don't think it's smart for us to associate ourselves with Elyse Contrand. At least not now. Adamo may know—hell, I'm sure he *does* know about her."

"Perhaps," Maggie agreed, "but I haven't mentioned the name Contrand. Maria only knows that we're looking for ancestors. That's our cover. As for the

Contrands, we'll have to find them on our own, as we did in the church cemetery."

"Yeah," Steven said dejectedly, "two tombstones, dating from the 1700s."

"One had no dates. It could have been your grandfather, the school teacher, but obviously the young priest knew nothing."

"Hardly wet behind the ears," Steven agreed. "We'll never learn anything until we find where the birth and death records are kept."

"We can ask Maria."

Steven scoffed at that. "How would she know when the priest couldn't even help us?"

"You said yourself he was hardly wet behind the ears."

"But at least he's associated with the church, Maggie. For God's sake. Use your brain." As soon as he'd given that rude advice, Steven tried to retract it, but Maggie wasn't intimidated in the slightest.

"I *am* using my brain, Steven. The priest is young and new to the area. Maybe he didn't know anything, or maybe he sensed something was wrong...."

"Or maybe he was afraid." Steven was thoughtfully silent for a long moment. "Yes, he could have feared recriminations from the military."

"Exactly," Maggie said. "It is by their largesse that the church continues to thrive. Obviously, Adamo is not a religious man. And in a military state—"

"I see what you mean," Steven said. "And you have an excellent point. I was out of line earlier. Sorry," he added.

It was a rather grudging apology, Maggie thought. But she also knew he rarely found apology necessary since he rarely admitted being in the wrong! It was a trait of Steven's that she'd become used to. No need to challenge it now.

"So we can ask Maria?"

Steven nodded just as the girl appeared.

"Here is one Melange and one Turkischer," she said. "As well I have brought a plate of pastries . . ."

Steven grinned at Maggie. She knew he was thinking of all the pastries they'd been served since arriving in Mendorra, and for a moment they were relaxed and easy with each other, just like a real married couple, Maggie thought, laughing at the same things.

"Is there something more I can bring?" Maria asked.

"No, but you can give us some information," Maggie said. "We are looking for our ancestors, you know."

Maria nodded brightly.

"But we cannot find the birth and death records."

"No, no," the girl agreed. "Not here, not in Bad Mendheim. Is too small."

"Then where?" Maggie asked.

"Across the mountains in Magris."

Steven groaned. "You mean there's no one around here who could help us."

"I do not think. Unless . . ."

"Yes?" Maggie asked.

"I will ask my father. Please wait."

With that she disappeared quickly, leaving Steven wondering what had brought on her sudden change of mind. He didn't have time to contemplate, however, for she was back with an answer.

Leaning over the table, she whispered, "My father says to go to the old priest. He lives not far from here on the Donnerstrasse."

"Donnerstrasse." Maggie repeated the number the girl gave her and then before she had time for a proper word of thanks, Maria had scribbled out the bill and gone off to wait on another table.

"I wonder if she knows what we're up to," Steven said.

"I don't think—"

Steven stopped Maggie's words with the pressure of his hand on hers. "*I* think we'd better get out of here before too many more people get suspicious of what we're doing."

Maggie looked around the little restaurant, but from what she could tell the patrons seemed much more interested in their coffee and pastries than in the two obvious tourists in their midst.

But once outside, she realized that they were, indeed, the subject of curiosity, not from the townspeople but from the soldiers, three of whom were headed toward them.

"Steven—"

"You're the actress, Maggie. Here's your big opportunity."

"Don't joke about this Steven. They're coming after us."

"Not *after* us, Maggie. Toward us. Remember, we're just two happy tourists. We have nothing to worry about," Steven assured her.

Maggie took a deep breath and tried to agree as the threesome approached.

"*Guten morgen,*" one of the soldiers said.

Maggie responded in German, noticing that he was no more than a boy, pink faced and barely old enough to shave. And yet there was something about his eyes that frightened her, something more serious than she would have expected from his youthful appearance.

He spoke rapidly, but Maggie managed to get the gist of his words and translate for Steven. "He says they notice we're strangers and want to know if they can help us. They also want to see our papers, the entry visas we got in Delphberg."

Steven nodded, reaching into his pocket. "You're doing great, Maggie." He pulled out the requested forms and handed them over.

The soldier studied them for a long time as if hoping to find some mistake. Apparently unsuccessful, he handed them back to Steven with a click of his booted heels and a few guttural words.

"He wishes us a pleasant trip," Maggie said, her heart finally returning to its normal rhythm.

"Smile and thank him," Steven advised, "and then just keep on walking the way we started. We can't turn back now."

Slowly, as if they had all the time in the world, they made their way along the curving, hilly Donnerstrasse.

"Are they following us?" Maggie asked.

Steven didn't answer right away, and when he did, his words confused her. "Stop here," he ordered, "and lift your veil."

"What?"

"Lift your veil," he repeated. "I'm going to pretend to remove something from your eye." When she did as he requested, Steven took out a handkerchief and dabbed at her eye, looking back toward the square they'd just left. "No one there. The street is empty."

Maggie lowered her veil, took his arm and they continued walking along the street. Its houses were old and large and generally in ill repair. Some of them had even been boarded up. "What was the address?" Steven asked.

"Twenty-two Donnerstrasse," Maggie told him.

"It must be the next one," he said, "but it looks deserted to me." Steven walked ahead toward the front doorway, searching for a number on the side of the house.

"But look, there's a gate to the garden." Before he could call out to stop her, Maggie had pushed open the creaking gate and stepped inside.

It was wildly overgrown with brambles and vines crawling up and around chipped and mildewed marble statues. Weeds and wildflowers had taken over the once neat plots and grew in wild profusion. Maggie made her way toward the rear of the garden where a small tumbledown summer house stood forlorn and neglected.

Maggie climbed the rotting stairs onto the porch and crossed to the door, which was open. As she stepped inside, a man materialized out of the shadows and grabbed her, putting one hand across her mouth, the other at her throat.

"Don't scream," he said. "Just call the gentleman in here."

Maggie struggled, trying to break free, but his grip tightened on her throat. "I do not wish to hurt you. But I will if you force me. Do as I tell you." He removed his hand from her mouth just long enough for her to shout Steven's name.

Chapter Eleven

"What the hell's going on here?" Steven asked as he stormed into the summer house. "Let her go."

The man gave Maggie a little push toward Steven before dropping his hands to his sides and stepping away.

Steven reached out and pulled Maggie to him. "Are you all right? Did he hurt you?"

Maggie shook her head. She was trembling all over, but the steady grip of Steven's hand on her arm was reassuring. She took a deep breath and answered. "I am all right, and I do not think he meant to hurt me. I believe he just wants to talk," she assured Steven, looking back at the young man.

To her amazement, she saw that he was smiling. "You are correct, Frau Englehardt. If indeed that is your name." He made a deep, mocking bow, his curly brown hair falling over his forehead.

"What do you mean—" Maggie began.

"Allow me to introduce myself," the young man interrupted with another flourish. His physique was trim and muscular, and he reminded Maggie of a dashing pirate with his handsome, clean-shaven face and eyes that flashed intelligent humor. "I am Anton Legel."

"Legel," Steven repeated knowingly. "Then the girl in the tavern . . ."

"You are very observant, Mr. Englehardt. She is my sister. And this is my half brother Wili. He is standing guard for us."

Out of the shadows stepped another man, older and heavier than Anton, his brown hair streaked with gray. He looked at them steadily but with none of his brother's apparent goodwill.

"So we've met your entire family," Steven commented wryly, "but I'm afraid that doesn't help explain why we're here."

"It's very simple. I know your true identity from Raymond."

"I should have guessed," Steven said with resignation, shooting one of his now-familiar doubting looks at Maggie.

"Yes, Raymond has told me everything," Anton continued, taking a step closer to Steven and observing him carefully. "And I can see that he is right. The family resemblance is remarkable."

"Oh, for God's sake," Steven said irritably, turning away.

Anton ignored his outburst. "It is difficult for me to understand why everyone hasn't noticed."

"Because everyone isn't looking for a resemblance," Steven said. "Only the few of you who're obsessed."

"Not obsessed," Anton said. "Just dedicated."

"To your cause," Steven said.

"Yes, our cause."

Steven looked down at Maggie again before asking Anton, "I suppose you're in the resistance."

Anton nodded.

"And I suppose 'cousin' Raymond told you I was on the way."

"He did."

Steven shook his head. "Even if I looked nothing like the Von Alders, you'd tell me I did to help your cause."

"It is possible that I would, but I do not have to because the resemblance is there."

"Well, I'm not here to help anyone's cause, Legel. I'm not interested in becoming a sacrificial goat." Steven pulled Maggie toward the door.

Anton's voice was thoughtful. "Spoken like a man who has had his fill of war."

"At last we understand each other," Steven said. "Come on, Maggie, let's get the hell out of here."

Before they could leave the summer house, Wili was at the doorway, blocking their exit, looking much fiercer than his brother. "I tell you to listen to Anton," he said. His bulk filled the doorway, leaving them no room for exit, and he casually fingered a long dagger in his belt.

Steven turned back to Anton. "You'd better know now, before this goes any further, that I'm not about to be threatened."

"I understand that," Anton responded. "Move away, Wili."

Reluctantly the big man did as he was told, but his grip remained on the knife's handle.

"I will not force you to stay and listen to me, but I will ask for just five minutes of your time." Anton called after them.

Maggie spoke then, prodingly. "What can it hurt, Steven? Five minutes is not asking very much."

"All right," Steven said with ill grace as they moved back into the little house. "But you better make the time count, Legel." -

"I will try my best," Anton said with great seriousness. "You have seen what happens to our country. Our men cannot find the work to support them and their families. Our women and children go hungry, and our old people wander the streets." His voice was low and compelling.

Steven couldn't deny what he was told; he'd seen it for himself.

"But there is more. Anyone who does not agree with Adamo and his practices is thrown out of his home or turned off his land. Look at this street." He gestured toward the Donnerstrasse. "The empty homes belonged to those who fought against Adamo, some out in the open, some—the more successful ones—subversively."

"Like your resistance forces."

"Yes," Anton replied. "We are still alive, still waiting for the right time. The others..." He shrugged. "They have been 'relocated,' or they have disappeared. We are all criminals to this government, because we share one hope." He looked at Steven with his eyes steady yet filled with excitement. "Our hope is to restore the monarchy."

Steven shook his head adamantly. "Sorry, my friend, but I can't do anything to help you even though I'm sure that Adamo is guilty of much, if not all, of your accusations. You have right on your side."

"That we do," Anton replied.

"But this isn't my problem."

Anton did not respond; nor did Maggie. They seemed to be waiting. Also waiting, but more menacingly, was the large man who had not moved from his place by the doorway, still fingering his knife.

Steven felt compelled to explain further. "Mendorra is not my country, and although I wish you well, I won't join in your battle. I am here to trace my family, my mother, Elyse Contrand."

Anton spoke then, excitedly, as if he had been waiting for Steven to speak those words. "That, my friend, is the crux of the whole matter. Elyse Contrand is the key. We believe your mother was secretly married to Prince Gregor, which makes you in direct line for the throne. If that could be known, our people would rally around you, fight for you, fight against Adamo."

"Don't even think about it, Legel. In the first place, I have no proof of a marriage between the prince and my mother. Secondly, even if I did, I don't support monarchy as a form of government."

"What? Do you know what you are saying?" Anton railed. "You have seen the suffering. You have said yourself that it is wrong—"

"Yes, I've said that," Steven agreed. "But I haven't said that I support your solution. America is my home, and about a hundred years ago, we fought the Revolution to free ourselves from a monarchy."

Anton made a dismissive noise deep in his throat. "Your family were not a part of that revolution. They were here, in Mendorra."

"But *I'm* an American," Steven said, "and for that reason alone, I'm not interested in your offer. So," he said with finality, "I'd appreciate it if you and your brother allow us to walk out of here without any further trouble. We will forget we ever saw you, and I hope you'll do the same for us."

"So," Anton snorted, "you are a coward, afraid to stand up for what is right."

Steven couldn't resist a chuckle. "That tactic has already been tried on me, and it doesn't work. This isn't my fight, Legel. I wish you luck, but there is nothing more to say."

"Steven—" Maggie began, not even sure what she wanted to say.

"Please, Maggie. Let's get out of here before this farce goes any further. The baroness is probably wondering what happened to us."

Wili quickly moved to block the door again, but Steven had had enough. "I'd hate to knock your brother off his feet, Legel, but I sure as hell will if I'm forced to."

"We shall see about that," Wili said suddenly, pulling himself up to his full height, standing with legs apart, hand on his knife, ready for whatever Anton asked of him.

"Don't call my bluff, Legel," Steven said, his eyes locking into the steady gaze of the young resistance fighter. "You might not like the results. So just ask your brother to move aside, and there'll be no trouble. That is, unless you intend to use the same tactics as Adamo."

At that, Anton lowered his gaze and gave a nod to Wili, who moved away with a grimace, allowing Steven the moment he needed to grab Maggie's hand and get out the door and across the yard before Anton changed his mind.

"Did you know about this friendly little meeting?" Steven asked as they hurried along the Donnerstrasse.

"No, I—"

"Maggie, don't take me for a fool. I've been party to enough of your schemes to recognize one when I see it."

"Really, Steven, I only knew about Maria because Raymond had given me her name."

"And her brother?" He pulled Maggie along beside him, not allowing her time to catch her breath and form an answer.

"Not his name," she wheezed.

He stopped then and turned to her. "But you knew he existed?"

She nodded, trying to slow her rapid heartbeat.

"And that he was planning a meeting?"

"Yes, but I did not know it would be today."

Silently he grabbed her hand and began pulling her along again.

"I have my mission, Steven," she panted. "Part of it is to help you find out about your mother, but the rest—"

"I know the rest, Maggie—to embroil me in some damned civil war. Let's just say that segment of your mission is over. You've failed, Countess. It's time for you to face that and give me some peace." With his fingers in a viselike grip on Maggie's arm, he hurried her along the Donnerstrasse and propelled them into the square almost into the arms of the three soldiers who had stopped them earlier.

Steven veered quickly to avoid a collision. "Fools," he said loudly. "They should watch where they're going."

He paid no further attention to the soldiers but headed Maggie in the direction of the Schloss. "We're going back and talk to the baroness—assuming she's managed to get out of bed. I want to know about this old priest and find out if he has the records we need for—"

He was interrupted by shouting from behind.

Steven and Maggie turned around to find that the soldiers were following them.

"Halt!" came the shout as the three soldiers ran toward them.

"What the hell do you suppose they want now?" Steven asked, unafraid but not unperturbed.

The young soldier who'd been Steven's nemesis all along began speaking rapidly in German as the other two grabbed Steven and held fast.

Steven shrugged them off, but they were back in a flash, this time with grips more appropriate to the strength of their captive.

Horrified, Maggie translated from the German. "Steven, he says you're an enemy of the state. They've been ordered to arrest you." Maggie's face was a mask of fear.

But Steven still couldn't believe this was anything but a charade. "Enemy of the state?" he repeated, almost laughing. "This is some kind of hoax."

"They say that you are plotting to assassinate Adamo," Maggie translated. She was still standing close to Steven, but no longer able to have physical contact with him because of the soldiers, holding fast to each of Steven's arms.

"Tell them it isn't true," Steven said. He'd stopped struggling momentarily, ready to try cooperation, logic, anything to get himself—and Maggie—out of this insane situation. "Show them my papers again."

Maggie spoke rapidly to the soldiers, shoving the papers at them and then listening in horror to their reply.

"Steven, they say your papers are a forgery. They are taking you to prison."

"Then they better think again," Steven said. With that he stepped to one side, tripping the young soldier over his outstretched leg and sending him crashing to the street. With his free elbow, he caught the other soldier in the gut, hard and accurately. With an agonizing groan, the man dropped to the street beside his fellow officer.

That left only one, an old grizzled soldier who was much the worse for wear. Steven barely had the heart to bring a right jab to his midsection and fell him completely.

He turned to Maggie, grabbing her hand. "Let's go—now, while we still have a chance."

But it was already too late. The replacements were crossing the square, more than a dozen strong. Steven knew that he was far outnumbered this time, and bravado would not be enough. He gave Maggie a shove into the crowd that had gathered nearby.

"Get out of here," he shouted as the soldiers surrounded him. "Get out and bring some help."

Maggie careened off one body after another, searching frantically for a familiar face—Maria, Anton, or even Wili—but she saw nothing except a sea of strangers, not one of them venturing forward to help.

She turned back to see Steven fighting against the terrible odds, his jacket torn, streaks of blood across his white shirt. But he was still on his feet, even while two of the soldiers attempted to hold on to him and another was pounding him in the ribs.

Finally, when she couldn't stand it any longer, Maggie screamed out, cursing the soldiers, yelling at the top of her lungs, "Stop it, leave him alone." She'd never been so afraid in all of her life, but she wasn't going to desert him.

Frantically she rushed back into the street, her arms flailing, beating at the soldiers. As the crowd pushed in closer, Maggie was crushed against one of the soldiers, who turned toward her, his arms raised. That's when Steven found a last burst of energy and threw himself into the man, knocking him sideways, as he cried out again, "Run, for God's sake, Maggie, run!"

"No," she cried, "I am not leaving you."

Gunfire sounded from the distance, followed by a moment of absolute silence as everyone stopped and looked across the square. More troops had assembled and were coming toward them, shooting into the air.

Then Maggie felt a strong hand on her waist, someone almost picking her up and pulling her back into the crowd. Once again, she flailed out, fighting for herself and Steven against the soldiers.

But it wasn't a soldier. It was Heinrich, towering over her. "Come with me," he said, pulling her away.

"No," she cried.

He held on tighter, forcing her out of the melee. "Yes, you will come, Frau Englehardt. Quickly, before they lock you up also."

"But Steven—" she protested.

"It is too late."

He propelled her down a side street where a carriage waited in the shadows. "We will return to the Schloss and the baroness. She will know what to do."

Before Maggie could answer, he had settled her in the carriage, climbed up beside her and cracked the whip to jolt them forward.

Maggie looked back to see Steven being marched across the square at gunpoint.

* * *

"My dear Margarette, you look as though you are faint." Baroness Sophie looked up from her coffee as Maggie charged into the morning room with Heinrich close on her heels. "Heinrich, ring for the smelling salts and—"

"No," Maggie gasped. "There is no time. Steven has been arrested."

"Arrested?" Sophie's scrawny hand clutched at her heart. "*Mein Gott,* what has happened?"

Heinrich stepped forward then, confirming what Maggie had said. "There were many soldiers, baroness."

"They beat him and—"

The baroness held up her hand, looking toward Heinrich, who nodded. "Then it is serious?" she asked of her butler.

He confirmed. "They will take him to the Mendheim prison as usual, baroness. After that..."

"After that?" Maggie cried, springing up from the chair where she'd flung herself. "There can be no 'after that.' We must get him out. Now."

"Sit down," Sophie demanded in a voice that Maggie hadn't heard before. It was clear, authoritative and almost youthful. "We need to think. Heinrich—"

"Schnapps?" he asked.

"Certainly not," the old woman replied. "This is serious business. Brew another pot of coffee and a cup for Margarette—and yourself."

Heinrich disappeared quietly, and Sophie stood up, leaning on her cane but less heavily than the day before. She moved across the room, additional wrinkles furrowing her brow as she frowned deeply. Finally she stopped before Maggie and asked, "What are the charges?"

"I do not know, I—"

"Of course you know," Sophie berated. "They must have given some explanation when they arrested him."

Maggie searched her memory. "Yes, they did. They called him an enemy of the state."

"So they are using that old charge. Meaningless but always convenient. What else did they say?"

"That he was plotting to assassinate Adamo." Maggie buried her face in her hands. "If they only knew."

"If they only knew what?" Sophie's eyes were bright with curiosity. "Is he with the resistance?"

Maggie looked up, tempted to tell Sophie everything, how they had hoped to solicit Steven for their cause and failed, and how he'd been arrested anyway. The terrible irony wasn't lost on Maggie, but she was not going to tell the baroness.

"No," she said. "My husband is not political at all. He does not care about Adamo. He does not even care about the monarchy."

The old woman moved back to her chair and eased herself down. "Sometimes I begin to feel youthful," she commented, "only to find old age getting in my way." She paused a moment, thoughtful, before speaking in a soft little voice. "He does not care about our monarchy, but he should care, should he not?"

"What do you mean?" Maggie asked.

"I noticed the resemblance last night at dinner. Of course, all the questions about Gregor only confirmed my suspicions."

"I have no idea what you are talking about," Maggie lied. "And I do not care." That much was true, she suddenly realized. "All I care about now is getting him out of prison."

"Of course." Sophie was still thoughtful.

"Raymond!" Maggie said suddenly. "We will get a message to him. He will send help."

"Raymond?" Sophie repeated with one of her familiar chortles. "What do you think that old man could do?"

"Well, he—"

"He has no power, none at all. No, anything we do, we must do ourselves. Ah, here is Heinrich with our coffee."

"If you do not mind, I would like a schnapps," Maggie said. Sophie could drink coffee to keep herself awake and functioning; Maggie needed something stronger.

"If *you* do not mind," Heinrich said, "I have anticipated your wish, Frau Englehardt, and brought this for you." He put a glass of schnapps on the table beside Maggie's chair.

With a grateful smile, she drank the burning liquid and immediately felt the warmth spreading through her. She knew it was giving her fool's courage, but it made her feel better.

When Heinrich left, Sophie leaned toward Maggie and said, "He knows the prison because they took his brother there once."

"And you got him out?" Maggie asked with hope in her voice.

Sophie shook her head. "Sadly, we waited too long."

Maggie jumped up. "Well, we cannot wait this time. Steven's situation is desperate!" she cried. "Please, baroness, help us." Maggie slipped to her knees by the old woman's chair. "If there is a way—"

The baroness reached out and touched Maggie's hair. "You love him very much, do you not, my child?"

"Yes," Maggie whispered. "I do, and I cannot lose him. He can not die...."

"He will not die," Sophie said with fervor. "Now, get yourself together, girl. We have plans to make."

Chapter Twelve

Steven paced up and down in his narrow cell like a caged animal. He'd been imprisoned for almost twenty-four hours and still had no idea why he was being held. His captors spoke little English, Steven's German was equally sparse, and communication with the soldiers had been futile and frustrating.

He'd done his best at a hasty reconnaissance of the surroundings when they'd dragged him to the prison, which was in the tower of a vast fort, probably one of the Mendheim family's fortifications in their endless wars with anyone and everyone who challenged them. The fort was further protected from attack by a wide river.

His cell was in a dungeon below the tower, a four-by-eight-foot space, dark and fetid, the damp ground its floor. A pallet passed for his bed, and a hole had been dug in the dirt for sanitary purposes. Near the cell door was a water basin, which was filled daily.

They'd taken Steven's jacket, all his papers and money, and left him with his boots, trousers and shirt before locking him away. He'd spent a sleepless night on the filthy pallet, and at dawn a tin plate had been pushed through an opening at the bottom of the door.

On the plate was a slab of bread and a bowl of unrecognizable mush that he refused—only to eat it a few hours later in desperation, not daring to breathe while spooning the food into his mouth for fear he would taste it.

At midmorning he'd been taken into a walled courtyard for exercise. There half a dozen other men walked the circumference of the yard in a single line, silently, heads down, looking neither to the right nor left. Steven had attempted to start a conversation with one of them but received no response, only a fleeting, frightened glance toward the armed guards, which told him what he needed to know. These men's spirits had been broken; they were afraid, and from what he could observe they had reason to be.

There were scars and even open wounds on their faces, hands and necks. Whatever skin was visible bore evidence of brutality. Steven swore silently to himself and vowed that he would be out of prison before anyone laid a hand on him.

But how? He could scale the eight-foot wall; that was no problem. Once on the other side he could make a run for the river. It was deep and fast-flowing, his way out. Except for the guards spaced at intervals along the wall, eight burly armed men to guard their seven straggly charges. He'd have to think of some way to create a diversion, and he certainly couldn't expect help from his fellow prisoners.

Steven spent the intervening hours between his morning and afternoon exercise period longing for the sight of the sky and smell of the springtime, the heat of the sun on his skin to temporarily ward off the clamminess of his cell. Once he escaped, he swore never again to put himself in the position of imprisonment. It was a hell worse than any he'd ever imagined, for just the deprivation of the outdoors was torture enough for Steven to whom a broad expanse of sky had always seemed his right. To have it taken away was an obscenity to him, and he cursed everyone responsible, including Maggie.

Yet he knew that she'd only been the impetus; he'd made the decision to come to this damnable country himself, and the sooner he was out of here the better.

Steven began pacing again, his mind working feverishly. Through his anger, he allowed a hope to sneak in that Maggie was hundreds of miles away by now, even out of the country, her wild schemes a thing of the past. It was a miracle that Heinrich had appeared and virtually kidnapped her. Otherwise, she could be here in Mendheim prison with him.

Steven's pacing continued as he tried not to give in to the nagging fear that the soldiers could have followed Maggie to the Schloss. He had no real idea what power, if any, the baroness still possessed. She might be only a figurehead, a silly old woman just like Raymond was a silly old man. Yet in neither case, Steven realized, would that silliness have prevented one of them from betraying him.

He stopped cold in his tracks. Obviously *someone* had been the betrayer. The soldiers wouldn't have singled him out with no warning; their job was difficult enough dealing with the rebels without picking on a seemingly innocent tourist. Yes, someone had turned on him, and maybe on Maggie, too. Now it was his job to get out of here and get himself—and Maggie, if she was still in the country—away from this place for good.

The opportunity came that afternoon, unexpectedly and not at all as Steven had planned.

It began with a commotion in the guard room at the end of the long dark hall. He heard a voice vaguely familiar, speaking angrily in German. Steven moved to the bars of his cell and peered into the darkness. Slowly his eyes adjusted to the dark and he made out the tall form of Heinrich, half-crouching so that his head wouldn't bump the low ceiling, a grotesque figure pushing a wheelchair.

It could only be the baroness, Steven realized, huddled in the chair, swaddled in shawls and blankets and wearing a Spanish black lace mantilla. So she had some influence after all, Steven thought.

"Leave me, Heinrich," she ordered in her querulous voice. "Go and wait with those guards who are peering down the hall and tell them to stop their eavesdropping. My words are for this traitor alone."

Steven heard the word "traitor" and smiled. So. She'd tricked them. She still had influence after all. Steven realized it was up to him to play along with her game and await whatever plan she had.

Unable to see more than the top of her head from his height, he leaned down and spoke softly. "I'm sorry, baroness, about any problems I've brought to you or your family, but I assure you that I've done no wrong."

"No wrong," she croaked. "Why, you are an enemy of the people, Mr. Englehardt, if that is your real name. And you must pray to God for help." With those words she raised her head to look at him.

As Steven bent close and peered into her eyes, his heart stopped in midbeat. Her eyes were deep and blue and very beautiful.

"Maggie," he whispered.

"Yes," she said, just as softly.

"For God's sake," he began. "You—" Unintentionally, in his surprise, Steven had allowed his voice to reach a high pitch.

Maggie scolded him, in the baroness's voice. "For God's sake, indeed, young man. Kneel down."

Steven remained standing, puzzled.

"Kneel down," she ordered again, "or I shall have a guard beat you to the ground." She signaled with her eyes toward the anteroom. Indeed, the guard who stood closest to them was watching and listening intently, and even though Steven and Maggie were speaking English, they still needed to watch every word and movement.

Aware of that, Steven dropped to his knees, his face and Maggie's now on a level. She pushed back the mantilla and he gave a start. Her lovely face was lined and mottled with age; only the eyes, the wonderful, clear blue eyes, gave any hint that it was Maggie not Baroness Sophie Mendheim who occupied her wheelchair opposite him. Her makeup, as well as her acting, was superb. He couldn't believe he'd been so completely duped.

"Pretty good job," he whispered.

"*Pretty* good?" she repeated. "Admit it, Steven, I am a wonderful actress."

"Granted," he said. Then the reality of the situation hit him, and he felt the anger rising again. "You're insane to come here. It's too dangerous. Get the hell out of this place and out of the country, which you should have done twenty-four hours ago."

Maggie ignored his comments and pulled a prayer book from beneath her black garments. "The guards have allowed me to bring this in with me," she said loudly. "It is my own personal missal, handed down through my family for generations. I suggest that we pray together from it for all your sins."

She leaned close to the bars and opened the book as if she were reciting a prayer and whispered, "We're going to get you out tonight. At sundown when you exercise. Go over the wall into the water. A boat will be waiting."

Steven started to ask a question, but the appearance of a guard in the hall forestalled him.

"You must pray constantly," Maggie intoned in her Baroness Mendheim voice. "It is only through prayer that you will realize your sins and receive forgiveness."

She thrust something at him in full view of the guard.

Steven, seeing the guard's inquisitive glance, tried to avoid the gesture.

She persisted. "No, take it. It is my rosary. Take it and use it. For if anything will save your life, it will be this."

Steven clutched the rosary in his hand as Maggie turned in her chair and gestured imperiously to the guard. "Find my servant, and send him to me. I have had enough of this place—and this traitor."

As the guard accompanied Heinrich down the hall, Maggie gave one of her very Sophie-like chortles and said, "Thank God for Felix Adamo and men like him who bring our enemies to justice. You," she said, pointing a quivering finger at Steven, "shall get just what you deserve."

And with those parting words she was wheeled grandly down the hall and out of sight.

Bravo, Steven thought. What a performance! Maggie *was* an actress. There was no doubt about it. He should have expected something like this, another performance to top all the ones that had come before. Even in the utmost danger, Maggie couldn't help but ply her trade. Well, she'd done her best this time, and Steven, as he unclinched his hand and looked down at the rosary in his open palm, couldn't help but be grateful to her.

The rosary was a beautifully crafted work of jade and pearls, no doubt old and valuable, but what intrigued him more was the wire that was woven into the chain of the rosary, a wire so fine and intrinsic to the rosary that it had been missed by the flustered guards upon the sudden appearance of the baroness.

Obviously, the baroness—or Maggie in her best role—retained both the family charisma and the power to intimidate and confuse the nervous soldiers.

Slowly, carefully, Steven pulled out the wire and curled it in his pocket. He smiled to himself. Maggie had judged correctly; he knew very well the uses of the garrote.

Just before sundown the guards came for him. Steven had wrapped the wire loosely around his wrist. He hoped he wouldn't have to use it, but he knew he would if it became necessary.

He joined the line of other prisoners walking the slow circumference of the walls. Instead of being frightened, for the first time since his capture, Steven felt alive, all of his senses ready, listening. Again he had that feeling of being on the edge of battle, and energy and adrenaline swept through his body. The guards seemed edgy, too, he thought, and they watched the prisoners carefully. It was in the air, Steven decided, a feeling of dangerous anxiety.

And then it happened, unexpectedly and dramatically—a loud explosion, followed by another and an-

other erupting from the town square on the other side
of the prison gate—whether cannon or gunshots, Steven
couldn't tell.

While moving away from the sound, he suddenly
knew the answer. It was dynamite. Someone, perhaps
Anton and his men, knew the advantages of a diver-
sionary tactic.

Like the prisoners, the guards had at first withdrawn
toward the back of the compound but were regrouping
and under their captain's orders unbaring the heavy
gate. Then, forming into some sort of order, they
moved out into the street amidst shouts and screams of
panic, leaving a few guards behind to round up the
prisoners and march them back toward their cells.

Except for Steven. At the sound of the second explosion he'd raced to a corner of the yard and crouched low
in the shadows formed by the last rays of the setting
sun. As the panic began, he felt suddenly very calm even
though he knew that he had only minutes, if not sec-
onds, to act.

And act he did. In the moment of stillness before the
panic, he'd gotten a foothold in the wall and readied
himself, waiting for the opportunity to summon his
strength for the climb.

His chance came when one of the prisoners pan-
icked, emerging from the comatose state Steven had
observed and going berserk. As the crazed man raced
around the compound, screaming hysterically, two of
the guards converged on him, wrestling the poor soul to
the ground.

Steven didn't wait for the obvious outcome. He was
ready to climb. But he'd been careless, not noticing a
third guard, who rushed toward him.

Before either prisoner or guard realized what was happening, they were face-to-face, the guard with his gun drawn, pointing at Steven's skull.

"*Halt*," he cried in a confident voice, his weapon steady in his hand.

But not steady enough. The quickness learned from a lifetime on the range paid off for Steven, who whipped out his wire and looped it over the guard's head as easily as he might have lassoed a calf.

One twist and the guard fell to his knees before Steven, who could have applied just the necessary pressure for the kill.

Instead, he relaxed his hold and with his knee kicked the guard backward, knocking him out instantly but not killing him.

Then he was over the wall, where he dropped to the other side and dove without hesitating into the icy river.

He swam underwater as long as his breath lasted and surfaced downstream, coming up quietly and treading water while he listened. In the courtyard on the other side of the wall, the commotion had ended. All was still, and Steven imagined the guards had managed to get their prisoners back inside. It would be a while before they realized he was missing and began to search for him.

Then he heard a sound, the soft plop of oars on water. Looking out into the darkness, he saw a boat, no more than a hundred yards away. He swam toward it.

Winded and chilled, he reached the boat and hooked one arm over the side, hoping that there were dry clothes available and that the oarsman, a slim figure in a felt hat, jacket and dark trousers, could speak English.

Steven reached out to be pulled aboard, calling, "Give me a hand."

This time the moment of recognition was instantaneous. He felt the softness of her hand and knew it was Maggie.

"What the hell?" he cried. "I thought I told you to get out of Mendheim."

"That is exactly what I plan to do," she replied testily, holding tightly to his hand. "Now help me get you into the boat and out of sight. With all those wet clothes you must weigh several hundred pounds."

Not bothering to argue the point, Steven managed with Maggie's help to lift himself into the bottom of the rowboat, where he lay, cold and clammy, gasping for breath as Maggie began to row, erratically, downstream.

"How did you ever get here, rowing like that?" he asked, sitting up and taking the oars from her. "They should have sent someone else. You should be out of the country by now."

"Well, I am not, and there was not anyone else to send."

"What about Anton?" Steven asked as he maneuvered the boat into the middle of the river where a wide trough rushed downstream, all but doing his work for him.

"It was Anton who created the diversion in town. You have him—and the rebels—to thank for that. They were willing to help even though you were less than interested in their cause."

"Now's not the time for a political lecture," Steven advised, finding a second wind and moving the rowboat swiftly away from the prison.

"There is a waterproof pouch with food and dry clothes if you want to change," she told him.

"No time now. I'll worry about that later. We need to get as far away as possible." He squinted at her through the darkness. "I figure you have a plan—you and Anton."

"And the baroness," Maggie added.

"Of course, the baroness."

"We are to row downstream, leave the boat on the opposite bank and head west toward Magris."

"Magris? Isn't that where the records of my birth are supposed to be?"

"Well, yes, but—"

"No, Maggie, we're getting out of this country. No more churches, no cemeteries, no archives. All that's over."

"Magris is on the border, Steven. We can cross over from there."

"There is also a north border, Maggie." The exertion of rowing was beginning to make Steven sweat profusely beneath the cold, wet clothes.

"It is too mountainous. The trek to Magris is bad enough, but it would be impossible to cross on the north side, and we cannot go toward Delphberg. There will be soldiers everywhere—looking for us. General Adamo knows what has happened by now."

"Which reminds me." Steven paused long enough to catch a ragged breath before continuing his rhythmic rowing. "Who turned me in? Do your rebels have any idea?"

"They can only guess. It could have been Raymond."

Steven shook his head. "Somehow, I don't think so."

"Maria. Or someone at the Schloss."

"Or Heinrich."

"Never," Maggie said. "He is devoted to the baroness, and she is prepared to defend the rebels with her last breath. I just hope she does not have to. I hope the soldiers do not question her." Maggie shivered involuntarily. "When we made our plans, we had to consult her because we may need to hide out at the convent in Magris, and the baroness knows the mother superior."

"The baroness does get around," Steven commented.

"But in the end, Anton told her that we had decided not to stop there. He invented an alternate route for us."

"She won't reveal the real plans."

Maggie nodded. "So far her position has protected her, but things can change."

"Yes, they can," Steven said, fighting the current to head toward the opposite bank. "How far downstream should we go ashore?"

"About a mile," Maggie told him.

"For God's sake, Maggie, we've traveled well over two miles."

"No, we could not have—"

"Was there a marker?" Steven asked.

"No, Anton said a mile. After that, there are rapids—"

Steven bit off an expletive. "Anton should have come himself. You should be away from here, out of the country just like I told you—"

He didn't finish the sentence. The rest of his words were swept away as a current caught the boat and spun it around. They were in the rapids already. He hadn't seen them coming in the dark, hadn't even known to look for them.

Steven began to fight the current, digging deeply into the water with his oars as he tried to make a diagonal cross of the river. But it was impossible. There was no choice but to go with the rapids, not trying to fight the surging, tumbling current.

Just holding the boat steady took all of Steven's strength, and he could feel the skin being stripped away from his hands as he fought to maintain a grip on the rough wooden oars. He couldn't afford to relax his hold even for an instant or the oars would be ripped from his hands, leaving the boat a victim of the capricious water.

He could feel the rocks tearing at the bottom of the boat and knew that he couldn't keep it afloat much longer, but the shore was only a few yards away, if only—

Then he saw through the dark waters what he had feared from the first moment the boat had hit the rapids. The river seemed to disappear, drop off into nothingness, and Steven knew that the rapids ended in a waterfall. Cursing Anton for not giving a better warning, cursing Maggie for not telling him soon enough—and for being here in the first place, he plunged the oars deep into the water and attempted to stop the forward momentum of the boat. Heading for the shore was no longer an option.

"Can you swim?" he shouted to Maggie over the increasing noise of the rapids.

"A little. Not well," she admitted.

He cursed again under his breath as he heard the fear in her voice. They didn't have long, for the closer they got to the heavy rapids and the waiting falls, the more difficult it would be to make it to shore, if they could make it at all.

"I'm heading for that outcropping of rocks," he shouted to Maggie. "I hope we'll go aground there, but whatever happens, if we hit the water, hold on to me. Put both hands around my waist and kick with your feet."

"What about the pouch?" she cried.

"To hell with the pouch. We're going to be lucky to come out of this with our lives." Steven thought of Sophie's rosary that he'd slipped over his neck, and its cool stones lying against his skin gave him comfort. He knew he'd need all of his skill—plus a small miracle—to get them safely to shore.

A side current caught them as the boat teetered and hovered on an upsurge of water. Steven, who knew only too well the dangers of the fast-flowing rapids on the Missouri and Colorado Rivers, was prepared for what would happen next. They weren't going to go aground on the rocks; they were going to be tossed in their midst.

He reached for Maggie and wrapped her arms around his waist. "Hold on," he shouted.

Just as he spoke there was a rasping, ripping sound as the sharp rocks tore hole after hole in the boat and began to break it apart.

Maggie hadn't expected the boat to disintegrate so quickly, ripping into huge splinters all around them before plunging them into the icy water. For a split second she forgot everything Steven had told her, letting go of him and flailing her arms around helplessly. Then, before he was swept away, she managed to grab on to his shirt, only to feel it rip apart in her hands as she was submerged.

The pressure in her lungs built instantly and violently until she could no longer breathe. She was going to drown—she *was* drowning.

Then Maggie felt Steven's hands under her arms, dragging her to the surface. She sputtered and gasped, spitting water, choking, almost vomiting and then, at least—breathing!

Steven wrapped his legs around her and his arms around the sharp angle of a protruding rock they'd been thrown against. The shore was a haven a few yards away. But there were rocks everywhere, rocks that were both dangerous and their only hope, for if they could manage to make it from one large outcropping to another and grab hold without being crushed, they could work their way ashore before being washed downstream and over the falls.

"Hang on to my legs while I turn in the water," he instructed. "Don't let go!"

Maggie wrapped her arms around Steven's calves and held on for her life, trying desperately to keep her head above water.

"Now reach up and grab hold of my belt," he told her. "I'm going to let go of the rock and start swimming. Hang on to me and kick like hell."

Steven headed diagonally across the river, and Maggie fought to keep her hold on his belt, kicking as hard as she could, hoping to help rather than impede his progress. But the current was their enemy as it rushed them downstream past the next outcropping before Steven had a chance to grab hold.

"No!" Maggie screamed out as she struggled against the current. It fought with the strength of giant, ravenous underwater hands, tossing them around at will and then dragging them under, deeper and deeper into the blackness below. Maggie held her breath as she was pulled beneath the water, but she never released the hold of her cramped, icy fingers on Steven's belt.

Then suddenly they were turned over in the current, and once more her head was above water. Maggie used that moment to pull all the air she could into her lungs just as they were hurled against another outcropping.

The rapids rushed all around them, but the rock was their salvation—just as the falls, now only a few yards away, could be their death.

"We'll make it," Steven assured her. "Take a big breath. Fill your lungs with air." With that he plunged again into the current and swam even more strongly than before. Then suddenly, miraculously, they felt rocks beneath them. Only a few more strong strokes and Steven shouted back to her, "I can touch bottom. We've made it."

They stood up, fell over and were flung a few more feet downstream toward the falls before managing to find the rocky bottom again and crawl toward the shore on hands and knees bloodied by contact with the rocky river bottom.

The embankment was steep, but for Maggie the climb up it was a welcome one, for it was on solid ground, over damp earth from which roots of overhanging trees protruded.

The bank above the river was lush and green. Maggie threw herself down on it with a great sigh, digging her fingers into the soil. Its deep, rich smell was one she would not forget through a lifetime, for it meant freedom.

Chapter Thirteen

Darkness had fallen and with it the damp chill of a mountain night. Maggie shivered and wished for their dry clothes and supplies, which had been lost with the boat.

She looked up at Steven, who stood above her, surveying the night sky. "Can we build a fire?" she asked. "I am so cold."

"No," he said sharply. "We can't take that risk. They may have sent a search party after us. Light from a fire would give away our position."

"But—"

"No, Maggie."

He was in charge. She had planned his escape—along with Heinrich and the baroness—risked impersonating Sophie to get word to him about the rescue, picked him up in the boat and come this far with him, only to be barked at now.

"I realize you're uncomfortable. So am I," he admitted. "But at least we're alive. No broken bones," he added, cataloging the results of their survival. "Only a few scratches and bruises."

He seemed to speak for them both, and Maggie refrained from mentioning that the gashes on her arms and legs from the rocks were more than what she considered "scratches."

"But it's all a small price to pay for survival," he said. "Now's the time to plot our next steps. Which way is Magris?"

Maggie looked up at the moon and stars, getting her bearings, and then pointed out a dark silhouette against the night sky. "East, over that mountain."

"Well, I guess that's where we're heading. As a fugitive, I don't have many options."

"I am sorry for what happened, Steven," she said. "I never expected there would be an informer."

"No, I'm sure you didn't, nor did Viktor. For that matter, he could be the informer himself."

"That is impossible," she cried. "Why would he have sent you all this way to have you arrested?"

"Arrested and put to death, I expect. That could have been his plan."

"Which he could have achieved without bringing you to Mendorra. He could have had you killed in Wyoming if he feared that someday you might find out your true birthright."

"Maybe he tried. Someone did," he reminded her.

"It was not Viktor. He—"

Steven cut her off. "Let's don't waste time talking about it."

His words were brusque and terse, and Maggie realized that he probably hated her for what she'd done to him, for bringing him to Mendorra. Suddenly she couldn't blame him. The whole grandiose scheme that she and Viktor had discussed in the comfort of his cozy parlor in Paris seemed a grotesque joke, especially now as she and Steven stood, wet and cold in the middle of a forest in a country where they were both fugitives.

"Are you ready to move?" Steven asked.

Maggie fought back tears, gritted her teeth and nodded. What she really wanted was to lie down, curl up and sleep for a night and a day, waking to a hot meal and a warm bath. What she didn't want was to set out on a long trek over a mountain to Magris.

"Then let's get going," he said. "We need to travel at night and find somewhere to hide during the day." He studied the terrain for a long moment, brushed aside intruding brambles and low-hanging branches, and then disappeared into the forest. With a deep sigh, Maggie followed.

Four hours later, Maggie began to think that she knew what hell was like. It was being tossed into an icy river and then having to follow a madman on an unceasing and painful march over a mountain.

Her feet ached, her back ached, and her legs ached; in fact, there was no part of her body that wasn't stiff and sore except for those parts that were numb. Undergrowth pulled at her clothing, and every few steps she stumbled over roots or dead tree trunks, falling more than once.

Steven had stopped to help her up each time but with rapidly decreasing concern, it seemed to Maggie. She'd decided not to mention the huge blister that was forming on her right foot, or that the toes of her left foot had begun to cramp. She imagined such a declaration would just further irritate him. Besides, she had vowed not to complain, no matter what, and she had long since managed to ignore the fact that her matted hair seemed to attract the night insects, which she swiped at unsuccessfully, and that her partially dried clothes were sticky and rough against her skin.

But she couldn't ignore the exhaustion that finally overcame her as they pushed farther and farther up the mountainside. "I have to stop, Steven," she called out finally, dropping onto a decaying log to rest.

Steven had other ideas. "If we stop now, we won't get started again. I know what I'm talking about, Maggie. I've been on enough forced marches in the army. You have to keep going."

Suddenly Maggie began to see red. "I do *not* want to keep going," she said from her firmly entrenched seat on the log. "I just want to rest, and for your information, I have not signed up for anyone's damned army."

Steven laughed, thinking that she certainly hadn't lost her spirit. "Come on," he coaxed, taking Maggie's hand and pulling her to her feet. "We're almost there, almost at the top."

And they were. Less than a hundred yards and they crested the mountain. Far below, too far, Maggie thought, lay the town of Magris, scattered lights in the windows of a few houses so late into the night.

"There'll be farmhouses outside of town," Steven said, "barns, sheds, somewhere we can sleep." He looked up at the sky. "We still have several hours until dawn. Come on, Maggie, don't give up on me now."

Like a sleepwalker, hardly knowing where she was going or even what she was doing, Maggie followed. With Steven's back as her guide, she let the downhill momentum keep her moving.

Just over an hour later, they discovered a path, overgrown but still discernible in the night, which was lit softly by a full moon. Steven followed the path, and Maggie followed Steven, trying to ignore the shining eyes of the night creatures watching from the shadows, putting one foot in front of the other and persevering.

A loud noise, made by what must have been a very large animal, caused Maggie to press closer to Steven, who didn't even break his stride. She tried not to imagine the size of the animal from which the noise emitted, even though bear-size was a very real possibility. Instead, she came so close that when he stopped she ran full force into him.

"Why did you stop? What is it?" she whispered, still imagining enormous wild animals.

"A house," he said, "there through the trees." He led the way into a tangle of pine and hemlock trees. The house lay before them in the darkness. No lights shone from the windows. No dogs barked. It was completely quiet except for the sound of crickets in the distance.

"It seems deserted, but I'll have a look. Wait here."

Before Maggie could object, he was gone, leaving her alone in the trees. Quickly she looked around, still having to assure herself that there was nothing out there larger than a night bird to threaten her.

Then she watched as Steven slipped along the stone wall of the big house that was nestled against the mountainside. She saw him peering into the windows, face pressed against the glass. There was no sign of life.

Then he bent down, picked up a rock and tossed it against a second-floor window, quickly hugging the wall, waiting.

Maggie, too, waited, fearful of hearing shouts or even gunshots. There was nothing but silence. The house, a stone manse three stories high, was deserted, probably by a prosperous family, Maggie decided, possibly enemies of Adamo, who'd fled to safety, or—she thought with a shudder—who'd been taken off to prison.

With a much larger rock Steven broke a window on the lower level, knocked out the remaining jagged glass, and signaled to Maggie before disappearing inside the house.

She slipped away from her place in the trees and was waiting and ready when he slid the bolts on the heavy wooden door and opened it for her.

The door creaked loudly, causing her to jump again. It had been a night of frightening sounds. Maybe now they were over for a while. "Are we safe here?" she asked.

"As safe as we'll be anywhere. The place is deserted, and it looks like the occupants left in a hurry without taking very much with them." In the light from the moon, Steven rummaged around and found matches and a candle.

In the candlelight, he surveyed the room—stone walls, huge fireplace, rough trestle table. "The kitchen," he said. "Maybe tomorrow we can turn up some food. But right now—" He headed across the room and Maggie followed him through a doorway to a smaller room.

"Probably servants' quarters. Not as fancy as the Schloss, but it'll do," he said as Maggie sagged against the wall, too tired to feel elation that they were safe, even if only temporarily, thinking of nothing but sleep.

Steven had put the candle down on a bedside table and given the mattress a hearty push. Dust rose up in the still night air, but Maggie didn't mind at all. At least it was a bed. She sank down on it gratefully while Steven opened bureau drawers and found blankets, even a quilt.

Then he pulled her to her feet. "Come on. Take off your clothes."

"I just want to sleep," she said. "My clothes are dry."

"And caked with mud." He handed her a quilt. "Undress, Maggie. I won't watch."

"I don't care if you do," she said tiredly, stripping off the stained and torn clothes and dropping them to the floor. Her eyes were half-closed, and she moved as if already in sleep, wrapping herself in the worn, soft quilt, and lying down on the bed, allowing her heavy eyelids to close. In a few moments Steven had pulled off his own filthy clothes. She felt the mattress move as he lay down beside her.

"There's only one bed," he reminded her. "I could look for another room, but I don't think it would be safe for me to leave you."

"It is all right," she said as he stretched out beside her. "I do not want you to leave."

Steven looked over at her. In the moonlight that streamed through the small window high in the wall of the room, he could see her face clearly. She looked young and more vulnerable than he'd ever imagined. For the first time since his escape, he thought of what Maggie had been through. More than he had, really, and certainly she was less used to hardship. He smiled to himself, thinking of her outburst about forced marches in army life. He'd lived through a war. This was Maggie's war. And he was proud of her for all she'd done, sorry she hadn't escaped when she had a chance, but no longer angry. She'd risked her life for him. How could he be angry?

"Maggie," he whispered, "are you all right?"

She opened her eyes. "Yes, Steven, I am all right, and I'm so sorry about all of this."

"It's over now, at least for a while." He slipped his arm beneath her shoulders and patted her awkwardly through the thick quilt.

All of the tiredness seemed to slip from her, in the most helpful and healing way, as tears cascaded down her cheeks.

He touched her face with his fingertips. "We're safe."

"For now," she said. "But we are still fugitives. There is probably a price on your head."

Steven nodded in the moonlight, still caressing her dirty, tearstained face.

"Adamo wants you dead. And it is my fault," she said suddenly, "for getting you into this, for making you do it."

"Shh," he whispered. "It's not your fault, Maggie. I'm a grown man, and I make my own decisions. We're partners, and I don't blame you."

"Partners?" she asked with a little sobbing hiccup. "Just look what your partner did to you!"

Maggie opened her eyes, their bright blue color clouded with tears. The henna rinse on her hair had faded to a deep strawberry blond. Automatically he reached up to smooth the tangles. This was certainly not the sophisticated countess who'd insinuated herself into his life at the Double E, this exhausted young woman lying beside him, her face now swollen with tears and exhaustion.

Steven found the words to tell her what he'd only allowed himself to think before. "You're a wonderful partner, Maggie. You're strong and brave and resourceful. You never give up."

"Stubborn," she added with a half sob and another hiccup.

"I have to agree with that."

Her eyes shot open again.

"Well, Maggie, you said it," he reminded her with a smile. "But you rescued me tonight. You saved my life, and I will never, never forget that."

She gave a little sniffle and said softly, her eyes closed again as sleep began to overcome her, "I rescued you..."

Steven drew her close and held her against his chest much as a father would hold a sleeping child. "Get some rest now, Maggie. Margarette," he whispered, *"Liebling."*

And then, his arms wrapped around her, Steven closed his eyes and he, too, slept.

Maggie thought surely it was a dream. The feel of a soft quilt around her, the smell of coffee in the air, the sensation of being warm and dry. She snuggled down into the softness again, only to be jarred by the sound of a pot clattering, followed by a muffled curse. Reluctantly she opened one eye. She was lying on a bed, a real bed, with the sunlight streaming around her.

Then she remembered everything, their escape in the rowboat to the cascading rapids; the chilling, rushing water that threatened to drag them down to its black depths; the shore slippery beneath their feet; the endless trek up the mountain to the chalet and safety.

Her memory was heightened by the aches and pains, minor, but still there—a throbbing in her head, a stinging sensation from the cuts on her arms and legs combined with itchy bug bites—all of which were incidental compared to the wonderful feeling of escape and freedom.

Sitting up, Maggie wrapped herself in the quilt as if it were a royal ermine stole and then climbed out of bed and stepped through the door into the kitchen.

Steven was there, standing at a big iron stove, pouring himself a cup of coffee. He was barefoot, and his trousers and shirt, which was open down the front, were bedraggled, his beard scraggly, but to Maggie he looked as wonderful as she felt.

He turned toward her, and she saw the long scratch on his neck and a bruise forming near his rib cage. "Good morning, Countess. Sleep well?"

"I had a marvelous rest. Honestly," she said with a smile, thinking of their last night at the Schloss and the fight that had kept them apart and kept her awake. That seemed a million miles away.

He was pouring another cup of coffee. Taking baby steps to avoid stumbling over the quilt, Maggie made her way to the stove and accepted the coffee gratefully.

"Where did you get it?"

"Oh, I'm very inventive. Made it out of blackberry leaves and bark, just like the Indians."

"Did you really?" she asked, dumbfounded.

Steven laughed. "No, Maggie. I found the coffee in the cupboard. Other staples, too—some of them even without bugs. Flour, baking powder, sugar, potatoes and lard in the cellar—"

"Why, that is marvelous," she exclaimed. "I will cook for us—after I wash up and drink this." She sipped the coffee, which was strong and black and tasted simply delicious.

"There's a pump outside and plenty of water. Oh, I raided the closet in the servant's room—the ones upstairs were empty so I guess our host and hostess got away with all their clothes," he added. "But I found that for you." He pointed to a gray shapeless garment flung over the back of a chair. "I don't think you and the cook are the same size, but it may be an improvement over the quilt you're wearing now."

Maggie laughed. "I am sure it will be."

"And I found this for me," he said, brandishing a straight-edged razor. "I figure it's time to get rid of the beard so I won't be as easily recognized."

"That's a good idea," Maggie agreed, "even though we'll be in hiding, anyway, won't we?"

"For a while. But I also have something to do." He paused because he hadn't completely formed his plan, but sometime during their escape—or maybe afterward, last night, when he saw Maggie drifting off to sleep beside him—Steven had made a decision.

"I'm going to find out the truth, Maggie."

"The truth?" She'd picked up the dress, adjusted her quilt where it had begun to slip and started toward the door. "About what?"

"About myself. My heritage. After all, that's why we're here, isn't it?"

"Yes," Maggie said softly. "But I thought you'd decided against any further search."

"Maybe I had. If so, I was wrong. I realize that now."

Maggie stood silently, looking at Steven, both relieved and frightened for him. It would be difficult—and dangerous. "Thank you, Steven," she said softly.

"For wanting to learn who I really am?"

"Yes, for that. And for yesterday... for getting me out of the river and across the mountain."

"That's what partners do for each other. I owed my escape to you. The least I could do was complete what you had begun." He smiled at her, and to Maggie that smile was like sunlight breaking through the clouds.

"Without you, I might have given up," she reminded him.

"Oh, no, Maggie," Steven replied. "You never would have done that. Maggie Hanson is too stubborn to give up."

She made a face at him and stepped outside into the glory of the morning.

The night sounds had turned to day music that refreshed and elated rather than frightened Maggie. All around her birds chirped, bees and insects buzzed, and squirrels chattered madly. Maggie walked along an overgrown path to the pump and washed as best she could, wincing slightly as she cleaned the cuts on her arms and legs. Then she pulled on the gray dress.

She couldn't help laughing aloud at the fit, which proved the cook was obviously half a foot shorter and a hundred pounds heavier than Maggie. The dress hung just to her knees and gaped in front so that she had to knot the material to keep from exposing her whole chest. The knot wasn't very stylish, but Maggie just shrugged. It didn't matter. Nothing mattered except that she and Steven had survived and were together, friends at last.

Face washed, hair slicked back and still damp, wearing the cotton dress, Maggie headed back to the house. At the door she paused and watched Steven. A shaft of sunlight bathed him as he sat on a stool at the kitchen table before a pan of hot water, lathering his face. The moment was perfect, Maggie thought. She'd caught him in a simple action but one that was intimate and personal and somehow gave her comfort.

The comfortable feeling was something like being married, she thought before pushing the thought away. No need to try and turn it into a husband and wife waking to a beautiful morning in the country. They had become friends; that was enough.

As Maggie went in, Steven looked up and grinned. "The unfortunate part is that I don't have a mirror so I may cut my throat, but I'm determined to get this damned beard off." He took a wild swipe at his face and Maggie cringed.

"You're going to cut your nose and chin, maybe even take off an ear before you get around to cutting your throat," she chided. "Here, let me." She placed the folded quilt on the table. "I know all about this kind of thing."

At his surprised look, Maggie explained, "Sometimes I used to give my husband his morning shave."

"Oh, yes. Of course," he said quietly, his eyes intent on hers as he handed her the razor.

Silently Maggie went to work, carefully shaving away his growth of golden beard. He closed his eyes, and she was glad to escape the scrutiny of those measuring, judging green eyes that often made her nervous. He saw too much, she thought, and it was difficult to keep her feelings hidden.

"This is pleasant," he said. "I ought to try it more often."

"Do not tell me that no one has ever given you a shave before, Steven Peyton."

"Barbers," he said lazily, "but no one as pretty as you."

He was flirting; Maggie knew it, and she let herself go and flirted right back. "What about your lady friends?"

He laughed at her question, and the movement of his jaw proved to be dangerous. She nicked him. "Sorry," she said.

"Just another battle scar," he responded lightly before opening his eyes and surveying her thoughtfully. "My lady friends, as you so charmingly put it, are usually more interested in their own appearance, their own pleasures, than to worry themselves about taking care of me. Besides, few of them would have gotten out of bed early enough to give me a shave." He closed his eyes again.

Maggie leaned forward and moved the razor across his cheek, actually delighting in the scraping sound it made as she shaved him, dipping the blade into the water between each careful stroke. They were so close that she could feel the heat rising from his body and mingling with her own. His chest was bronzed and muscular, splashed with golden hair that shimmered in the sunlight.

He opened his eyes and looked boldly at her, and Maggie realized that with the knot on her dress she hadn't quite achieved the purpose of completely covering herself. The tops of her breasts were exposed to his gaze.

She made no move toward modesty, aware that she wanted him to see her; she wanted him to touch her, just as she wanted to reach out and touch him, run her fingers down his chest, across his flat brown nipples, along the lines of his rib cage. She wanted to feel his skin, smooth over the hard muscles, warm in the morning sunlight. She wanted to massage his aching muscles, touch him, comfort him, and she wanted Steven to do the same for her. Maggie's thoughts were dangerous and erotic—and very persistent.

Her eyes met his and she forced herself to question him. "These friends of yours sound rather selfish." She slid the razor along the line of his cheek.

"Selfish, indulgent, but always beautiful."

"I am not surprised," she said, wishing now that she'd never brought up the subject of Steven and other women. The thought of him touching someone else, making love to another woman, was odious to her, but something dark and perverse made her go on.

"Did you have a—lady friend," she said with a smile, "in Cheyenne?"

"Nope."

"Oh?" Maggie was doubtful as she concentrated on shaving the delicate area under his chin.

"Surprised? Well, I have to admit there were a few, but the women in Cheyenne who weren't married were ready to *get* married. Whereas the ones in Chicago and Kansas City where I did business had a more fun-loving attitude."

"Do you have something against marriage?" She moved the blade along his throat.

"Not when a beautiful woman has a knife at my neck," he teased, grabbing her wrist and moving the razor away. "Have you finished with me?" There was something very suggestive in the question, Maggie thought.

She nodded. Maybe she'd just imagined the inference. His face was clean shaven again; he was as handsome as the first time she'd seen him, but something in the lines of his face was tougher and leaner and more dangerous-looking than the man she'd first seen on the train.

Maggie dipped a cloth in the warm water, squeezed it out and carefully put it over his face, her thoughts still on the difference in Steven then and now, a difference that intrigued her and drew her to him.

"So I get the full treatment," Steven mumbled from under the cloth.

"Of course. Always the best for Mr. Peyton." She was leaning over him now, and although he was unable to see her, Maggie knew from the sound of his breathing that he felt her closeness. She didn't move away but remained close, and after a few moments removed the cloth gently, lifting the corners, wiping away the remaining bits of soap on Steven's face and shaving one spot she'd missed by his ear.

He was looking at her with intense eyes that wouldn't let hers look away. There was a stillness in the room, a sense of something about to happen.

"There. *Now* I have finished with you." She repeated his earlier suggestive words. They hung heavy in the air.

Once more Steven reached out and grabbed her wrist. "Oh, have you?" he asked insinuatingly, his lips curving in a grin.

Maggie nodded.

"Then I'd say you've played another good part, that of a very skilled barber. Even though your dress isn't exactly designed for the role."

Maggie glanced down to see that the knot she'd made had come loose, and one shoulder of the dress had slipped down her arm, exposing part of her breast and the tip of her nipple. She reached for the troublesome sleeve, but Steven's hand was there first.

"Let me." Slowly, still holding her wrist with one hand, he trailed the other up her arm, pushing the sleeve to her shoulder. "There," he said, moving his hand away and then laughing aloud as the sleeve immediately slipped down again. "I guess it's a hopeless task," he admitted through his laughter.

Maggie started to step away, but he held on to her wrist. "Don't you want to feel what a good job you've done?"

"It looks fine," she said, hating it that her voice seemed so shaky and hoarse, hating herself that just standing near him made her legs weak and her stomach beat with the wings of a thousand butterflies.

"I want you to touch me," he said.

Maggie's ragged breath caught in her throat as he lifted her hand to his face and laid the palm against his smooth cheek. When he released her hand, she started to pull it away, but the warmth that had enveloped her was so overwhelming that she found herself unable to do so. It was as if a magnet held her to him. She couldn't fight against it; she could only move with it, downward, tracing the line of his jaw, across his chin to the other smooth cheek, and then upward to his temple.

Still drawn to him, unable to pull her hand away, she ran her fingers into his thick hair, as their eyes met, locked together. Then it drew her closer until their lips were no more than a millimeter apart.

He reached for her, and Maggie knew that Steven was the magnet that had held her, the undeniable force that brought them together.

She heard a clattering sound as the razor dropped from her hand onto the stone floor. And then he kissed her.

His tongue invaded her mouth, circling her tongue, probing against the silken recesses of her mouth, setting her on fire. Maggie took his tongue into her mouth deeply and sucked on it, all the while making little sounds of savage delight deep in her throat. She wanted him, she loved him, and there was no need for any force to hold them together now. Their own physical desire was enough.

Steven was struggling with her dress, pulling it down over her shoulders, away from her breasts. She flung back her head to expose her neck and breasts to him, wanting him to touch and kiss her, to set her aflame and then quench the fire with his body.

His lips traced paths of heat along her throat, to the hollow of her breasts, to her nipples, hot and swollen. She wound her fingers in his hair, pulling him even closer, making him part of her.

"You're setting me on fire," he murmured, echoing her own thoughts. "I want you so much... feel how much, Maggie," he said, guiding her hand between his legs. She felt the thick, throbbing bulge beneath the rough cloth of his trousers and pressed her hand against it, delighting in the evidence of his need for her.

"I want you, too, Steven," she whispered. "I want to make love to you."

"Yes," he said, "yes, Maggie."

"The bed—" she began, her voice weak with passion.

"No bed," he told her. "Here and now." He stood, spread the quilt out on the table and lifted her up, in one motion pulling her dress down over her legs and setting her on the low hardwood table.

Maggie reached out, and her fingers fumbled with the buttons of his trousers until her hands found and caressed him, feeling him grow. She heard his groan of pleasure, felt his kisses along her neck, his tongue darting bursts of sensual delight in the softness of her ear.

As he kissed her, Steven spread her legs apart and with loving fingers found the soft center of her desire. He touched her until she cried out with pleasure and need, and then with his hands around her buttocks he pulled her closer and closer until he could enter her and fill her warmth with his need.

Hardly able to believe what was happening, Maggie clung to him fiercely, arms around his shoulders, legs outstretched as he moved within her, slowly at first, watching her face, watching the surprise and pleasure, listening to the little moans that came from deep down in her throat.

Then the moans turned to cries of passion as he grabbed the edge of the table and plunged deep within her, moving faster and faster, almost fiercely, until their dual pleasure spiraled into wave after wave of sensual excitement.

Maggie fell back on the table, her hands holding tightly to his strong wrists, fingers digging into his flesh, wanting more than the pleasure he gave her, wanting to be one with him, part of him. And when they found that moment of rapture that made them one, she felt as though she would burst with joy.

Hot, sweaty and satiated, they clung to each other for a long time, not speaking, until Steven moved away and stripped off his trousers. Then he wrapped her in the quilt and picked her up, carrying her to the little room where they had spent the night.

Gently he put her on the bed, spread the quilt out and lay down beside her. "I've thought of this so many times, Maggie," he whispered. "But," he added with a smile in his voice, "I never thought it would happen again, especially not on a kitchen table in a chalet near Magris."

Maggie laughed softly as she reached out to touch his face, the beautiful face that she loved beyond all others. "I never thought it would happen at all," she told him. "I thought you hated me."

"Hated you? How could I ever hate the woman who's everything to me." He drew her close. "That's better," he said. "Now I can feel you, all of you."

She smiled, contented, and ran her hand down his arm, loving the feel of his passion-damp body next to hers.

"Oh, Steven, I feel so peaceful, so happy." Then she laughed again. "How can that be? We are wanted by the military, we have no clothes, nowhere to go...."

"We have each other, though, and that's gotten us through before. It will again." He took a lock of her hair and let it slide through his fingers. She looked so small and vulnerable, he thought, innocent and wise, shy and seductive. He felt that if he knew her forever, she'd still be a mystery to him, and that only made him want her more.

"I'm bound to you, Maggie," he said slowly, "by all that we've gone through together and more."

She took his hand and raised it gently to her lips. "I know, Steven. I feel that way, too."

"Making love to you, knowing you so perfectly, being part of you..." He paused, searching for the right words. "Everything is different with you."

Maggie was afraid to speak, afraid of breaking the spell by telling him that she loved him.

"I can't make any promises," he went on, "because they'd be false ones. I don't know if we can get out of this mess or not, and if we do, I don't know what will happen to me. Or us."

"I want no promises," she told him. "All I want is right now. You and me in this funny bed in the servant's quarters." She propped herself up on one elbow and gazed down at him. "Remember what you said in the hotel?"

Steven groaned. "I said a lot of things, Maggie. Please don't hold me to any one of them."

"I am holding you to this one, Steven Peyton," she teased in mock sternness. "You said if you were to be swept away by passion it would have nothing to do with the surroundings—"

He raised up and kissed her gently. "And everything to do with the woman." He dropped his head back and laughed. "Well, I was right about that. A kitchen table's a hell of a lot different from the bridal suite."

"A lot more inventive," Maggie said, cuddling back beside him.

"Not to mention more athletic. Which has made me hungry, woman," he added. "I want something to eat—"

"Potato pancakes?" she asked. "A Mendorran speciality."

"Exactly, and I am going to need lots of them to keep my strength up."

Maggie pretended she didn't know what he meant. "Whyever in the world?"

"I'll be needing more energy for the afternoon."

She looked at him with wide-eyed innocence. "What is so special about the afternoon?"

"We're going to spend it in bed." He punctuated each word with a kiss. "Instead of on a kitchen table. And in bed we'll improve on this morning's activities."

"Well, maybe we can improve on the setting, but not on what happened there."

"Wait and see. We'll go more slowly so we can savor each moment, so we can improvise ... innovate ... invent." As he spoke, Steven took his thumb and rubbed it against one of her nipples. As he increased the friction, he watched her face change and soften, her eyes deepen with desire. She squirmed beside him. "Steven... if you don't stop, we'll never get any food—"

"Do you really want food now?"

Her breath came in little gasps as his hands made dual assaults on her sensitive, tingling body. "I thought you wanted—"

"I want everything. But in the right order. First you..." He kissed her thoroughly. His mouth covered hers, and Maggie let herself slide into the erotic web he wove.

Half an hour later, they struggled from the bed, running nude into the afternoon sun, washing each other with icy water from the pump, splashing, romping and laughing like children.

Steven caught Maggie and held her against him, both of them out of breath. "How can we be so silly?" she asked, "when there is so much evil all around us?"

"But that's just it," he replied, looking down at her. "Don't you see, Maggie? The more danger, the more we fear losing, the more precious that makes every moment. I don't want to waste one moment of this day. You learn that in war, not to anticipate but to savor and enjoy each minute of your life. Like this."

He began to kiss her, pulling her body close to his, her breasts rubbing against the hardness of his chest, her thighs pushed against his, and Maggie felt the familiar heat of need and desire surge through her. Steven was right; this could be their only day together, and like

Steven she would not let one moment of their new-found joy be wasted. She would love him for today and not think about tomorrow.

Chapter Fourteen

Early the next morning they set off for Magris, and even after their three-mile trek into town Maggie still couldn't control her giggles at their attire. Steven was wearing his water-stained, tattered trousers and shirt, and an old suede hunting jacket he'd found in the kitchen closet. A slouch felt hat completed his costume. Unable to find any firearms, he carried instead a stout walking stick and a kitchen knife as their only means of protection.

Upstairs in the chalet, Maggie had rummaged through an old trunk Steven had overlooked and come up with a bright dirndl skirt and a blouse, but this time they were much too small, which Steven had not missed.

"You'll call attention to us in that, Maggie," he'd told her. "Not that I don't approve heartily, but maybe you should cover up."

She obliged by adding a shawl and scarf and miraculously turning herself into a peasant woman, arm in arm with her husband on a shopping trip to town. It had been her insistence that they could carry off such a ruse that convinced Steven to make the trip by daylight.

Despite their appearance, they were better off than the average peasant, for Baroness Mendheim had wisely sewn currency into Maggie's pockets before she left the Schloss, and now she and Steven each had money hidden in their clothes, a very generous amount. They would need it for food and extra clothing, and—more importantly—to offer bribes if that became necessary.

They had inadvertently picked market day in Magris, which attracted everyone from the surrounding area. As Maggie and Steven neared the little village, the road became clogged with wagons, people on foot and riding astride farm animals. Children ran in and out among the adults, and contributed to the festive feeling in the air.

"This crowd is good camouflage," Steven said in a low voice so no one would overhear his way of speaking. He'd have to depend on Maggie to do their negotiating, for there was no doubt that Adamo's soldiers would be looking for a tall bearded man who spoke English with an American accent. Even without the beard, he fit the rest of the description perfectly.

Maggie was the first to notice the spire of a small Romanesque church behind the city wall. "There is the Convent of the Sisters of Hope, just as Sophie described it." She pointed out two nearby buildings of white stone with red tiled roofs. "Theirs is a cloistered order and—"

"And the mother superior is Sophie's old friend. I remember," Steven said. "A safe haven if we need it." He made a mental note of the narrow path behind the convent, disappearing into the hills. On the other side was the border, well guarded, he suspected, very near and yet very far away. But he had other business to attend to first. "Somewhere in this town could be the record of my identity," he said to Maggie.

"We will find it," she assured him as they followed the crowd into the main square where they mingled, walking from stall to stall, buying fruit and cheese, bread and a bottle of wine before settling themselves on a bench near a fountain in the public park.

"We are much safer not to go into restaurants," she said. "Someone might ask you a question—"

"Which I couldn't answer." Steven took a last bit of cheese and looked around the park while they finished their lunch. "Lots of soldiers," he noted. "Doesn't surprise me since this is a border town, but there're a hell of a lot more here than in Bad Mendheim."

A little nervously, Maggie began to pack up the remains of their lunch in a basket she'd bought. "Do you think they are looking for us?"

"Could be." Steven got to his feet. "Come on, let's see if we can find the town hall. Should be one of these buildings around the square. I want to start right away looking through the birth records."

They'd just left the park when Steven suddenly stopped, leaned down and kissed her blatantly, paying no attention to the smiles of passersby.

Surprised at first and then delighted, Maggie returned the kiss. "Not that I mind," she said as they continued along, "but what was that for?"

"Because I thought you needed something to calm your nerves. And because you're beautiful, the sun is shining, and we're together."

They walked along slowly, and Maggie found she couldn't keep her thoughts to herself. "I wish . . . I wish we could stay here always."

"In the park?" he teased.

"No, in the mountains, in the chalet. I wish we really were a couple who'd come to town for a day of shopping." She began to imagine their life together. "Tonight we would return home, and I would cook."

"And we'd make love again," Steven said, joining in the dream.

"Yes, and later we would close up the house, put out the fire, and go up to bed, just like ordinary people."

Steven took her hand and brought them both back to reality. "But we wouldn't be ordinary people, Maggie. We'd be pretending; we'd be acting. Haven't you had enough of lies and pretense?"

His words made her think of the Schloss and their evening in the baths. "I have had enough of the lies, but it would not be like that. We would just be pretending, both of us, that we were someone else. That would not be so bad, would it, Steven?"

She'd been half joking when she started the conversation, but now Maggie realized they were both serious.

"Being with you at the chalet would be wonderful, Maggie, but not real. I need my life back," he said. "Hell, I need to know who I am and what my life really is. Pretending can never be enough for me."

There was no blame or criticism in his words, but somehow Maggie felt it. When hadn't she pretended or acted, she wondered? As a child she'd made believe that her aunt and uncle were really her parents, and from the age of seventeen she'd played roles both onstage and off. With Steven she'd played many parts, which she regretted now.

Then it came to her, clear and certain as the sunshine. There was no pretense when she was in Steven's arms. Being with him was her reality, and she never wanted to lose it.

They walked on silently around the town square, each lost in thoughts for a brief moment until they noticed again that the square was alive with soldiers. There were two coming toward them, almost upon them when Steven put his arm around her and pulled her back into a doorway, kissing her again.

"That kiss was not quite as spontaneous as the first one," he whispered as the soldiers passed by.

"They did not seem suspicious," she told him.

"I know, but we can't be sure how long this ruse will last. That's obviously the town hall," he said, indicating a building half a block away, surrounded by soldiers. "Do you think we should risk it?"

Maggie looked across at the squat brick building. "I have a better chance than you," she said. "I could pretend Elyse Contrand was my mother or my aunt." The word "pretend" caught in her throat.

"I don't know," Steven said worriedly.

"We could go back to the chalet and try again tomorrow," she suggested.

"It'll be the same—but with less of a crowd for us to get lost in. No, the search begins today. And ends today. I hope. But let's walk around first and look in the shops. Something doesn't feel quite right."

He didn't tell her what he was really thinking. Perhaps soldiers never lost their sixth sense, but he could feel it, danger lurking. He'd let down his defenses once before, when he was caught in Bad Mendheim. He wouldn't do it again.

They walked slowly along the crowded streets, peering into shop windows, stopping to look at a vendor's wares. Then he felt Maggie stiffen beside him. "Wili—

over there!'' She made a move to walk toward him, but Steven held her back.

"Let's just watch for a minute."

They stood in the crowd as Wili cut across the square past a group of soldiers.

"He is being very bold," Maggie whispered.

"Wait," Steven advised. "Something's going on."

As they watched, Wili mingled with the crowd, circled back toward the soldiers, looking around, hands in his pockets, as if he didn't have a care in the world. Unseen by the big man, Steven and Maggie continued to observe him as he took one hand out of his pocket and dropped something at the foot of one of the soldiers before ambling on.

The soldier bent down, ostensibly to speak to a child carrying a balloon, but they both noticed the extra movement as he scooped something up from the path.

"A note?" Maggie asked.

Steven nodded imperceptibly.

"But why?"

"I don't know, but we're going to find out."

He and Maggie made their way through the crowd, keeping Wili in sight. Before they'd gone more than a few yards, they realized that the soldier who'd picked up the note was ahead of them, also following Wili.

"Rendezvous," Steven said, slowing his step. "I'll bet on that."

Maggie felt her insides constrict with the cold hand of dread. "Maybe the soldier is a spy, maybe he is giving information to Anton and the rebels."

"Maybe," Steven said, "but I doubt it. I imagine the information is going the other way."

They reached the side street and turned down it, walking slowly but determinedly, even though this part of the town was less crowded than the square, causing Maggie to feel vulnerable and exposed.

Halfway down the street, Wili ducked into a tall brick house. Within moments the soldier reached the house—and walked right past it.

"We were wrong," Maggie said.

"Wait," Steven advised again, slowing his pace.

The soldier had doubled back and was standing in front of the house, looking carefully to his right and left. The few people who'd been in the street had walked on, and they were left alone with the soldier.

Maggie could hear her heart thumping. He was looking right at them! Her first instinct was to turn and run, but Steven prodded her on, slowly toward the soldier.

Any moment he could step forward and arrest them, Maggie realized in a heartbeat. If that happened, she knew they would never be lucky enough to pull off another escape. If that happened, they were doomed.

The pressure of Steven's hand was firm on her elbow, his steps steady and sure guiding her. She had no choice but to keep walking.

They were almost beside the soldier now, and Steven was speaking softly, his voice barely audible, even to Maggie. But she heard a word or two. "Talk to me...in Mendorran...lovingly...just a whisper."

She understood, found the words and spoke them softly in his ear. "I love you, darling, I love you very much."

They were passing the soldier as she spoke, and Steven gave her a kiss on the cheek. A few feet more and they were past him.

She risked looking back to see the soldier, after a quick glance at them, survey the street once more before stepping inside the house. Maggie let out a long sigh of relief.

Daring to quicken their steps, they reached the corner and turned, moving quickly away from the center of town back toward the mountain.

"By the way, Maggie," Steven ventured at last, "what did you say to me back there?"

"I said—" She hesitated. This wasn't the time. Maybe it would never be the time. She couldn't predict that, but she knew she couldn't tell him now. "I said we were having soup for dinner."

"A good peasant woman taking care of her man," Steven told her with a laugh.

But the laugh was not long-lived. There was trouble all around them, and they both knew it. "Do you think Wili is a traitor?" Maggie asked. "Was he the one who betrayed us in Bad Mendheim?"

"There's one way to find out," Steven said grimly. "Find Anton. He may have sent Wili on a mission to meet with one of Adamo's men. If not, Anton needs to know what his half brother is up to. It sure as hell doesn't look good."

"But if Wili's a traitor, then why hasn't he turned Anton in?" Maggie asked, running a little to keep up with Steven's long gait.

"Good question. I don't know. He may be waiting for the right moment, a time to bring down the whole rebel army, not just Anton." Steven was thoughtful for a while before adding, "Whatever's going on, this isn't the time to be searching for my birth records. Anton has to be found."

Maggie heard the commitment in Steven's voice and realized how much he'd changed from the man she'd met on the train racing across the American continent toward Wyoming.

"That means returning to Bad Mendheim," Maggie said.

Steven nodded.

"Should we go back to the chalet first? We'll need to take something warm for the mountains."

"Not 'we,' Maggie," Steven said firmly.

"What do you mean?" She tried to stop, but he urged her on.

"I'm going back. You're not."

"Steven!" This time she stopped in her tracks. "What makes you think that you can run off and leave me now?" She didn't give him a chance to answer. "I am going with you."

"No, you're not, and for a very good reason."

"To keep me out of danger?" she asked. "I have risked danger every minute—on the river, just now when we followed the soldier..."

"I know that, Maggie," he attempted.

"And I did not let you down. In fact, you might not have been able to fool them without me."

"I know that, too," Steven admitted. "This has nothing to do with keeping you out of danger. God knows, there's danger everywhere, especially here in Magris. If Wili sees you, I wager he'll turn you in without a qualm." Steven put his hands on her shoulders. "Listen to me. You and I are the only ones who can tell Anton about Wili. If something happens to me, then it's all up to you. We're in this together, Maggie. That's why we have to separate."

"I don't want us to be separated, Steven. I can't bear the thought."

He put his arm around her, and they started walking again. "It has to be this way, Maggie. We both can't go charging back to Bad Mendheim. Admit it. I'm right."

"I know you are. And I'm so proud of you, Steven, for what you're doing."

"Don't try to make me a hero, Maggie. I have no choice."

"You could walk away, cross the border, and leave all this behind," she told him.

"No man could do that and live with himself," Steven replied.

After that they were silent, Steven formulating his plan, Maggie waiting for him to tell her what would happen next.

Finally he did. "You can't stay alone at the chalet so we're going to have to depend on the baroness and her connections."

"The convent?"

"Yes," Steven said. "Another woman cloistered there shouldn't arouse any suspicions."

"All right," Maggie agreed. "Let's go to the convent and find out how friendly Sophie really is with the mother superior."

Mary Therese, mother superior of the Convent of the Sisters of Hope, was less than friendly, far less than welcoming. She looked down her patrician nose at Steven and Maggie, who'd come knocking at her door with what she considered a farfetched tale.

After seating them in straight-backed chairs in her office in the convent, she made her pronouncement in perfectly enunciated English. "I find it very difficult to believe that my old friend Sophie would have sent you here for sanctuary. There is certainly no reason to imagine that I would be involved in activities counter to our government.''

Steven narrowed his eyes and studied Mary Therese carefully. It was she, not the baroness, who had the cool patrician look of an aristocrat. The mother superior was tall and slender, her pale, almost translucent face unlined, her blue eyes clear and bright. When she spoke, the nostrils of her strong-bridged nose flared slightly, and after each sentence her lips pressed together in a thin, determined line. Her gray habit and the white starched wimple around her face enhanced the mother superior's looks.

Steven watched her closely, trying to read her real feelings, which he hoped were different from her words.

When he didn't immediately respond to the mother superior's query, Maggie plunged in. ''Baroness Mendheim was very kind to us during a difficult time. Due to no fault of our own, we are being hunted by Adamo's soldiers, and Sophie—the baroness—assured us that you would give us sanctuary here, Mother Superior.''

Mary Therese laughed softly, showing the first signs of creases in the porcelainlike skin of the woman who was close to Sophie's age but seemed decades younger. Her bright eyes focused on Steven although she was responding to Maggie's question.

''Sophie is very generous with my convent, is she not?''

''She is a generous person in many ways,'' Steven said, shifting his weight in the straight-backed chair.

Mary Therese lifted her chin slightly without taking her eyes off Steven.

''She is also trusting,'' Steven added, certain now that he understood what was in the very intelligent nun's mind. "For example, she had no fear that we might be spies for Adamo, trying to trick her into acts against the state. Perhaps you are not so trusting."

Mary Therese's eyes wavered only slightly. "I am not certain that I understand your meaning," she said.

"I mean that you may need proof of our sincerity." Steven reached into his pocket and pulled out the rosary that Maggie had given him in prison, Sophie's rosary. He laid it on the table. "This belongs to your friend Sophie. Perhaps you recognize it."

Mary Therese lifted the rosary, letting the pearls and jade beads run through her fingers. "I remember when she got it. We were in convent school together in Delphberg. Best friends, if that seems possible. Sixty years ago," she mused aloud. "It is one of Sophie's lifelong treasures."

"She gave it to us," Steven reminded her.

"Or you took it," Mary Therese challenged.

"Her lifelong treasure? How do you think that's possible, Mother Superior?" Steven looked at her long and hard. "When she wore it at all times around her neck? Do you suppose we killed her for it?"

Mary Therese crossed herself and murmured a prayer.

"You would know if your friend had died," Steven told her. "I imagine you have your ways of finding out everything. Somehow, word would have reached the convent."

Mary Therese nodded. "Yes. I would know if my friend were dead," she agreed. "But the rosary—she would not have parted with it easily."

"Unless she thought it might save lives. *Our* lives, Mother Superior. And that's what I'm asking, not for myself but for Maggie, Margarette. She needs sanctuary while I go back to Bad Mendheim.''

Mary Therese folded her slender hands on her office desk. "You are an intelligent man, Mr. Englehardt, and you understand that I cannot immediately put my trust in everyone who comes to me. There are spies everywhere. I thought perhaps you were one of them, sent by Adamo to learn what the sisters in our convent were doing for the cause of freedom.''

"You were right not to trust us until we gave you proof,'' Steven said. "Adamo has many cards up his sleeve.''

"I do not understand.''

Steven laughed. "I admit to being a gambler, Mother Superior. It's an expression which means your general is full of tricks.''

Mary Therese nodded sternly at that. "He is an evil man, and none of us who believe in justice will rest until he is removed. Meanwhile, we do what we can, hiding rebels, taking care of their wounds, sharing our food.'' She smiled at Maggie, a smile that made her porcelain face suddenly quite warm and human. "And of course we shall take care of Margarette. She will be easy to hide. Another nun among so many. But you must work for your keep, Margarette.''

"I shall do whatever you ask, Mother Superior,'' Maggie said gratefully.

Mary Therese rose to her feet, her long gray skirts rustling around her legs. "Then I shall tell Sister Angela that you are here, and she will begin preparations. You can trust her as you trust me. She and I try to keep our activities against Adamo from the other sisters for their own good. Such knowledge can be very dangerous. But I know that you understand our caution.''

Steven rose to his feet. "You're not only generous but wise," he said. "It means so much to know that Maggie will be safe while I'm gone."

The nun paused at her office door. "No one will be truly safe until Adamo is gone, but we shall do our best. If you will stop by our kitchen, the nuns there will prepare food for your journey. You will need all of your strength for this venture."

"My deepest thanks for everything."

Her face broke into another beautiful smile. "Perhaps you and Margarette would like to use my office to say your farewells. God go with you, Mr. Englehardt, and return you safely to us."

She swept out of the office with a regal and determined air.

When the door closed behind her, Maggie stepped into Steven's arms and held tightly to him. "I don't want you to go. Can't we forget this idea?"

He squeezed her tightly. "You know better than that, Maggie. I have to find Anton and tell him what's going on with Wili. I only hope I can convince him."

"You can," she said adamantly. "I know you can, and then you'll come back to *me*. Soon. Please, Steven." She turned her face up to his.

"I can take care of myself," he assured her. "I'm very good at that."

"No, you're not," she shot back. "You need me to help you and look after you."

Steven threw back his head and laughed, and the sound of his laughter made Maggie more desperate than ever to hold on to him. "You, my dear, are the one who got me into all this to begin with." He kissed her lightly.

"And got you out," she reminded him.

He kissed her again, much more thoroughly. "That you did, but this time I won't get caught. This time I'll be more careful, and I *will* come back to you."

"I want you to swear," she said, clinging to him. "Swear that you'll come back."

He held her tightly against him. "I remember last night," he whispered. "Do you remember, Maggie?"

She felt her body tingle with desire at the memory. "I will never forget," she said.

"I'll be thinking about that while I'm gone, looking forward to another night making love with you. That's enough to keep me alive, enough to bring me back."

"Swear, Steven."

"I swear," he said.

Tears were flooding her eyes when she looked up at him. There was no way she could deny any longer what was in her heart. She spoke the words in English that she'd whispered to him on the street. "I love you, Steven." Her heart was in her throat, waiting for his answer that didn't come. Finally she covered her sadness with another pronouncement. "If I lost you, I couldn't bear it."

"You won't lose me, Maggie. Didn't I swear?"

For a moment she thought he was going to say it, tell her that he loved her. But his mood lightened when he said, "Surely there's more trouble in the future you can get me into. I don't want to miss out on that."

"Don't tease, Steven. This isn't a joke."

"I know that, Maggie. Trust me, I'm no fool." He rubbed his thumb along her cheekbone gently, tenderly. And then he wiped away her tears, but more drained from her eyes to replace them. "What we have is too good to throw away. Trust me," he repeated.

Maggie took his hand and pressed it to her lips. She wanted to hold him forever, safe here with her. "I will try," she whispered.

He kissed her one more time, wondering when they'd be together again, wishing he could imprint the memory of her lips on his. Then he said, "I have to leave now. I'll be all night on that mountain." Reluctantly he removed her arms from around his waist and stepped away.

Maggie saw the rosary on the mother superior's desk and picked it up. "Take this," she said. "Please, for protection. Please." She tried to put it into his hand.

"No, Maggie," he replied softly. "You keep it as a talisman that I'll be back." He wrapped her fingers tightly around the rosary. "I'd like to think of you keeping it for me."

He dropped a final kiss on top of her head and then turned and was gone.

Maggie leaned against the door, her face stained with tears, clutching the rosary in her hand. Finally the tears stopped and she wiped away their tracks with the back of her hand, straightened her scarf and shawl, and went in search of Mary Therese.

Chapter Fifteen

Twenty-four hours later, just at sundown, Steven made his way into Bad Mendheim, looking very different from when he'd left. Gone was the stylish, well-dressed, bearded aristocrat who'd been a guest at Schloss Wolke. In his place was a slouching, shambling man, whose dirty clothes gave off an odor of perspiration and mountain dampness.

He limped along the back alleys of the town, trying to look like a peasant after just a bit too much to drink, winding his way home. He'd chosen sundown to make his approach, since the soldiers changed shifts then and the confusion would give him the best chance to avoid an overzealous guard.

He sank into the shadows of a doorway across from the back of the Café Legel and settled against the wall to wait. He had no idea how long it would take, but he had all night, and eventually she'd have to leave.

Half an hour passed, and then an hour. Steven heard the clock strike in the town square and shifted his weight from one aching leg to the other. He'd been this tired before, after a roundup, even after a marathon card game in his private railroad car. But never from walking across a mountain. He grinned to himself and thought ironically of how much walking he'd done in the past week, too damned much for a cowboy. What he wouldn't give for a horse, even the oldest and most swaybacked on the Double E.

He hadn't thought about home in a long time; events had been moving too quickly, but he still missed the Double E, missed Bert and Faye and wondered if he'd ever see the ranch again.

The back door of the café opened, and he tensed, watching as one of the cooks, a short, slight man, disappeared into the black night, heading toward the street. Steven settled himself, his eyes readjusting to the darkness, and let his thoughts turn to Maggie. He hadn't allowed himself to think about her as he'd made his way back to Bad Mendheim; that would have been too dangerous when he'd needed all of his senses to be alive to what was going on around him. He needed those same senses now, but he couldn't resist the images of Maggie that infiltrated his mind, couldn't resist the smile that again grazed his lips.

Maggie in a convent! That was something to contemplate. He imagined she was playing her role to the hilt. He'd like to see that. He'd like to see *her,* he admitted; he ached for her. She'd been his ally during the past weeks, and through the long, wonderful night at the chalet, she'd become a real part of him. Steven remembered her face when he'd said goodbye, thought of the way she'd clung to him. And told him that she loved him.

And what had he done? Walked away. He couldn't say the words she wanted to hear; he couldn't tell her that he loved her and then leave. That was the coward's way. When he said those words, he wanted to be with her, holding her, showing her his love. And he would, he determined. For now, all he could do was say it aloud. "I love you, Maggie," he whispered into the blackness. "I love you."

Then the door opened again, and Steven stiffened, leaning forward to watch. The girl was young and slim, and her hair glowed ebony in the light that followed her from the café. She was wearing a shawl and carrying a basket as she started down the alley past him.

With a lightning-quick move, he grabbed her, looped one arm around her waist, clamping his other hand over her mouth. He lifted her off her feet as he pulled her into the shadowy doorway and spoke in a hoarse whisper. "Don't say a word, Maria. Not a word. I have a knife, but I don't want to have to use it."

She struggled wildly in his arms, dropping the basket with a thud into the alley. Steven only tightened his grip, his lips close to her ear. "Hold still, Maria, and listen to me. Listen." He gave her a shake, and she quieted in his arms. He could hear the quick, frightened gasps of breath and the terrified thudding of her heart.

"I want to see Anton, and I want to see him tonight."

Frantically she shook her head.

He turned her so he could look into her face. "It's Steven Englehardt, the man you sent to Donnerstrasse. You had a reason for that, just as I now have a reason for finding Anton."

She relaxed a little then, her body collapsing against his.

"Now listen to me. I'm going to take my hand from your mouth—but," he warned, "I'll put it on the hilt of my knife, and if you scream, I'll sink the blade into your heart. Do you understand that?"

She nodded once, her eyes wide with fright.

Gingerly Steven moved his hand and slipped it to his waist, fingering his knife. Maria stood quietly, not daring to breathe.

"Do you recognize me now?" he asked.

She nodded again.

"You can talk, quietly," he told her.

"You are alive," she struggled for the words, unsure of her English and afraid to speak beyond a whisper. "We do not know. We think possible you go over the falls."

"I'm alive," he said brusquely, "but your brother may not be for long unless I talk to him. You know where he is, don't you?"

She stood immobile.

"Maria, where is he? You know," he insisted.

"I know," she repeated. "I go now to take him his dinner."

"Forget that," Steven ordered. "Tell Anton I need to see him tonight. Alone."

"He does not—"

"Alone," Steven repeated. "And tell him not to let anyone know. Not your father or your mother or your brother. No one. Do you understand?" He gave her a shake.

"Yes," she whispered. "I understand. I go now. Please."

He released her, and she stumbled slightly before bending down to collect her basket.

"Forget that," Steven said.

"Please?" She didn't understand.

"Don't take the basket. I need it more than Anton." Then he reiterated. "Twenty-two Donnerstrasse in one hour."

"One hour," she repeated.

Steven could make out her expression in the dim light of the alley and could tell she was terrified. He hoped that he could trust her to take his message to Anton and Anton alone. If not—if she didn't understand him or if she told someone else, he and Anton were as good as dead.

There were soldiers at the corner of Donnerstrasse and the square, and after looking over the situation, Steven withdrew back into the shadows of the alley. He'd have to find another route to his rendezvous with Anton. He cursed himself that he knew so little German; if he were stopped, even for questioning, he'd be a dead man.

Doubling back down the alley, Steven discovered a path through two low buildings that opened onto the street. He turned left and began walking, slowly, head down until he came to a house that he calculated was just behind 22 Donnerstrasse.

A gaslight burned on the front porch, but otherwise the house was dark. He'd have to take a chance that the owners were either asleep or away. He walked past the porch toward the backyard.

A dog barked from inside the house and stopped him in his tracks. Crouching low, he waited in vain for the insistent barking to stop. As long as his scent was in the air, the dog showed no signs of letting up. Frustrated, Steven could neither turn back nor go on. The barking continued. Finally he could stand it no longer and yelled out at the dog, conjuring up one of the few German words in his vocabulary, *"Stillen!"*

To his surprise, the dog stopped barking, began to whimper softly and then was quiet.

He waited for sounds that would tell him others had been disturbed by the barking and were coming to investigate. Five minutes passed. Then ten. Nothing. He'd already decided his next move, and without hesitating again, he made it, ran for the backyard, scaled the stone wall and dropped into a clump of blackberry vines on the other side. He could feel the prickles on his hands and face as he pushed through, looking for the summer house, hoping he'd dropped into the right yard.

Then he saw it, just ahead beyond a line of low shrubbery. He crept closer, conscious that his footsteps on the dried leaves and grass echoed in the walled garden. He hoped there would be no one there to hear them. Except Anton.

Reaching the house, he sank down in the shadows to wait. Scarcely had he hunkered down when he heard a low laugh behind him. He didn't even bother to turn around. He knew who it was.

"Well done, Mr. Englehardt. Or shall I just call you Steven?"

"Steven will do," he answered, rising to his feet.

"Unless I'd been lying in wait for you, I never would have known you were here. Good work."

"I'm not auditioning," Steven replied. "I've come to talk."

"Then let us talk," Anton said. "You are as safe here as anywhere. And I understand that you took my dinner. Shall we share, or have you already eaten it?"

Steven grinned and began to pull Anton's dinner from his pockets. "Bread and cheese, an apple, a pear."

"No wine?"

"I drank a little but had to leave the bottle behind."

The two men sat on the steps of the summer house and quickly dispatched the meal.

"Now we talk," Anton said.

Steven took a deep breath. This wasn't going to be easy, but there was nowhere to start except at the beginning.

"Maggie and I were in Magris two days ago, and we saw a man, someone we recognized, arranging a rendezvous with one of Adamo's soldiers."

Anton's eyes were bright with interest. "Go on, tell me about this man."

And Steven did.

Anton Legel didn't believe in staying in one place for too long. Perhaps that was the secret to his success of remaining alive. Tonight he slept in a cave high in the mountains; tomorrow he might be found in a hayloft on one of the farms whose owners were friendly to his cause. He had learned to trust few people; one of the people he trusted most was his half brother Wili, son of Anton's father and his first wife.

Anton and Wili bent low over a map on the ground. They studied it by the light of a flickering fire. The cave was dark and smoky; impenetrable shadows reached out from the farther dark recesses of the cavern. They spoke quietly in German.

"The garrison at the head of Lake Kranich? That's where we're making our attack?"

"That's it," Anton said. "If we take the garrison, we take the supplies, the weapons."

"But you said the attack would be at—"

"We've talked of many attacks, made many plans, but I believe this is the best. It will happen in two days."

"Two days?" Wili questioned. "There hardly seems time to—"

"There's plenty of time," Anton said. "Our men are ready and tired of hiding. We'll mass here and here." He jabbed the map with his forefinger. "Now I need for you to do what you do best, my brother. I need for you to keep watch on the garrison and report back to me." Anton rose to his feet and looked deeply into Wili's eyes, eyes so like his own. "Will you do that for me?"

"Of course, little brother. Haven't I always done what you've told me?" He turned to go, but Anton called him back.

"No farewells? No good lucks?"

Wili caught him in a great bear hug. "When did Anton Legel ever need luck? He has everything, doesn't he? The love of his family, the adoration of the people—"

"Then I wish us both luck, Wili. May God be merciful to us."

Anton followed Wili to the mouth of the cave and stood drinking in deep drafts of cool mountain air as he watched his brother disappear like a shadow among the pines. Then with a deep heavy sigh he turned back. "You may come out now."

Steven stepped from the darkness at the back of the cave into the smoky light.

"You heard?" Anton asked.

"I heard, but I didn't understand."

"I forgot," Anton said with a sad smile. "I gave him the false information that we were attacking the garrison. Instead, we ride to Delphberg, and take over the palace, the Parliament and the police. If you're right and Wili is a traitor, then Adamo's forces will all be concentrated at the garrison. We will ride almost unchallenged into the city."

"If I'm wrong?"

"Then I am leading my men into a suicidal mission, am I not? Adamo's troops will still be in Delphberg, and we will have one hell of a fight on our hands." Suddenly Anton was very quiet. Then he said, "I do not wish for my brother to be a traitor. I do not wish for you to be right, and yet I feel that you are right."

"I understand what you're going through, Anton. But I saw what I told you."

"I know that you did. I know because Wili is a man who wants more than he is capable of acquiring. He is not a leader, and because of this he is jealous of me. Because of this he betrays me. And in betraying me, he betrays all of us in the resistance."

"I'm sorry, Anton."

"I cannot think about it. There is much to do."

"Yes, there is, and I wonder if you're prepared," Steven said. "What kind of fighters are your men?"

"The best," Anton responded defensively. "Tough guerrillas, mountain fighters. If they have no guns they will fight with swords; if they have no swords, with their knives. If no knives, sticks. They will never surrender."

"How many are there?" Steven pushed.

"Not enough," Anton replied honestly.

Steven didn't have to think before he asked the next question; he'd already given it much thought. He may even have known before he left Maggie: he was going to join the rebels, not as pretender to the throne, not as Prince Gregor's son or Karl's grandson, just as a man who suffered at the hands of Adamo.

At one time, Maggie would have welcomed the decision, but he knew it would be different now, now that she loved him. And that's why he hadn't been able to tell her.

"How would you like another volunteer?" he asked Anton.

"You?" Anton's look was unbelieving.

"I know something about fighting, and I have a very personal score to settle with General Adamo."

"Because of Prince Gregor?"

Steven shrugged. "I've heard rumors that Adamo caused the prince's death many years ago...."

"He wanted no challenge to his power. King Karl was malleable but Gregor... he was a strong man. Adamo had to dispose of him—and of Elyse and her son—before he could take over." Anton looked speculatively at Steven.

"I know what you're thinking. But my reasons for wanting Adamo out have nothing to do with my possible connection to royalty. You have to understand that, Anton."

"Even if you are the heir—"

"It's not important," Steven emphasized.

Anton seemed to find that hard to believe.

"My birthright is still unknown, and I can't even think about it now. But my reasons for wanting to oust Adamo concern the present, not the past. He had me arrested and thrown in prison without a hearing or a trial. I'm sure he's done the same with scores of others. I refuse to be treated that way, and I'd like to settle things with him... face-to-face."

Anton threw back his head and laughed. "And when you do, I hope I am there to see the fireworks."

"If I join the rebels you will be," Steven said. "Am I in, Anton?"

The rebel leader reached out and clasped Steven's hand in his. "You are now officially my lieutenant."

"I was a captain in the Grand Army of the Republic."

Anton laughed again. "Here, I am in charge, not General Grant. We have no uniforms, but I think I can find some clothes for you that at least will be—clean," he said, eyeing Steven's garb.

"I don't give a damn about the clothes," Steven said, "but I do have one request. Find me a gun and a horse. If I have to walk into Delphberg, I'll never make it."

Maggie knelt by the narrow single bed and let the beads of Sophie's rosary slip through her fingers. It had been a long time since she'd prayed, really prayed, but tonight all the faith she'd ever had was focused in her prayers for Steven. The words were simple. "Keep him safe, and bring him back to me."

Her emotions were more complex. During the day, which seemed interminable, she worked at the convent under Sister Angela's instructions. Mother Superior wanted to keep her segregated from the other nuns, and so the tasks Maggie was assigned were by their nature solitary and lonely.

She'd spent hours on her knees scrubbing the stone hallway of the convent. Later she'd worked in the garden, weeding and picking the first crops of lettuce, squash and eggplant. She hadn't minded the hard work, the hard earth—or stone—beneath her knees. They kept her body occupied, but her mind had been free to wander and think about the past months.

Why had she and Uncle Viktor thought it would be so simple, this ingenious little plan? Slip Steven into the country, let him find his heritage, tell the rebellious citizens that he was their rightful ruler, and they would overthrow Adamo. Then Steven would rule.

It was a fairy tale, she thought bleakly, a pitiful, foolish plot thought up by an old man living in the past and a young woman with unrealistic dreams. Instead of the traditional happy ending, she and Viktor might have led Steven to his death.

And Steven was right. She had lived too long in a world of pretense. Now she was facing the consequences.

"Sister Clare! Sister Clare, you must slow down."

Maggie, who'd been lost in her thoughts, finally paid attention to the stout little nun running along beside her. "I'm sorry, Sister Angela. I guess I'm just anxious to get to town."

"You'll only attract attention to us if you rush ahead like that," Sister Angela scolded. "Nuns are meant to be decorous and deliberate. We walk slowly and thoughtfully."

"Yes, Sister," Maggie said meekly, lowering her head slightly and trying to do as her companion asked.

A small smile curved Maggie's lips, however, as she thought that Sister Angela's complaints might have more to do with short little legs and an extra twenty pounds of weight than with the rules of the convent.

At first the starched white wimple surrounding Maggie's face had been an irritant, but now she found it an asset. If she dropped her head slightly, taking on the sisterly pose, her face was practically hidden. Sophie had done well when she suggested the convent as a haven. Maggie's disguise as Sister Clare was perfect. She only prayed that Steven was faring as well.

Sister Angela had no patience and even less knowledge of Maggie's thoughts. She only knew that they could be making a mistake. "I'm not sure you should even be coming to town," she fussed. "It could be dangerous."

"It won't be dangerous at all," Maggie reassured. "Besides, you couldn't come to town alone, could you? There are convent rules to be observed."

"That is true," Sister Angela responded. "But remember, if anyone asks you a question, remain quiet and let me answer. Even though your German is excellent, you know nothing of the convent and our practices. I will answer," she decreed, "and you will look . . . penitent," she decided, after groping for the proper word.

Maggie smiled and replied demurely, "Yes, Sister." The nun was a delight, Maggie thought, bossy and scolding on the outside, kind and loving and thoroughly understanding beneath her starched exterior. She'd shielded Maggie from the curious eyes of the other nuns, and somehow she'd gotten permission for them to venture into Magris. Now Maggie wondered if she could persuade the little nun to take part in another, more dangerous mission.

The town square came into view, and they headed for the small frame post office standing at the corner across from the town hall. Maggie looked longingly at the brick building of the hall as she followed Sister Angela into the post office. The line was long and the wait seemed more interminable because the postmaster seemed to spend most of his time gossiping with each of his customers. At last Sister Angela presented her letter.

"Ah, the weekly report to the mother house in Delphberg," he said, placing the stamps carefully onto the letter. "Where is Sister Paula today? She usually comes with you."

"She wasn't able to make the trip today," Sister Angela said, reaching for her change. But the postmaster wasn't about to let her get away so easily. He asked the status of the convent's crop of blueberries, which were sold to the public each July. He chatted about the recent lack of rain and its effect on the local farms; he mentioned that many of the soldiers had been withdrawn from Magris.

Maggie's ears perked up, and she hoped that Sister Angela would question him further. Instead, the nun thanked the postmaster and turned to walk away, but her lack of interest didn't stop him.

"It seems they are massing for an attack. I have heard they move down toward Lake Kranich. Of course, that is only a rumor."

"Whatever the reason," Sister Angela said in finality, "it is good to have them out of town."

"I agree with you, Sister Angela. Furthermore," he continued, "I understand that they never did apprehend the escaped prisoners they were looking for."

Maggie and Sister Angela paused.

"I also heard they were dangerous," he said. "A man and a woman." He looked speculatively at Maggie, who quickly lowered her head. "But one can never know. These are rumors only."

"And we will not listen to them," Sister Angela proclaimed. "Come, Sister Clare, it is late." And with a beneficent smile for the other customers waiting in line, she swept out of the post office, trailed by Maggie.

"I would have liked to hear more about the troops moving down the mountain," Maggie said. "I wonder if Steven . . ."

"Keep your wonderings to yourself," Sister Angela advised.

"Do you think the postmaster is a spy for Adamo?"

Sister Angela considered that for a moment before answering. "No, I believe he is on our side—against Adamo—but this is much too dangerous to talk about."

As they crossed the street, Maggie took the nun's arm. "I have an important favor to ask of you, and before you refuse, please hear me out."

"No, I must not," the nun replied. "I can tell by the tone of your voice this is something which is best left unsaid."

"You're wrong, Sister Angela," Maggie admonished. "It's not of any consequence to you and the convent."

"Then why do you seem so nervous?"

"Because of the importance of my request, not the danger. It's not dangerous at all. I only want a little time—five minutes, no more—to go into the town hall and look up some records."

They stopped in the shade of a newly blossoming tree. Its scent enveloped them, causing Maggie to hesitate for a moment as she tried to balance her task against the everyday life of Sister Angela and the other nuns. This was something that transcended their godly work. To explain that would not be possible. She decided instead to trivialize.

"Why would you want to look up records in Magris?"

"My family..." Maggie said, hating herself for lying to her newfound friend.

Sister Angela studied Maggie's face carefully, and before she spoke, Maggie realized that she hadn't fooled the little woman. "My dear friend, I know you are not telling the truth. Yet I can tell from your eyes that you are desperate to have this information." She spoke slowly and carefully in her well-phrased German with its local Mendorran accent. "You know that Mother Superior would object to our doing anything she was not aware of."

"Then I can tell her when we get back to the convent," Maggie said.

"But first you must tell me. The truth. Do you trust me?" she asked.

"Of course I trust you. I just don't want to endanger you."

Sister Angela laughed then. "Do you not think that I am already in danger for what I have done to help our rebels?"

Maggie nodded in understanding. "I will tell you," she said quietly. "I want to look up records, but not for myself. For Steven. There is reason to believe that he might be connected to the royal family, that his mother Elyse Contrand might have been married to Prince Gregor."

Sister Angela's gray eyes sparkled with interest. "Our beloved prince?"

"Yes," Maggie said staunchly.

"Then we must go at once and see what we can find." She was fidgeting with excitement. "But let me do the talking. I will say that I need information for a friend. That is not entirely untruthful," she defended.

"No," Maggie agreed. "Thank you, Sister," she added, taking Angela's arm as they started up the steps to the town hall.

At the door, her heart began to pound wildly, not in fear of the soldier standing there, but at the thought that in a few minutes she might find out the truth about Steven.

The soldier gave them a cursory glance and went back to his flirtation with a young girl who was selling pastries from a basket. Maggie followed Sister Angela down a long hall to a room filled with row after row of huge, dusty ledgers.

"What year?" Angela whispered. "What year was he born?"

"Eighteen forty-one," Maggie whispered back as an ancient man shuffled out from among the shelves that housed the equally ancient tomes.

"Sister Angela, what a most pleasant surprise," he wheezed. "How may I help you today?"

"You can look something up for me, Herr Capen. Something quite simple. Just a birth date."

Chapter Sixteen

At the head of his troops, Anton Legel rode into the city of Delphberg with little resistance. The small band of soldiers guarding the garrison outside the city had been easily dispatched, and the few soldiers and policemen patrolling the streets quickly turned themselves in to the rebels.

The victory, which brought joy to his ragtag army of rebels, brought sadness to Anton.

"So," he said to Steven as they dismounted outside the People's Palace. "You were right. My brother took word of the attack at Lake Kranich to Adamo. Obviously, the general has moved all of his troops there. The city is ours."

"Yes," Steven agreed. "Delphberg belongs to the people now. That news will spread quickly throughout Mendorra. But I know that the victory has been won at a great price to your family."

Anton nodded. "They will carry the sadness with them forever. It will temper everything that we have won, and my father may never understand."

"And you?" Steven asked.

"I will always feel some guilt that my brother could not achieve the leadership he desperately wanted." He turned and looked up at the palace. "It seemed to come to me so easily," he said.

"You were born to this task, Anton," Steven told him. "It's destiny. There is nothing you could have done for your brother."

"I know that. I also know Wili was a coward at the end. And yet I feel no anger toward him, only pity."

"What will happen to him, I wonder? Will you bring him to trial?"

Anton shook his head. "I have no need. When Adamo finds out that his information is wrong and that we hold Delphberg, he will turn on Wili like a snake on a mouse. My brother may be dead already."

"I'm sorry, my friend," Steven said.

Anton straightened his sagging shoulders. "We don't have time for sorrow now. We need to marshal our troops, recruit others to join us, and march toward Lake Kranich. Adamo will be on the way to retake the city, and we cannot let that happen."

"I hope you don't plan to meet them in the open?" Steven questioned.

"No. There's a pass through a narrow valley just west of here, and that will be where we attack. My men only have one fight in them, I believe, and I want that fight to count."

"Then let's ride," Steven said, swinging onto his horse and giving a resounding yell.

At Anton's astonished look, he laughed. "Something I picked up from the other side during our Civil War. Maybe I can teach it to your men. That ought to get Adamo's soldiers thinking."

"I should scold you and Sister Angela both," Mother Mary Therese announced, "for your unauthorized visit to the town hall."

Sister Angela tucked her head, but Maggie was less repentant. "A visit which accomplished nothing," she said.

"That isn't the question."

"It's a fact, nevertheless," Maggie continued, unintimidated by the stern face of the mother superior across the office desk.

"Perhaps you will tell me the purpose of your unsuccessful trip," Mary Therese challenged.

"Well, we—"

"Go on, Margarette."

"We—that is, I—wanted to locate the birth records for 1841, the year that Steven was born, it is said, to Elyse Contrand and Prince Gregor Von Alder."

Mary Therese's eyes narrowed almost imperceptibly. Then she glanced at Sister Angela. "Were you aware of the reason for your visit to the town hall, Sister?"

The little nun ducked her head again, nodding vigorously.

"Then I must chastise you both again for being so foolhardy."

"Mother Superior—" Maggie began.

"Silence." The word was spoken with such authority that nothing would have induced Maggie to add another syllable.

"I will ask the questions now, and you will answer them, Margarette," she ordered.

"Yes, Mother Superior."

"There is a rumor that Steven Englehardt is Prince Gregor's son?"

"It is more than rumor. My uncle Viktor Beitel—and many others—know this to be fact. There is, unfortunately, no writtten proof. That is what I was searching for."

"And someone had removed the record book for the year of his birth?"

Maggie nodded.

"That someone being General Adamo?"

"I am sure the general didn't personally take away the book."

"Of course not," Mary Therese said. "He would have sent one of his underlings. But if, as you say, Steven is the prince's son, Adamo would be sure to have had all evidence destroyed." Mary Therese no longer seemed to care about Maggie's breach of convent rules. Clearly she wanted to hear everything Maggie had to report.

"Herr Capen said the book had been missing for years. He is trying to reconstruct some records with help from the townspeople, asking doctors and midwives about births, checking church registers, but he is having a difficult time."

Mary Therese stared off into space for a long moment. "Yes, indeed. Church records. Perhaps we have something here. We would have no birth records, but baptisms—"

"And marriages!" Maggie said with a burst of enthusiasm.

"Yes, yes!" Sister Angela inserted but not before she was silenced by a look from the mother superior.

"Our convent church is an old one. Who knows what registers we might find."

"Oh, Mother Superior—" Maggie began.

"Do not be too hopeful. Our priest, Father Michael, has been here only a few years, but he still might have something for us to see."

"That would be wonderful," Maggie said.

"Yes, Saint Stefan's Church is—"

"Saint Stefan?" Maggie asked. "That's the name of the church?"

"Well, of course," Mary Therese replied. "I thought you knew."

"No," Maggie said. "I never even asked." Saint Stefan. It had to be. She had an overpowering conviction that the truth about Steven's heritage was somehow contained in the church that bore his name. "I'll go right now," she said, getting to her feet. "I'll ask Father Michael—"

"You will not go anywhere," Mary Therese ordered in a voice that again brooked no argument. "You will wait right here until I talk with Father Michael."

"Yes, Mother Superior," Maggie mouthed.

"I can ask just as well as you to see the entries for 1841. You will only call attention to yourself and raise more questions."

"Yes, Mother Superior," Maggie repeated.

"And please, stop saying, 'Yes, Mother Superior' to me."

"Yes, Mother—I mean—"

Sister Angela let out a giggle that brought a stern, silencing look to Mary Therese's face.

"Between the two of you—" she said, not bothering to finish her sentence. "I need only warn you, Margarette, that the fewer people who know about you, the better. Father Michael has enough problems without a fugitive on his hands who is in search of the birth records of a supposed member of the royal family. Wait for me here," she told Maggie. "And Sister Angela—"

"Yes, Mother Superior?" the little nun replied, this time suppressing her giggle.

"I believe you have your prayers to attend to."

With that, Mary Therese rose from her desk, advising Maggie, "Just stay calm, my dear, and if you need something to occupy yourself, you, too, might say your rosary beads. I'm sure all of us could do with a little extra prayer."

She swept from the room, followed closely by Sister Angela.

Feeling reprimanded but at the same time elated, Maggie pulled the beads from the deep pocket of her habit. She tried to pray that the Mother Superior's search would be successful.

But as she fingered the rosary, Maggie's mind drifted away from her prayers to Steven—Steven standing in the dewy morning at the chalet, the rising sun illuminating his golden body as he washed at the pump. It was a moment she'd tried not to think about, a moment after their long night of love, when once more they were about to begin a trek that would end they knew not where.

It had ended at the convent, and now Maggie was alone, with only the memories of that never-to-be-forgotten night. If she closed her eyes very tightly she could bring his image back, another image of Steven sitting opposite her in the chalet kitchen, drinking coffee, talking softly. Or Steven getting up from bed in the night to cover them with a blanket and then lying down again beside her, keeping her warm with his body.

It was that last image that brought tears to Maggie's eyes. She blinked them away and quickly returned to saying her beads.

The moment that Mary Therese stepped into the room, Maggie felt her heart sink. "You found nothing," she said. It was more an observation than a question.

"Oh, we found something," Mary Therese replied, a troubled look on her face. "We found that one of the pages had been torn from our church registry. The missing page, of course, was for several months of 1841."

"We were so close," Maggie said with despair.

"Yes, very close. First the records gone from the town hall, and now the missing page..." Her voice drifted off as she settled herself back at the desk.

"Do you think Adamo removed it?" Maggie asked.

"No," Mary Therese answered immediately. "No, I don't. Here at the convent, if he or his men had come and rifled through the church, we would have heard about it. Such an action would not have gone unchallenged. I believe someone else took the page and hid it for safekeeping."

"The old priest?"

"Yes, Father Jacob was devoted to the royal family. He would have risked his life for them."

"If only we could talk to him," Maggie said.

"My dear child, he has been dead for many years, and whatever knowledge he had of the missing page went with him. I am afraid you've come to a dead end in your search."

Maggie sat in silence, but her mind was calculating wildly and rapidly. Her search was by no means over, she thought. It was only beginning.

Maggie waited until the convent was quiet. Up and down the hall, candles flickered and went out, and everywhere there was a deep heavy silence. In the darkness of her little cell, Maggie slipped on her habit, fumbled for her candle and stepped out of the room, barefoot on the cool tiled floor.

She crept down the hall toward the main foyer. Passing one of the rooms, she heard a sudden sound of someone waking. She pressed herself against the wall, frozen motionless, wondering what sort of story she'd have to concoct to explain her presence here in the middle of the night.

She could feign sleepwalking, or even admit to the urge for a midnight raid on the kitchen. Maggie stifled a giggle at the thought. Then the waking nun seemed to settle down and once again all was quiet.

She passed the mother superior's office, crossed the wide stone entrance hall and slipped the great lock at the convent's front door. To her, it sounded like the clanging of Big Ben. Again she froze, waiting for Mary Therese to swoop down on her, but the convent was silent and sleeping.

Outside in the cool night air, Maggie slipped across the courtyard toward the sanctuary of Saint Stefan's. The Romanesque arches loomed eerily above her as she approached the heavily carved wooden doors. She closed her hand around the bronze doorknob and turned. Or tried to. Nothing.

Maggie's heart sank. She hadn't thought that it would be locked. Frustrated, she tried again, this time using her shoulder to push against the door as she jiggled the knob. To her relief, the door swung open, and she stepped inside the church, engulfed by darkness and the powerful aroma of incense.

She reached into her pocket for matches and her candle, which gave off a wavering light. Raising the candle, she looked around the little church. This wasn't going to be easy, not at all. The church was filled with statuary and icons; there were literally hundreds of places where something could be hidden. But she wasn't going to give up now. It was more than a premonition guiding her. It was a deep faith that somewhere in Saint Stefan's Church lay the answer to Steven's parentage.

More than that, Maggie felt sure Father Jacob had hidden the missing page and that he'd hidden it in a place where it could be found—but only by the right person, someone protective of Steven and his birthright. Maggie was such a person; she merely had to solve the puzzle and come up with the answer: Father Jacob's hiding place.

It wasn't going to come to her magically, out of the blue. She'd need to search and hope that something would trigger the answer. Slowly, methodically, she began.

She started in the most obvious place, the huge statue of Saint Stefan that stood in the church's sanctuary. She examined every inch of the marble statue and its pedestal. Unless it was concealed beneath the statue, which she couldn't move, the page wasn't there.

Maggie spent two more hours, on her hands and knees when necessary, covering every square foot of the church. Still, there was nothing, no paper, no sign of anything to give her a clue to Father Jacob's hiding place.

In one darkened corner of the nave, she paused at the baptismal font, studied the shell-shaped basin, and above it the carving of a baby. The object intrigued her; it seemed to be carved in a different style from the rest of the statuary. The babe's face was sweet and cherubic. She held up her candle and tried to decipher the words carved beneath the child.

They were illegible. She held the candle closer, but still she was unable to make out the letters. Finally she reached out with one hand and traced the first letter. *"S,"* Maggie said aloud, moving on to the next letter and then the next. *"T, E..."* Her heart began to race. *"F..."* She knew the rest. *A* and *N*. It was a statue of Saint Stefan as a child! Maggie's heart raced, and she was sure she'd found the answer.

"Father Jacob," she whispered. "I believe I know where you have hidden the record of Steven's birth. Guide me to it, please. Guide me to it."

Maggie felt behind the font, beneath it. She looked for a hidden panel that might open. She found nothing. Frantically she moved her hands down the marble pedestal. There were no niches, no openings.

Using her shoulder, she tried to move the statue. It was heavy but seemed to budge a fraction of an inch. Summoning up all her strength, she tried again. Her bare feet dug into the cold stone floor of the church; her hands and arms ached with the effort. Her back stiffened, and then she gave one final violent push, and the pedestal slid across the floor.

With a great sigh of relief, Maggie stood up, holding her candle low to the floor, studying the random stones. Then she fingered each one, searching for the stone she knew would be loose. It had to be there!

Again and again she pushed at the stones until finally one of them seemed to move beneath her hand. She looked around for something to use as a lever, finally pulling off a loose board from the altar rail, saying a silent prayer she hoped would absolve her of any sin connected with the desecration.

With the board, Maggie moved the stone away. Beneath it was a folded sheet of paper, yellowed with age.

With trembling fingers, she picked it up, unfolding it carefully for fear the paper would disintegrate in her hands.

Reaching for her candle, which she'd placed beside the statue, Maggie held it close to the paper. There, written in a spidery hand, the ink slightly faded, was a list of names and dates. Baptisms. Marriages. Funerals. The years was 1841. Rapidly her eyes scanned the list until she came to the entry she'd been searching for all these months.

"Married January 3, 1841, Elyse Elinor Contrand and Gregor Von Alder..."

The ceremony had been held in this church, secretly, Maggie imagined.

Her eyes skimmed down the page. Then she turned it over. Nine months later another line:

"Baptized this day, September 7, 1841, Stefan Karl Von Alder..."

With a little sob, Maggie folded the paper and put it in her pocket. Using the board again, she replaced the stone, moved the pedestal to cover it and then left the church as silently as she'd entered.

The rebel forces, now officially named the People's Army of Freedom, fell upon Adamo's soldiers like wolves on a herd of sheep. Out of the steep walls of the cliffs they came, yelling, shouting, brandishing their swords, firing with rifles and pistols.

The fight was short and brutal. Many of Adamo's forces surrendered, offering their services to the rebels. Those who did not and still lived were summarily taken prisoner.

At the end of the day, a scout roared into Anton's victorious camp and slipped from his sweating horse.

"Adamo and a few of his guards are trapped in the gorge two miles east of here. They will not last long."

Without a word, Steven and Anton mounted their horses and, followed by a handful of men, rode toward the east. At a narrow gash in the pass, the rebels paused. Down below them in the valley, Adamo and his men tried to make their way to safety, but their journey was destined to end before it began.

Anton, Steven and the men watched as a contingent of their rebel army raced after the soldiers, cornering them in a cul-de-sac, quickly victorious.

Except for one rider, who, on his fleet horse, backtracked and passed the rebels, heading out toward freedom. Anton turned in his saddle and looked at Steven. "He is yours, my friend."

With that, Steven dug his spurs into his mount and charged down the incline.

General Adamo raced through the gorge, looking back to be sure no one followed, only to see a rider bearing down on him. Whether or not he knew who his adversary was, Steven couldn't tell, but he'd slipped his gun from its holster and begun firing, wildly and at random, the shots coming nowhere near Steven, who pressed on.

Then, his gun emptied and tossed aside, Adamo bent low in the saddle and urged his horse on. Steven kept coming, riding straight toward his adversary. He kicked the stirrups aside, held on to the saddle with his knees, and as he passed Adamo gave a mighty leap, bringing the general to the ground with him. Their bodies lurched and rolled over, and then both men were on their feet, facing each other, hands up, prepared to strike. "No guns, Adamo," Steven cried, "no swords. Just fists." He was filled with a wild anger, a lust to kill,

to destroy. His head swam with it. He had a split second to look into the face of the man who, it was said,
had killed his father and caused his mother to flee. He
had a sudden urge to know the truth, but first, the man
facing him had to be brought to his knees.

Fists flying, they lunged into each other, but the big,
heavy man was no match for his younger, stronger op-
ponent. Steven hit him again and again, and when
Adamo finally fell to the ground, his face torn and
bleeding, Steven grabbed him by the shoulders and
pulled him up.

Holding him at arm's length, he finally asked the
question that had plagued him subconsciously for so
long. "Tell me, Adamo, tell me that you killed him."

Adamo just stared back, dumbstruck.

"My father, if he was my father. Did you kill him?"

"I don't understand—"

Then Steven hit him again, connecting perfectly.

"No more, no more!" the general cried.

"Then tell me. Was he my father?"

"I don't know. Yes—he was. There is proof, but it
has been destroyed. Now only rumors remain—"

"And you killed him to quell the rumors?" Steven
was shaking so hard he could barely hold on to the battered man.

"No, it was not me. It was the others."

"What others?" Steven drew back his fist to hit
again, anger consuming him. This time, when he connected, the general crumpled in a heap. "Get up, do you
hear me, get up and tell me who—"

A strong arm reached out and pulled Steven away.
"He is unconscious, my friend," Anton said. "He will
tell you nothing for a while."

"But I must know," Steven insisted.

"You will know—we will all know everything, but not yet, not now."

"Then I'll beat it out of him."

"And kill him?" Anton asked, pulling Steven aside and beckoning to one of his men. "Take the general away."

"No," Steven said, rage boiling up in him, not just for what happened more than thirty years ago, but for the more recent injustices—the dictator who sent assassins to look for him in Wyoming, who had him imprisoned and who held a freedom-loving country in his thrall. "We'll make him talk!"

Once more, Anton restrained Steven. "A few more blows, and he is a dead man. We need him alive so he can be tried in a court of law. Then we will learn everything. Then justice will be done. Do you understand, my friend?"

The blood rush of hate cleared from Steven's head and he nodded. It was over. Really over. Adamo and his remaining contingent were prisoners to be rounded up and taken back to Delphberg. The rebel forces were victorious.

But for Steven there was so much more, the admission that he was Gregor's son, and what that could mean to him—to all of them.

"You must come with us," Anton advised. "Come to Delphberg, and there we will march Adamo through the streets to prison. You need to be with us then—and later, for his trial. It will mean much to us, Steven."

Steven knew what the proud soldier meant, but now that it was over, he couldn't stand the idea of waiting around. Somehow, suddenly, it didn't matter whether it was Adamo or one of his henchmen who murdered Gregor. His father—and now he knew what he'd al-

ways known, deep down, that Gregor was his father—
was dead. Had been dead for more than thirty years.
Whoever murdered him would pay. Nothing else mattered.

"Steven—"

Nothing else mattered except Maggie.

"Are you coming with us?"

Steven shook his head. "No, I have somewhere else I
need to be. Can I take my horse?"

"Small payment for what you've done." Anton
grasped Steven's shoulder warmly. "Come back soon,
Steven. We have much to discuss about what has happened—and what is to come. The future of Mendorra."

Steven nodded and climbed wearily onto his horse.
There was so much on his mind, and yet it all boiled
down to a single thought. Maggie.

Chapter Seventeen

Maggie struggled along the path toward the chalet. The trip down with Steven had been easier than the climb back, and there was an apprehension now that she hadn't experienced before, even though they'd been uncertain of the future. At least they'd been together.

Now Maggie was alone. He would come back. She knew he would. But their future was as uncertain as ever.

Mother Superior had ordered her to stay in the convent until his return, but for once Maggie had stood up to her. She was going to wait for Steven at the chalet. Whatever happened, they deserved this time together.

The fighting was over. Throughout Mendorra, the bells sounded in jubilation that Adamo had been overthrown, and the People's Army of Freedom was victorious. She'd heard that Anton had been proclaimed interim president until the Parliament could meet and take action on a new government.

Maggie shifted her backpack, which was filled with food from the convent, and thought about the yellowed paper tucked inside her pocket. The information on that paper could change the history of Mendorra. And she was the only one who knew it existed.

That same information could also change the course of her life when she showed it to Steven—if she showed it to him. She would make that decision later, Maggie decided as she trudged on.

The chalet lay waiting for her in the morning sunlight just as she and Steven had left it. Slowly she walked through the downstairs rooms they had shared, touching the kitchen table where they had sat together and sipped their morning coffee, smoothing the bed where they had made such passionate love. They had spent only a short time here in the chalet, but her return seemed like coming home.

She unpacked the food that the nuns had sent with her and set about cleaning the rooms until they shone. She scrubbed the old wooden table and hung the sheets and blankets out in the mountain breeze to air. She picked wildflowers that grew near the chalet, blue gentian, edelweiss and delicate columbine, filling cracked pitchers and glasses with their ephemeral beauty, decorating the cottage for Steven's return.

Maggie pumped water into a wooden bucket, heated it and bathed, wishing she had something beautiful to wear, but there were only the clothes she had borrowed from the chalet. She tied the shawl around her waist, hoping that would make the costume a little more festive, rubbed gooseberry juice on her lips to pinken them, and sat in the sun to dry her hair.

She ran her fingers through the squeaky-clean strands and rubbed vigorously with a towel so that her hair was dry and shiny just as the shadows began to lengthen and the day drew to a close.

Still she waited, ensconced on a big rock in the overgrown front yard of the chalet, growing more uncomfortable as the afternoon sun hovered on the edge of the mountain, but determined not to go inside. He would pass by here, and surely he would know she'd be waiting, but Maggie didn't want to take any chances. She would be here, in full view of the path, when he approached.

She had expected him to be on foot, and when she heard the hoofbeats, slow and steady, coming up the path, she felt fear at first and then, shielding her eyes against the setting sun, elation.

She saw him in the distance, a tall figure on horseback making his way toward her. She started to run to him, her heart catching in her throat, her blood pounding wildly in her veins. She wanted to call out to him, but there was no breath left to speak his name. Winded and elated, she opened her arms as Steven jumped from his horse and caught her up in his strong embrace.

"Don't cry, Maggie," he said, feeling her tears on his face. "It's all over, now. I'm back, and we're together."

She threaded her hands through his hair, pulling his face close, touching him, feeling him, aching for him. He kissed her over and over, murmuring her name against her mouth.

"God, Maggie, I wondered if I'd ever hold you again."

"Oh, Steven, I've missed you so much." She reached out and caressed his cheek and ran her fingers along his lips. He was here. He was real.

"I'm back for good," he said, "and we're going home, Maggie, home to Wyoming."

Steven put an arm around her waist and steered her toward the chalet. The horse followed docilely behind and then paused to crop grass in a shady spot.

"Anton—Adamo—" Maggie said. "Tell me what happened."

"Anton is fine, very busy trying to get Parliament back in session." He paused and looked down at her. "You know that we were victorious?"

"Yes, Steven, I know."

"I've never seen men fight like these Mendorrans. It was an honor to stand beside them. You should have seen—" He broke off. "Have you heard about Adamo?"

She shook her head.

"He's in jail, where he belongs. There'll be a trial, a fair one, where he'll be given a chance to speak for himself."

"Unlike you," Maggie said.

"Yes," Steven replied.

Maggie heard his news with mixed feelings, relief that the injustices perpetrated during Adamo's reign of terror were finally over, but wariness that Steven seemed to have become such a complete Mendorran. And yet it couldn't have been otherwise. He was an honorable man, and he had fought to preserve the country's honor. Now she wondered how much his heritage had come to mean to him.

"I'm glad," Maggie said, and she was, even though she knew that Steven had been changed by the events of the past few days.

"We're all glad," Steven said, "glad that it's over."

Was it really over? Maggie refrained from voicing that question, asking instead about Anton's half brother. "Was Wili a traitor?"

Steven nodded. "Adamo had him killed."

"I'm sorry," Maggie said.

"So am I. So are we all." Steven was quiet for a moment as they approached the house, still holding each other. "But I don't want to talk about that. I want to talk about you—how beautiful you are, how warm and sweet and exciting."

He took her in his arms, running his hands up and down her arms, across her breasts, along her neck. "All I want to do is touch you and kiss you."

He leaned over and drank heavily from her lips, kissing her with a well-remembered passion, his tongue teasing hers.

Maggie reveled in his kiss, in his touch. The feel of his arms around her, the solid muscles of his chest against her demonstrated the pure strength of his embrace and made her weak and dizzy with longing.

For a moment Maggie gave herself over to her happiness, and then she stopped, feeling completely selfish. He'd been on horseback for hours; he would certainly be tired and hungry.

"I have food and wine, and the bed is all ready for you to rest. I washed the sheets and—"

He never let her finish. "Do you think I want to sleep or eat now, when you're in my arms? No, Maggie, I want no food, no wine, no rest." He picked her up and walked through the open door of the chalet. "All I want is you."

Maggie laughed aloud, and in the laughter she heard more than amusement or delight, more even than joy. She heard desire. "And I want you, Steven, more than ever."

He didn't answer as he strode through the little kitchen, kicked open the bedroom door and carried her to the bed where so recently—and yet so long ago—they'd last made love.

Next to the bed, Maggie slid from his arms and stood beside him, her hands fumbling at the buttons of her blouse. But Steven's hands were more sure, swifter, as he undressed her, his fingers sending little sparks of fire across her skin.

When he was finished, and she stood naked before him, Steven spoke at last. "Now undress me," he whispered as he stood, filled with desire, before her.

He helped her when Maggie's fingers became too clumsy, guided her hands as she pulled off his shirt and trousers and tugged at his dusty boots.

Then they were lying on the fresh-scented sheets, surrounded by the flowers she'd picked, touching each other as hungrily as if they'd been apart for years rather than days.

"I've waited so long to feel you like this again, Maggie," he whispered. "To touch you." His fingers found her breast, her nipple taut with excitement. He was gentle, teasing, rolling the pink rosebud lightly between his fingers.

Deep inside Maggie felt a warm, delicious wave of desire begin to flow through her muscles and veins as every fiber of her body yielded to Steven.

He kissed her again and again, his lips moving lightly across her face, kissing her eyelids, her nose, her cheeks, her chin. All the while, Maggie touched him and caressed him, running her fingers up and down the smooth hard muscles of his back, adoring in the feel of his skin next to hers. She wanted to melt into him, become part of him.

Steven's mouth was doing extraordinary things to her, sliding down along her neck to her breasts. He captured a petal-pink nipple in his mouth and sucked greedily, sending intense ripples of pleasure from her head to her toes. She arched against him, begging for more with her body, as her fingers dug into his shoulders.

Greedily Maggie pulled Steven's lips back to hers and kissed him again and again. She traced the outline of his lips with her tongue, caught his bottom lip between her teeth and nibbled, tasted, drank the sweetness of his mouth, exploring in and out while Steven groaned in agonized pleasure at the touch of her fiery tongue. And while her mouth held him prisoner, she used her hand to touch his manhood, soft as velvet, hard as iron.

She looked up at him and smiled. "I love you, Steven."

"I love you, Maggie, more than you can imagine." Not yet satisfied with his exploration of her, hungry for more, Steven moved his lips across her rib cage, nibbled on the line of her hipbone, and then found the aching sweetness between her thighs. As she held him, he tasted her, and together they gave each other the intense pleasure only two lovers caught up in such passion could give. Maggie's breath came in long tremors of pleasure. She felt loved and desired; she felt as though her whole world were opening and expanding into the universe.

"What do you want me to do?" Steven asked, still doing everything she thought she could want.

Yet there was more for them, and Maggie answered boldly, "Show me, Steven," she cried, "show me your love."

His face swam above her, the face she loved more than all others. She wanted to be joined to him, be part of him, if not forever, at least for now.

She reached out and touched him as he prepared to enter her, and then she moved her other hand to her own soft center of desire and opened it for him, for them. Eager to take him inside her body, Maggie guided him until it was no longer necessary, until they were joined.

He moved slowly, waiting for his rhythm to match hers, bringing their bodies into harmony. There were no words, only little cries of pleasure as they were bound by more than the physical need that impelled them, more even than their desire to please each other.

It was as if each had discovered a missing half, a part that had been lost and now was found. And when at last their release came, bathing their bodies in mutual pleasure, they laughed aloud in joy and completeness.

Neither wanted it to end and so they held each other, taking comfort from the shared warmth of their love, holding on until the sky darkened and the night birds began their lonely calls.

"Are you cold?" Steven asked, covering Maggie with a sheet that had twisted around their legs.

"How could I be cold with you to warm me?" she asked in reply.

Then, after a moment, he tried another question. "Are you hungry?"

"No," she said.

Another pause, and he admitted, "I am."

Maggie laughed. "I knew that."

"But I'm too lazy to get out of bed."

"Me, too," she said, leaning her head against his chest. She twined her fingers in his and then brought his hands to her lips. "I'll get up and make some dinner for us," she said finally as she stirred.

He stopped her. "No," he said. "I'd rather be hungry than have you leave me."

Maggie felt a little thrill of satisfaction. He loved her as she loved him. Everything was perfect. And yet it wasn't. They needed to talk, had to talk.

"Steven—"

"Yes?" He kissed her eyelids softly.

Not yet, Maggie thought. Not yet. She wanted to share this time of bliss a little longer, to continue the wonderful sunlit afternoon that had led to the perfect dusky twilight for another few moments, moments that she'd be able to remember and cherish forever.

"I'm hungry, too."

He laughed.

"But I don't want to get up, either. I want to stay here—forever."

Steven raised an eyebrow at the sudden intenseness in her voice that just before had been so lighthearted. "I don't think we can play house much longer," he observed. "The owners will probably return now that Adamo is defeated."

"Yes," she said, "and there'll be no more playing." She was aware that it was approaching, the time when she'd have to decide what to tell him. She couldn't avoid it.

"No more make-believe, Maggie?" Steven chided lovingly, his face still curious at the sudden change in her emotions.

"No more," she said. But her head was aching with what she knew, and what she was going to do about it. If she told him of the records she'd found, she could lose him forever. He was a man who believed in all that was right and just. She'd known that all along. He wasn't the kind of person to walk away from his duties. Or from a country that needed him, a country he loved.

Maggie sighed deeply.

"Maggie?" Steven leaned up on his elbow and looked down at her. "What is it?"

"Nothing," she said, thinking how easy it would be to leave it at that. She could pretend she'd never found the hiding place in the church.

Yet she couldn't lie to him. Once, maybe she could have, but it wasn't possible now. She loved him too much to ever lie again.

Maggie wrapped herself in the sheet and sat on the edge of the bed, her face turned away.

"There is something," he said.

"Yes."

"Tell me." He reached out and touched her shoulder, and that made it so much more difficult.

"Let's just say I have to face reality like everyone else." Maggie struggled to control the quivering edge in her voice.

"And what's that reality?" He ran his finger down her back.

"I . . . I'm not sure." It was time to tell him, to show him the paper, but she sat there immobile, paralyzed by the thought.

"How about this for reality?" Steven asked, still lying on the bed behind her. "How about coming back to the Double E and marrying me?"

Maggie felt her whole body change, tensing at the suddenness of his words while glorying in them.

"I know it's not the kind of life you're used to, living on a ranch in Wyoming, but I love you, Maggie, and I don't see how we can live apart. Not after all this. I need you—"

But Maggie hadn't heard anything past his first words. She turned around to look at him. "Marry you?" she asked.

"Of course. Is that so preposterous?" His voice seemed unsteady, unsure. "Maggie?" he prodded.

She shook her head. Why was he making it so difficult? Every word he said and every moment she waited made her decision that much more painful. He'd asked her to marry him, and that's what she wanted most in the world, but he'd asked it just when she was prepared to tell the truth. The irony of that twisted like a knife in her heart. She felt guilty because she didn't want to tell him, angry because she knew she must.

Steven took her hand, the puzzled look invading his eyes. "You love me. I know you do. What is it, Maggie? You don't want to live in Wyoming?"

"No, that's not it."

"Then what?" He raised his voice, angry and confused, and Maggie pulled away, shaking her head. Her hair flew wildly around her face. "Then what?" he repeated.

"I love you more than life, Steven, but I can't marry you. At least—you can't marry me."

"Why the hell not?" He sat up in bed.

"Because," she said, the words torn from her. "Because royalty can't marry commoners. Because an actress can't be queen of Mendorra—"

Steven threw back his head and laughed. "Now I know you're joking. You had me worried for a minute."

"I'm perfectly serious, Steven." The tears had begun to form on her eyelashes.

He reached over and shook her gently. "Listen, Maggie, the battles are over, Adamo is in jail, and Mendorra is free. That's what matters. Nothing else."

When she spoke, her voice sounded very small. "Even if... even if there's proof of your parentage, proof that Gregor was your father?"

"What proof? Did you find something in Magris?" Steven's eyes darkened.

Still wrapped in the sheet, Maggie got up and crossed the room, lifted a flower vase on the table and removed the yellowed paper. "I found this at Saint Stefan's Church." She thrust it toward him. "Your parents were married there. Your *parents*," she repeated emphatically, "Prince Gregor Von Alder and Elyse Contrand. You were christened there."

Steven took the paper from her hand. "I can't read it," he said. "I need a candle."

She rummaged around, found a candle in a holder by the bed and lit it. Steven slowly unfolded the paper. His face was expressionless, his eyes narrowed. When he finished reading, he looked up at Maggie standing above him, her face pale in the candlelight.

"It's true, Steven. Gregor was your father, Karl your grandfather."

"It seems so strange to have it verified."

"What do you mean? You never believed—"

"Not until yesterday. I didn't tell you everything, Maggie. But I was the one who got to Adamo first. I forced him to tell me the truth."

"You knew all along?" Maggie dropped down beside him on the bed.

Steven nodded. "This paper is just the written proof of what Adamo admitted to me. I wanted to kill him for what he did to my family. At first. Then I realized my hatred was not about my ancestry. I never knew my father or my grandfather. They're only names to me. It was about a country Adamo tried to destroy for his own glory. Now it's over. That's all that matters."

"But you're a Von Alder, Steven. There is nothing for you to do now but show this to Anton and Raymond and go before Parliament—"

"To ask them to make me king?"

"Of course, Steven. The people want the monarchy restored and the Von Alders on the throne. It's your duty."

"Do you really believe that?"

"I believed it for so long. Uncle Viktor told me again and again that what we were doing was right—I still believe it," she added weakly.

"No, you don't. Not anymore. And neither do I. Let me tell you what I believe, Maggie." Steven stood up and walked a few steps away before turning back to her. "I believe that Mendorra deserves to be a republic—or a democracy—whatever the people and Parliament decide. I've done my part—my duty," he added with a smile. "And I don't believe they ever have to be told who I am."

Maggie felt a surge of relief at his words. Then her heart sank. "Adamo knows," she reminded him.

Steven laughed. "I think that's one person we can count on never to reveal the truth."

"But what about that?" she asked, indicating the paper in his hand.

"Is it the only evidence?"

She nodded. "Everything else was destroyed."

"Good." He held the yellowed paper toward the candle flame.

"No!" Maggie cried out.

Steven stopped. "What is it, Maggie?"

"You *are* the rightful heir to the throne. It's wrong to—"

"Wrong for whom, Maggie? Not for the country, not for the people. And certainly not for you and me."

She felt a sudden thrill of fulfillment—for her and for Steven. He'd said those words himself. But the thrill was mixed with a belief in Steven's destiny that had been instilled in her for so long, through her uncle Viktor. She had no right to interfere with that destiny. "You can't give up the throne—"

"Can't I?" Steven asked with a faint smile curving his lips as he held the paper to the flames and watched until it began to crinkle and burn.

Maggie watched, too, mesmerized as Steven dropped the blackened paper to the floor, where it turned into an insignificant pile of white ashes.

"There was never any choice, my darling Maggie," he said softly, turning to her.

It was over, Maggie realized as she sank back beside her beloved Steven. "I almost didn't tell you about the evidence," she said. "I thought I'd lose you if you knew, but I had to tell you." When she looked at him, her eyes filled with tears. "I love you so much, but I couldn't live a lie. And yet you knew all along."

"Yes, I knew, but I couldn't live a lie, either, Maggie. And it would have been a lie for me to stay in Mendorra without the woman I love. I want to go home and take my wife with me."

"That's what I want, too, Steven. What I've wanted all along."

"Do you mean that, Maggie?"

"Of course." She looked up at him, puzzled.

"A sophisticated woman, a renowned actress used to Paris and London and all the capitals of Europe—"

"Who spent her happiest moments in a little room tucked away in the Mendorran mountains. Yes, Steven, I can adjust. The plains of Wyoming will suit me just fine. As long as you're beside me."

"I'll always be beside you," he said, kissing her thoroughly. "But if you get a case of cabin fever, there're trains running regularly to Chicago, New York—and San Francisco."

"I've been to San Francisco," she said, nuzzling against his chest, "but I'd love to see it with you."

"I'll take you there," he said. "And you'll love it even more," he added, sweeping her up into his arms again and whirling her around the room.

"Steven—"

"You'll love everything about being Mrs. Steven Peyton."

With one more dizzying twirl, they collapsed onto the bed again. Steven rolled over, Maggie in his arms, kissing her mightily. "But first you must promise me—"

"Yes?"

"Two things."

"All right," she agreed quickly before changing her mind. "Well, maybe."

"Maybe?" he asked in mock fierceness.

"Let me hear them first before I promise." Maggie was only teasing. She was so happy, she'd promise him anything.

"First, you're never to mention the paper I just burned. Not to anyone. Not Anton or Raymond or even Viktor."

"Not Viktor?"

"Especially not Viktor. If he finds out, he'll never leave us alone."

"You're right," Maggie said. "I won't tell him, but I hate to lie."

"You won't need to lie. Just say all evidence has been destroyed. That's the truth."

Maggie considered that for a moment, thinking about the dream Viktor had carried with him for so long.

"His country is free, Maggie," Steven prodded. "That's all that counts. Nothing else. Now swear that you won't reveal what we know."

"I swear," she said. "What's next?"

"Marry me."

"Yes, yes!"

"Here, now—as soon as we can find a priest."

Maggie shook her head adamantly. "No," she said. "I won't promise that."

"You won't?" Steven faked a disturbed look.

"No, I want to be married in Paris with Uncle Viktor there. We owe him that much."

"You drive a hard bargain, Maggie. But I agree." Then with authority, he said, "We leave for Paris tomorrow, the first leg on horseback over the mountain."

Maggie groaned.

"Then we'll board a train, traveling first class in our own compartment."

"That's more like it," Maggie said.

"In the meantime, we'll spend one more night in our borrowed chalet, a night that neither of us will ever forget."

Maggie curled up beside her lover. "Then our real life will begin."

"Yes, no more counterfeit marriage." He kissed her neck and she cuddled closer. "No make-believe honeymoon. We'll travel Europe together, and this time we'll actually *be* Mr. and Mrs. Steven Peyton," he added with a laugh.

"I'll have a real husband, real children—"

A look of stunned delight flickered over his face. "Children? Are you—"

Maggie giggled aloud. "No, at least I don't think so, but anything is possible."

Steven wrapped his arms around her. "Yes, anything is possible when we're together."

"Everyday," Maggie said, settling happily against him. "For the rest of our lives."

* * * * *

JAYNE ANN KRENTZ

A two-part epic tale from one of today's most popular romance novelists!

Dreams
Parts One & Two

The warrior died at her feet, his blood running out of the cave entrance and mingling with the waterfall. With his last breath he cursed the woman— told her that her spirit would remain chained in the cave forever until a child was created and born there....

So goes the ancient legend of the Chained Lady and the curse that bound her throughout the ages—until destiny brought Diana Prentice and Colby Savager together under the influence of forces beyond their understanding. Suddenly they were both haunted by dreams that linked past and present, while their waking hours were filled with danger. Only when Colby, Diana's modern-day warrior, learned to love, could those dark forces be vanquished. Only then could Diana set the Chained Lady free....

 Available in September wherever Harlequin books are sold.

JK92

HARLEQUIN
Romance®

**Harlequin's Ruth Jean Dale brings you
THE TAGGARTS OF TEXAS!**

Those Taggart men—strong, sexy and hard to resist...

There's Jesse James Taggart in **FIREWORKS!**
Harlequin Romance #3205 (July 1992)

And Trey Smith—he's **THE RED-BLOODED YANKEE!**
Harlequin Temptation #413 (October 1992)

Then there's Daniel Boone Taggart in **SHOWDOWN!**
Harlequin Romance #3242 (January 1993)

And finally the Taggarts who started it all—in **LEGEND!**
Harlequin Historical #168 (April 1993)

**Read all the Taggart romances!
Meet all the Taggart men!**

Available wherever Harlequin books are sold.   DALE-R

Harlequin® Historical

**IF YOU THOUGHT
ROMANCE NOVELS
WERE ALL THE SAME...
LOOK AGAIN!**

**Four exciting Historical
romances every month**

Each month, authors like Ruth Langan, DeLoras Scott
and Dallas Schulze whisk you away to another time
and place....

And don't miss our annual Historical Christmas Story
collection, which will be sure to have you stringing up the
mistletoe—this year featuring Bronwyn Williams, Maura
Seger and Erin Yorke.

But there's more! In July 1993, we're celebrating the Fifth
Anniversary of our launch with a Western Historical Story
collection, three of the most exciting, rough-and-tumble
love stories ever set in the Wild West. Be sure to join in
the fun!

HARLEQUIN HISTORICALS—
A touch of magic!

HHT